Grave Mistake

Don't Call Me Hero
Book 5

Eliza Lentzski

ISBN: 9798512909997
Imprint: Independently published

Also by Eliza Lentzski

Don't Call Me Hero Series

Don't Call Me Hero

Damaged Goods

Cold Blooded Lover

One Little Secret

Grave Mistake

Stolen Hearts

~

Winter Jacket Series

Winter Jacket

Winter Jacket 2: New Beginnings

Winter Jacket 3: Finding Home

Winter Jacket 4: All In

Hunter

http://www.elizalentzski.com

Standalones by Eliza Lentzski

Lighthouse Keeper (forthcoming)

Sour Grapes

The Woman in 3B

Sunscreen & Coconuts

The Final Rose

Bittersweet Homecoming

Fragmented

Apophis: Love Story for the End of the World

Second Chances

Date Night

Love, Lust, & Other Mistakes

Diary of a Human

∽

Works as E.L. Blaisdell

Drained: The Lucid (with Nica Curt)

To C

Prologue

William Desjardin was dead. I'd said the statement over and over again in my head. I was familiar with death, but that didn't mean I was at ease with it. The sudden permanency of it would be forever startling. You would never see that person again, never get to talk to them or ask them questions. They'd never tell you another joke or share another secret. They were just gone. One minute my buddies were laughing and celebrating after a successful directive; the next, they'd been obliterated by an undetected IED as if they'd never existed in the first place.

My parents hadn't raised me to be religious, and the concept of an afterlife had never caught on during any of my tours abroad. Plenty of Marines carried religious paraphernalia with them—a holy book, a rosary, a picture of their god—but just as many carried a lucky rabbit's foot or some other good-luck charm. I considered them all the same.

Julia's suitcase was packed in the trunk of her Mercedes. I'd watched her fill the luggage with meticulously folded blouses and pencil skirts. The more outfits she packed, the more I wondered if she planned on coming back. The postal mail had been put on hold. She'd asked a neighbor to keep an eye on her condo and to water the houseplants in her absence.

I'd been surprised she hadn't put up more of a fight when I insisted that I come along with her to Embarrass. I didn't own proper luggage, so she'd let me borrow one of her suitcases.

I'd informed Captain Forrester that there'd been a family emergency. Stanley and Sarah would hold down the fort while I was away. I kept the details sparse.

Julia's Mercedes idled at a stoplight. Embarrass, Minnesota was just over three hours away, a straight shot north on I-35.

Talk radio played quietly in the background. Julia's hand rested lightly on the automatic shifter in the center console. I put my hand on top of hers and squeezed.

I was in it. I was there for her. She may not have been ready for marriage or babies or whatever that next step looked like for us, but I wanted her to know that I was there for her—for better or for worse. And I hoped that for the time being, that would be enough.

Chapter One

"How did Embarrass get its name?"

"Hmm?" hummed the woman in the driver's seat.

I twisted slightly in the leather upholstered passenger seat to face her. The oversized sunglasses obscured the upper half of her face, hiding her expressive caramel-colored eyes and her dark, manicured eyebrows. She'd chewed off most of her bright red lipstick over the nearly three and a half hour drive from the Twin Cities. When she wasn't engaged in banal conversation with me, either her top or bottom lip had been trapped between her upper and lower rows of teeth.

"Embarrass," I repeated myself. "Where did the name come from? Was there a Mr. Embarrass?"

Julia shook her head with barely a glance in my direction. Her eyes were trained on the stretch of open highway in front of us. "It's French. French fur traders named it after the Embarrass River. *Riviere d'Embarras.*"

Her tongue didn't stumble on the accent, which made me

wonder if she knew the language. It wouldn't have surprised me; she was just about the most accomplished person I knew.

"*Riviere d'Embarras.*" I tried to make my words sound like hers, but with less success. It sounded more like *river duh bare ass* out of my untrained mouth.

"It translates to River of Obstacles," she told me. "In French, *embarrass* means to hinder or to complicate. The river is narrow and shallow, which made it hard to navigate in their birchbark canoes."

"River of Obstacles," I quietly contemplated.

The name of the township and its namesake river seemed all too appropriate. I had sought the northern outpost as a break from the high-stress policing of Minneapolis, but instead of finding refuge, I'd fallen in love with a complicated woman and had uncovered an embezzling scheme that traced back to the small town's distinguished mayor. Julia and I had successfully navigated our relationship despite the twists and turns we'd encountered, but not without capsizing our vessel a few times.

When Julia didn't continue her history lesson, I returned to staring out the passenger window.

When we'd left Minneapolis, the fall colors had been past their peak. But two hundred miles due north, the season was just starting to hit its stride. Deep reds, rich oranges, and vibrant yellows painted the horizon along the interstate highway. I wasn't one of those people who went wild about fall—apple picking, flannel shirts, and pumpkin spice everything—but even I could admit how pretty the season could be, especially in northern Minnesota.

It was the kind of road trip I'd rather be taking for recreational reasons though. I imagined convincing Julia to get on the back of my Harley Sportster and we'd ride at our own pace, on our own schedule, stopping now and again to stretch our legs or grab a meal at a rural, roadside diner. Julia would look devastating in skinny jeans or maybe even leather pants. And I'd make her wear a helmet no matter how much she complained about it messing up her hair.

We'd take that trip someday, I told myself. But for the moment, I shelved the imagery of Julia on a motorcycle to pay better attention to the real thing beside me.

"Has Embarrass ever dealt with a homicide before?" I wondered aloud. "Will they seek outside assistance?"

Julia's features became contemplative. "I'm not sure. As city attorney, I didn't deal with those kinds of crimes. Minor infractions only. Excessive parking tickets, vandalism, theft," she listed. "Or I was defending the city or its employees when they got sued."

I nodded, remembered how magnificent she'd been in the courtroom when she'd defended David Addams after he'd been sued by a local businessman who'd gotten caught serving alcohol to minors. Everyone in the court room—even the judge—had been in awe of her talent, among other things.

"They still haven't found my replacement as city prosecutor," she remarked. "It's hard to attract talent all the way up here."

"Unless you're a police officer with PTSD," I couldn't help observing.

Julia tilted her head in acknowledgment before continuing. "The person serving in the interim in my old position is a solid temporary solution, but I can't see him being ready to try anything more serious than parking infractions."

"Plus, Embarrass only has a couple of cops," I noted. "Who knows if they were able to hire someone for third shift after I left. They might call up the County to help out, but more likely Chief Hart is getting assistance from the BCA—the Minnesota Bureau of Criminal Apprehension. The division was created for these exact situations," I said, thinking aloud. "They'll send over agents from a neighboring field office and use the crime lab in St. Paul."

"I didn't know that. It's awfully handy having a cop in the house," Julia mused.

I shrugged. "I do what I can."

We came upon a faded wooden sign in need of a fresh layer of paint. I could still make out the words that had welcomed me the first time I'd driven my motorcycle into town only a handful of months ago. *Embarrass, Minnesota. The Cold Spot.*

I couldn't help but recall the chilly reception I'd originally received from the people of Embarrass. I'd arrived in the small, northern town as an unproven stranger, knowing no one beyond Larry Hart, chief of police, and his wife, Marilyn. My dad had been friends with Chief Hart since childhood, the two having grown up together in my hometown of St. Cloud, Minnesota.

A strange feeling of nostalgia swept over me as we passed familiar Embarrass landmarks. The stately Victorian home that served as a bed and breakfast where I'd spent a night when I'd first arrived in town; Stan's diner—where the restaurant's namesake held court at a u-shaped countertop and locals occupied red vinyl stools; City Hall—the cream-brick building that housed the city's various municipalities and police department; the local grocery store that made me realize I didn't know how to cook; the church where Grace Kelly Donovan went to mass every Sunday with her parents; the laundromat and the second-floor apartment that had been my home for two months.

We continued past the concentrated main street businesses and turned right at a four-way stop. Another five miles out of town brought us to the red brick home with the blue door and stately white columns where Julia's grandparents had once lived. The house—a mansion, really—had become Julia's own home once she'd returned to Embarrass after her brother Jonathan's death.

6

Among the dense forestry and sprawling farm lands, the columned mansion just didn't fit in. A farm house or a log cabin wouldn't have earned a second glance, but Julia's home looked architecturally out of place. The home seemed to have that in common with its owner. After attending college and law school in Minneapolis, Julia had had a hard time assimilating back into small-town life, although I wasn't convinced she'd ever felt like she'd belonged. Her discomfort had earned her a reputation among the town as standoffish and unapproachable—the antithesis of Midwesterners who were typically known for their friendly and earnest openness. Luckily, I hadn't originally met Julia in Embarrass, or she might never have given me a second glance.

I stared out my car window at the sprawling home. "It looks bigger than I remember," I spoke aloud.

I typically had visited Julia's mansion at night when I was on duty. The imposing home looked even larger in the daylight.

"That's what she said."

Julia's retort was routine instead of playful. Her mind must have been too full to make room for the juvenile joke.

Julia parked in the half-circle driveway in front of the stately home. I climbed out of the passenger side and stretched from the road trip. I was only twenty-eight years old, but the combination of cooler weather, sustained inactivity, and my military injuries made my body feel at least a decade older.

I retrieved our suitcases from the rear trunk and dragged them up the short front stoop while Julia unlocked the front door. She had packed one of her larger suitcases for the trip, which had produced an uneasily joke from myself about if she was planning on coming back to the Twin Cities after her father's funeral.

We hadn't been together long enough to go on an actual vacation together. We'd gone out of town together, but it had been for another funeral—Geoff Reilly's funeral in Fargo, North Dakota. I had been witness to too much death for a lifetime, and I'd attended two funeral services in as many months. The first, the funeral service of another former Marine who'd been in the same squad as me, and the other, a young woman who had taken her own life from shame, guilt, depression, and a misguided scheme that her toddler daughter would benefit more from a life insurance policy payout than actually having her be in her life.

I rolled the suitcases over the small bump in the entryway and paused in the front foyer to remove my boots.

"You don't need to do that," Julia stopped me. "Your shoes are probably cleaner than the floors."

The marble floors looked immaculate as ever to me, but the house had been closed up for several months.

I retied the laces on my boots and straightened. My gaze swept around the familiar interior of Julia's home. The grand foyer with its lofted cathedral ceiling and impressive crystal chandelier. The white marble floors and inlay medallion. I instinctively knew the closed door to my right led to Julia's den where I'd find stiff, yet cozy furniture, an oversized fireplace, and two crystal tumblers inside an ornate built-in cabinet. I wondered if the bottle of bourbon was still there, too.

I let Julia take the lead. I followed her deeper into the home with our suitcases rolling behind me. Julia's heels click-clacked against the tiled floor, and yet the house was still eerily silent, a fact exacerbated by the drop cloth covering most of the furniture. The detail produced a haunted effect throughout the home. Mixed memories flooded my mind of the various encounters that had taken place in the luxurious house.

We passed the grand staircase that led to the second floor master bedroom with its oversized, dark wooden furniture. The central hallway opened up to the kitchen and a high vaulted ceiling. An impressive L-shaped island dominated the space, second only to the back wall that was nothing but windows.

I whistled under my breath. "Yep. Still intimidating."

Julia smiled warmly at my reaction. "I miss this kitchen every day."

I planted a fake scowl on my face. "Well now you're making me jealous. How can I compete with a farm sink and a pot filler?"

"I'm sure you'll think of something, dear."

I lifted the suitcases that flanked me. "Want me to bring these upstairs and we can unpack?"

Julia glanced at her watch. "That can wait. I know we just got here, but I'd really like to see my mother."

"Has anyone told her what's going on yet?" I asked.

Julia shook her head. "No. The staff at the assisted living facility has been waiting for me to get here. Her nurse thinks it's best if I'm the one who tells her about my father."

Julia pinched the bridge of her nose and her dark eyes shuttered. It was the body language of a woman accustomed to being in control, trying not to feel overwhelmed. This trip was so much more than planning a funeral. Julia wasn't just burying her father; she was gaining custody of her mother as well. Either one of those things could have been overwhelming on their own, let alone having to deal with them simultaneously. And I knew how her brain worked. Julia was obsessively organized. She would never be satisfied unless both duties were handled with the utmost care and with attention to every small detail.

"How do you eat an elephant?" I offered.

Julia's hand stayed in place, but she opened one eye and trained it in my direction. "What?"

"How do you eat an elephant? One bite at a time," I explained. "I know your To Do list is only growing, and it feels like you can't possibly do it all, but the good news is, you don't have to do it all at once, and you don't have to do it alone."

Julia opened her mouth. I knew it was her habit to not ask for help, not even from me. She was proud and stubborn and self-sufficient. I was all-too familiar with the combination of qualities because I was the same way.

"What are the most urgent things on your list?" I cut her off before she could get started on the excuses.

"I need to see my mom," she said. "She's been temporarily placed in a nursing home at the outskirts of town. There's not really another option for her right now, but I want to make sure she's comfortable."

I nodded gravely. "And then what?"

Julia released a long, loud breath. "And then I need to meet up with the funeral director to make arrangements for the wake and the burial."

"Okay. And what else?"

Julia gestured to the stainless steel appliance in the corner of the room. "The refrigerator is empty."

I immediately perked up. "Great. It sounds like we've got a plan. Go visit your mom and meet with the funeral director. I'll take care of the groceries."

I grabbed onto Julia's hand to stall what I was sure was another list of excuses. "Let me do this one small thing. You'll actually be doing *me* a favor. Otherwise I'll go crazy with not being able to help."

The framing of my statement coaxed a small, knowing smile from Julia's lips. It was a small thing—a small victory, that smile—but it was something. "Okay," she allowed. "I'll let you go grocery shopping."

I tugged on the hand I held and pulled her closer. "I mean it,

Julia. You don't have to do this alone. I know you're used to it, but we're a team."

Her eyes shifted low and she toyed with the bottom hem of my Henley shirt. "I know," she reluctantly capitulated. "But I'm not very good at this sort of thing."

"You're right. You're not," I readily agreed. "But that's what I'm here for. Let me lighten your load," I urged. "I can do more than be good in the bedroom."

Julia's nostrils visibly flared. "Miss Miller."

There was an exaggerated bounce in my step as we left Julia's house for her parked Mercedes. The feeling was fleeting, however. My hand paused on the passenger door handle as a realization sank in: "We only have one vehicle."

My shoulders slumped forward. I instantly deflated. I'd been so excited about the prospect of being able to help Julia, but because we'd driven to Embarrass together, there wasn't a second car for myself to run errands.

"I'll grab my father's car from his house and you can take the Mercedes," Julia offered.

I cocked my head. "Are you sure? I bet I could call Grace Kelly for a ride."

"You've driven my car before," Julia pointed out.

It wasn't what I had meant, but if she didn't object to driving her deceased dad's car around town, I wasn't going to make a big deal about it either.

It was a short drive from Julia's rural mansion to the Embarrass home where she'd grown up. The two-story home was set back on a little hill with concrete steps carved into the earth. The red brick home with blue shutters was far more modest than Julia's countryside estate, but it was still one of the larger homes within the city limits.

Julia parked her car in the center of the two-car wide driveway. Yellow police caution tape still sealed the front door of her parents' home. I hadn't considered that the house might still be an active crime scene.

I reached across the center console and lightly touched her arm. "Do you want me to call Chief Hart or David? You shouldn't go in there without a police escort."

Julia continued on as if she hadn't heard me. "Isn't that what you are, dear?"

She exited the car, leaving me to scramble after her.

"Julia, you can't go in there," I called out.

Instead of walking towards the front entryway, however, she strode toward the attached two-car garage. She pressed a series of numbers into an exterior keypad and the electric garage door began to lift.

"I don't have to go in the house," she explained. "My father keeps his keys in his car. *Kept*," she corrected herself. "My father *kept* keys in his car."

I stood to one side of her car while Julia entered the garage. The two-car storage space was filled with cardboard boxes and storage containers. A set of golf clubs leaned against one wall. I felt torn between my loyalty to her and my dedication to the badge. Technically, we probably shouldn't have been on the property at all, but no one had thought to barricade the driveway or the garage.

Julia opened the unlocked driver's side door of a charcoal grey Jaguar. Her upper body disappeared as she leaned inside. I continued to wait outside, nervously crossing and uncrossing my arms. My attention vacillated between Julia and the street out front as if I expected David Addams to drive by at any moment in the police department's dark brown squad car.

Julia reappeared, jingling a slim ring of keys in one hand. "My mother always hated that he kept a spare set under the driver's side visor," she said. "His inflated ego thought no one would be bold enough to steal the Mayor's car."

My heart rate started to return to normal, but the open garage door still felt like a giant target.

Julia's heels clicked on the black pavement as she returned to me. "Do you need money for groceries?"

I resisted the urge to roll my eyes. "No, I don't need money. I'm not your kid."

She frowned. "I'm sorry. I'm nervous."

"Nervous? About what?"

"Seeing my mother." Julia wrung her hands in front of her body. "I don't know what she's going to be like. Does she understand what's going on and why she's not in her regular house?"

I clasped onto her worrying hands and held them steady. "She's going to be *so happy* to see you." I held her uncertain gaze and said the words with as much conviction as I could muster.

Julia wet her lips. "How do you always know exactly what I need to hear?"

I had no answer, so I shrugged. So much for being good with words.

Julia let out a shaky breath. "Okay. I've been delaying for long enough. Time to do this."

"I could go with you," I offered again.

Julia shook her head. "No. I appreciate the offer, but your presence would probably just confuse my mother more, and my meeting with the funeral director should be brief enough."

I nodded, admittedly relieved. I didn't do well in hospitals, and I was even less comfortable in assisted living facilities. Plus, I would only sit awkwardly at the funeral home; would Julia really want my input on picking out her father's casket? I felt far more confident with my grocery store task.

"I'll see you back at the house," she told me. The words seemed to be for her own benefit, reassuring herself that the challenging day would soon be over.

She pressed her lips to mine in a deep, yet chaste kiss. When we parted, she ran the pad of her thumb over my mouth to remove any lipstick she'd left behind.

"Call me if you need me," I urged. "Really."

Her lips ticked up in a small smile. "Thank you, dear."

After exchanging keys, Julia began the slow walk back towards the open garage door. I opened the driver's side door of her Mercedes and paused to watch. Her arms hugged at her thin frame, her head tilted towards the ground, and her forehead furrowed in thought.

"You've got this, babe," I called out in encouragement.

Julia stopped and turned back to me. "Cassidy, promise me you'll buy at least a few vegetables?"

"Kinky," I shrugged, a playful grin on my features, "but okay."

Chapter Two

My cart had a squeaky wheel. Three of the grocery store cart wheels glided seamlessly across the speckled, probably asbestos, tiles, but the fourth defiant wheel twisted around in the wrong direction, announcing my presence with its rhythmic squealing sound. Out of all of the carts I could have selected, of course I would have found the damaged one. Damaged things tended to find each other.

Even without the squawking cart, my presence in the Embarrass grocery store had garnered a few curious stares. I didn't run into anyone I knew, but as I picked over the produce I had promised Julia, I could feel the extended glances of other shoppers. I was a familiar face, no doubt, but they couldn't quite place how they knew me.

Thanks to my former neighbor, Grace Kelly Donovan, my arrival in Embarrass the previous spring had literally been front page news. When I'd resigned from the police department a few months later, I hadn't stuck around long enough to learn what had been written about me. I did wonder though—would most residents remember me as Detective Cassidy Miller, Navy Cross recipient? Or was I better known as the police officer who had failed to get the former mayor prosecuted for his crimes?

Julia herself had left an even more dubious legacy in town. Instead of city prosecutor, homegrown protector of Embarrass' civil and criminal codes, she was probably the villain of her story—the beautiful, aloof woman who had put her family before her civic duty.

I didn't linger in the grocery store any longer than I needed to, and it hadn't taken much time to cruise up and down the grocery aisles. It would probably take me longer to check out than it had for me to fill my cart with food. The lines weren't long—it was midday on a weekday when most people were at their jobs—but the grocery store clerk was in no hurry to complete my purchase.

I stood in the empty checkout line and watched the slow movement of the rubber conveyor belt. The cashier hadn't greeted me when I'd first started unloading my cart, so I felt no pressure to initiate small-talk. She was also in no hurry to finish the transaction based on how slowly she scanned my produce. Julia typically took care of the grocery shopping back home. She claimed it was only because her work schedule was more flexible than mine—she set her own office hours—but I had always suspected she didn't let me shop for fear that I'd stock the pantry with Little Debbie Snacks.

I didn't have any place to be, but the slow pace of the checkout clerk made me gnash my back teeth. Instead of focusing on the elongated pauses between each item being scanned, I looked over the magazine covers on display in the aisle. Headlines bellowed about the latest celebrity scandals, urged me to try a new fad diet, and counseled me on tips to find and keep a boyfriend.

Nestled among the national periodicals was a stack of Embarrass' weekly newspapers. I picked up the top copy and, curious, flipped open to the end pages where I suspected the obituary section might be. Only a few names and corresponding images were listed beneath the block, sans serif type, so it didn't take long to find the entry I'd sought: William Joseph Desjardin. I found no photograph of the former mayor, but his obituary was listed first among the other entries—credit to his status in town or merely a coincidence of alphabetical order.

The obituary was scant on details about the man's death. It identified that he had died in his Embarrass home, but the text didn't explicitly identify that he had been killed. I wondered who'd written the obituary. Julia hadn't mentioned writing any announcement, but then again, I didn't know who was typically responsible for those kinds of things. Had Grace Kelly written it? Or someone else employed at the newspaper? Had they asked Julia if she'd wanted an image of her father in the paper and had she declined?

"Are you going to buy that?"

I looked over the top of news pages to see the grocery clerk staring expectantly at me. She'd finished scanning all of my items while I'd been reading about the mayor's death.

"Uh, yeah. Sorry." I dropped the copy of Embarrass' weekly newspaper onto the grocery conveyor belt.

"Do you have a Saver's Card with us?"

"A what?"

The checkout clerk didn't try to hide her eyeroll. She punched a series of numbers into the cash register, and I watched the already low-priced grocery bill slash even lower.

"Oh, uh, thanks," I awkwardly appreciated.

"Sure thing," came the woman's monotone reply. "Paper or plastic?"

My groceries hadn't yet been bagged, but I suspected if I

wanted to get out of there before the sun set that I would have to bag them myself.

~

I stared into the antique, full-length mirror in one corner of Julia's bedroom. It was one of the only pieces of furniture that hadn't been covered with a protective drop cloth. A thin layer of dust covered the long pane of reflective glass. I used a rag to clear a solid path down the center of the mirror. I paused in my task to inspect the woman staring back at me.

I had twisted my long hair up into a bun to keep it out of my face while I cleaned. I was due a haircut. My wavy blonde hair was as long as it had been since I'd joined the Marines. The color was a little duller as the days became shorter and the sunshine less plentiful. My cheekbones were a little less visible, my face a little rounder, a little more full. Unlike my eight-year stint in the military, I now sat behind a desk most days and Julia's culinary talents assured that I ate well.

I didn't know when to expect her back, but I would feel satisfied if I could make even a small dent in the housecleaning. The memory of her earlier comment about the dirty floors had given me a new purpose once I'd returned from the grocery story. I found everything I needed to make Julia's house sparkle and shine in a closet in the second-level laundry room. I put the sheets from the master bedroom in the washing machine. I removed the drop cloths from their respective pieces of furniture and dusted everything else that hadn't been covered. Area rugs had been vacuumed, mirrors had been polished, and wooden floors had been swept. I might have been taking away a task that could help Julia retrain her energies—cleaning could be cathartic —but at the same time I knew she wouldn't really be able to focus on the reason we were in Embarrass if there were dust bunnies under the bed.

I hadn't receive any updates from Julia throughout the day on her progress or when she expected to be home, but I tried not to let her radio silence bother me. Neither of us were too attached to our cellphones, and Julia had far more important things to concern herself with than checking in on me. The rational part of my brain insisted on that, at least. The more sensitive, selfish, and emotional parts expected more from her.

As the hours passed, still without any word from Julia, my annoyance heightened and I turned to more arduous cleaning tasks. I washed windows; I vacuumed out her Mercedes; I detailed the grout in the shower stalls. I was on my hands and knees, scrubbing the kitchen floor, when I finally heard the front door open and close.

The clock on Julia's gas range indicated it was just past 6:00 p.m., but the sky outside appeared much darker. The days were getting shorter, a fact emphasized by being farther north than usual.

"Cassidy?" I heard Julia's call.

"In the kitchen," I hollered back.

I heard the punctuated click of her high heels on the hardwood floor as she made her way to the back of the house.

I tossed the cleaning brush into the suds-filled bucket and leaned back on my knees to inspect my work. The tile floors hadn't really been dirty to begin with, but now they gleamed under the recessed lighting. My knees, however, were far less satisfied. I'd ignored their silent protest for too long and doubted I could stand up on my own without a dramatic performance.

Julia's heels struck against the kitchen's marble flooring.

"Shoes!" I all but barked.

My girlfriend hopped backwards onto the wooden floor of the

hallway as if she'd discovered that the kitchen floor was made of lava.

"Sorry," she mumbled, sounding a combination of embarrassed and alarmed.

She slipped out of her heels and left them in the hallway. "Permission to enter?" she posed.

I grunted as I gingerly climbed to my feet. I stretched out my legs and felt the dull ache radiate across my kneecaps. "Permission granted."

"You've been busy," she observed as she re-entered the room.

"You got pizza?" The sight of the cardboard pizza box tucked under her arm was nearly enough to make me forget my petty annoyances.

Julia set the slightly stained pizza box on the kitchen island. I bit back another sharp protest. I'd cleaned the granite surface earlier and now there would be pizza grease on it, but I didn't want to be the nagging housewife.

"I figured neither of us would feel like cooking tonight," Julia explained the unexpected indulgence.

"I've got boneless chicken breasts marinating in the refrigerator."

Now it was Julia's turn to look surprised. "You do?"

"I thought I could make dinner for you tonight," I shrugged.

"I'm sorry," she frowned. "I didn't know. I didn't mean to ruin your plans."

"It wasn't an official plan," I deflected. "The chicken can chill out until tomorrow."

"And you cleaned."

"I *started* to clean," I corrected her. "The sheets are in the dryer, but I still have to make up the bed. And I haven't gotten to the powder room down here, although I did clean the master bathroom. I swept and I vacuumed, but I might go into town tomorrow to see about renting a carpet cleaner—."

With one quick and purposeful step, Julia closed the distance between us until her nose nearly bumped against mine. She tenderly cupped my face in her hands and tilted her head to the side. I was the one to erase the final breath.

I had expected a long, languid kiss, but Julia pressed her mouth hard against mine. The kiss was bruising, as if she wanted to kiss *through* me. The intensity momentarily stole my breath. Her fingers tugged and pulled at my trapped hair like she wanted to scratch a hole in my head to crawl into. I tried to match her ferocity, but found myself struggling to keep up.

I gently pried her hands away from my aching scalp, but she only moved on to grip the front of my shirt. She twisted the cotton material until I heard the fabric strain. It was an old t-shirt, nearly see-through from wear and multiple washes, but I hadn't thought to bring many similarly casual clothes with me on this trip. I wasn't going to say as much to Julia, however. If anything, it would only spur her on to tear the t-shirt in half. No one told Julia Desjardin what she could or could not do.

The pressure of her lips softened just enough that I was able to hijack her momentum. Her stockings on the kitchen floor provided little leverage; barefoot, my foundation was far sturdier. With my lips still pressed against hers, I pushed her against the kitchen island.

My mouth left her painted lips, but only to softly pepper kisses against the long column of her neck.

"I wish you would have called," I murmured into her skin.

Julia held onto the back of my head as I worked my way down to her collarbone. "I know. I'm so sorry, Cassidy," she breathed. "Time got away from me. I really didn't intend to be out so late."

I flicked open the top buttons of her Oxford shirt. "You're forgiven."

"Because I brought pizza?" I could hear the knowing smile in her words.

I continued to free each individual button until her shirt hung open in the front. I peeled back either side, revealing the delicate lace bra underneath. "Am I that transparent?"

"That all depends, darling—which one of us are you more excited to eat?"

My eyes flicked over to the abandoned pizza box. The gesture didn't go unnoticed; Julia grabbed my chin and jerked my attention back to her.

"Don't make me jealous of fast food, Miss Miller," she throatily warned.

I grinned to let her know I was only teasing. I stroked my hand down the center of her chest, between the valley of her bra-encased breasts, and down the flat plane of her stomach. I deftly unfastened the front of her dress pants: first the sliding hook and then the hidden inner button.

We hadn't been intimate in this way since Julia had learned about her father's death. She'd tried to fuck me on a pool table in a Minneapolis dive bar, but nothing since then. She hadn't initiated sex after that and I'd been too careful, too worried about coming across as insensitive about the situation, to do anything either.

I wasn't sex crazed or a nymphomaniac, but I'd missed her. I knew it would take time for her to properly grieve the death of her father, despite their estrangement, but I took Julia's current encouragement as a sign that things were returning to normal.

"Hop up on the counter," I husked.

I saw Julia's quizzical eyebrow, but she obeyed my request. Her legs swung back and forth from her perch on the countertop's edge.

I stood between her parted thighs and didn't resist the impulse to bury my face between her breasts. A quiet moan tumbled past my lips from the sensation of her perfumed flesh, her soft skin, and the rough texture of the lace demi cups. Julia massaged her fingers against the back of my scalp, a departure from the earlier digging and scratching.

"Why do you feel so good?" It wasn't a question I intended to be answered.

I licked a line between the swell of her breasts. Her skin was faintly salty from the long day of travel and errands. I dipped my head to kiss her lower, eager for the opportunity to taste her in other, more intimate places.

Julia lifted her backside off the countertop and helped me shimmy her dress pants over her hips and down her legs. I was lucky to discover that her nylon stockings didn't go all the way up. It would have been an enjoyable challenge to rid her of the pantyhose, but it was one less barrier to reaching my final destination.

Only a thin layer of satin and lace remained.

I held onto Julia's naked thighs in either hand and subtly spread her legs wider. I bent at the waist and nudged my nose against her panty-covered sex. I smiled at Julia's initial noises; her hips bucked forward and she reached for me. She took purchase of my hair tie and yanked. My long, chaotic waves tumbled free from the former containment of the elastic band, and she raked her fingertips through my loose hair.

I bit down gently on the inside of her thigh, just beyond the panty line. It was no longer bikini season, so I didn't worry about leaving a mark. I sucked at the tender flesh, moving with the involuntary twitching and jerking of Julia's leg in my refusal to be separated from her. I sucked and bit until I was satisfied with the red and purple bruise my efforts had achieved.

Julia looked down at my handiwork. "Pleased with yourself?" she mused.

I licked my lips. "That was for me," I admitted. "This next part is for you."

I pushed the center panel of her underwear to the side and ran my middle finger the length of her slit. I stroked her up and down, coating the tips of my fingers with her arousal. I sank a single finger into her warm, wet opening and heard her contented sigh. I withdrew my hand completely and sucked the same finger into my mouth. I rolled my tongue around the digit and groaned at her taste.

I repeated the motion again: my middle finger deep and hard into her sex, navigating around the narrow swatch of satin and lace. I heard her breath hitch in her throat. I removed my hand and offered it to Julia. She grabbed my wrist in both hands and brought my finger to her mouth. Her tongue flicked against the tip before she sucked the entire thing into her mouth. Her tongue worked on the length of my finger, cleaning it of her juices. My eyes nearly crossed when her painted lips tightened around my knuckle and she sucked hard.

The action pulled something basic and primal from me. I pulled my fingers from her mouth and forced her underwear to the side. I wrapped my free arm around her torso and pushed two fingers into her tight, clenching channel.

Julia leaned back and her legs splayed apart. I furiously pistoned my fingers in and out of her pussy. I had been promised a feast, but I wanted to fuck her. She grabbed the tops of my shoulders, and I felt the bite of her fingernails through the fabric of my shirt. There were no more jokes or double entendres exchanged. There was just me fucking her.

Her breath hitched again and again each time I bottomed out. My knuckles repeatedly struck against her pelvic bone; the hickey on her inner thigh wouldn't be the only thing she felt in the morning.

"Cassidy."

I'd thought her nearly incapable of forming words until I heard the strained plea.

I slowed my fingers just enough to rub the pad of my thumb across her neglected clit. The hands at my shoulders tightened as did her clenching thighs at my sides.

"Cassidy." My name came out a strangled cry. "Please, oh please."

I curled my fingers inside of her and her noises grew louder. I rubbed her hooded clit in small circles. Julia's head fell back and her lips parted. Shuddered, staccato breaths tumbled from her mouth. In a luxury condo above a busy city like St. Paul, I might have missed the change in her breathing. But in a remote country home outside of Embarrass, Minnesota, they were all I could hear.

A low moan, akin to a wail, followed. Her sex noticeably clenched and unclenched around my fingers as an orgasm ripped through her body. Julia clawed at my shoulders until her head rolled forward and her upper body sagged in place.

I eased my fingers out of her underwear and returned the material to its original position. I was still hungry though—starving, really—and I greedily sucked on my Julia-painted fingers.

Julia's chest heaved up and down. "It seems," she breathed heavily, "this house brings out the best in you."

I pressed a cocky, yet pleased kiss to her lips. "And we're just getting started."

～

We reheated the takeout pizza and ate it in the formal dining room. I'd insisted that cold pizza was just as good as the original, but Julia was determined to have a civilized meal that night, not frat party leftovers. There were overhead lights in the formal dining room—a chandelier hung over the long wooden table—but we lit candles instead, and occupied one end of the stretched, elegant table.

The long-stemmed wine glass I twisted between my fingers was more like a crystal chalice. Paper towels doubled as napkins and the pizza box was probably soaking a grease spot into the dining room table. The meal was a perfect representation of our relationship. It shouldn't have worked, but somehow it was the perfect combination.

I ran my fingers along the fine edge of the crystal wine glasses Julia had set out for dinner. "It's funny," I said, thinking aloud. "I typically hate rich people. And here I am, in love with you."

Julia arched an elegant eyebrow. "Is that really funny?"

"Not funny 'ha ha,'" I conceded, "but funny, like, interesting or ironic."

She hummed in thought. "Why do you hate rich people?"

"I mean, 'hate' is probably a strong word," I confessed. "But I imagine most of them didn't have to work hard to earn their money; it was given to them. And they typically don't care about anyone but themselves," I unabashedly opined.

"I think you've just described me, darling," Julia mused.

"No. You're different."

"Am I?" she posed. "I didn't personally earn most of my wealth. Like you said—it was given to me. And we all know that I care very little for other people unless it somehow serves to my advantage."

"That's not ... that's not entirely true." Although there was some truth to her words, I felt obligated to defend the woman I loved. "You've gotten a lot better."

Julia smiled and tilted her wine glass towards me in salute. "Thank you, dear. I *am* trying."

"How did it go today with your mom?" I asked.

I hadn't had an opportunity yet to ask about her errands. I'd been too distracted when she'd gotten home, first by her dirty shoes on my clean floors and then by her fingers and mouth.

The smile on Julia's face was replaced with a wistful frown, and she set her heavy wine glass back on the table. "I couldn't do it. She was already so upset about being in that place instead of her home; it would have been too cruel to pile on that her husband was dead."

I rested my hand on top of hers and squeezed.

Julia sat a little taller in her chair. "Tomorrow. I'll tell her first thing tomorrow," she vocally vowed. "The nurses and orderlies know they're not to speak to her about his death until I have."

"How is she doing in general? It's been a while since you last saw her," I observed.

"Joy, her regular nurse, says she's been about the same," Julia noted. "The doctors have categorized her as having moderate dementia, which is the longest stage of the disease. Memory issues become more severe—you might forget your address, your personal history—but as the disease advances, the brain damage will become worse until she has problems communicating or keeping up with conversations. And then that," she sighed deeply, "can manifest any variety of emotional responses from violence to depression to paranoia."

I always felt guilty when the topic of Julia's mother came up. My own mother was healthy as a horse and I took that health for granted. I wasn't estranged from my family, but I also didn't make a concerted effort to make them a part of my life.

"Do you ever regret leaving all of this?"

Julia looked over her wine glass at me. "That's a complicated question."

"Is it?" I naïvely asked.

"Professionally, sometimes," she admitted. "You know I've gone back and forth about being a public defender. It's rewarding to offer proper legal counsel to people who otherwise couldn't afford it. I know I'm doing good," she said with a resigned sigh, "but this idyllic job of working with clients who've only committed minor infractions ..." She trailed off. "The writing's on the wall. They want me to take on bigger criminal cases, and I don't think I'll ever be okay with that. Maybe once upon a time I could have been a heartless criminal lawyer. But not now."

"What changed for you?" I asked.

She raised an eyebrow. "Is that a serious question?"

"I guess so?" I shrugged.

She licked her lips. "Being in love."

I felt her answer vibrate through me.

"Have you thought more about Melissa Ferdet's job offer?" I asked.

In the wake of Julia successfully defending the initial suspect in my latest cold case, her public profile had only grown. It had caught the eye of a powerful Minneapolis law firm where she'd once interned and later had been a junior partner. That career had been derailed by her brother Jonathan's death, which had brought her back to Embarrass. She was back on the firm's radar, however, with a lucrative job opportunity that promised she'd be able to take on worthy *pro bono* cases of her choosing.

The more I thought on it, the more ideal it sounded. The only issue was time; she already worked long hours as a public defender. This new job would demand even more.

Julia's eyes dropped to her wine glass. She ran a single finger around its rim. "There really hasn't been time." Her voice was no more than a whisper.

I could have piled on—I could have pressed her to talk to me about her mindset regarding the job opportunity—but she'd taken enough bites for one day; the elephant would still be there in the morning.

～

I love that moment when your feet and bare legs hit freshly laundered sheets. I wiggled my legs beneath the top sheet, enjoying the feel of Julia's high-thread count cotton sheets against my bare skin. I kind of felt like doing a snow angel motion in the center of the mattress. Prior to my relationship with Julia, I'd never paid much attention to bedding. I wasn't as bad as some of my guy friends though, who didn't bother to make up the bed and inexplicably slept on a naked mattress with only a ratty comforter to cover up with. I'd come to appreciate—because of Julia—that some things shouldn't be skimped on: bedding, toilet paper, and laundry detergent.

I looked in the direction of the *en suite* bathroom when the door opened. Julia emerged, looking fresh faced and makeup free. She'd exchanged her clothes from the day for a dark purple silk robe that stopped just above her knee. My eyes threatened to pop out of my head when she slipped the robe off her shoulders and hung it over the edge of a wooden chair in the room.

The lilac-colored nightgown she wore underneath was downright sinful. My eyes swept over the scalloped edge that hugged the top swell of her bra-less breasts. The silk baby-doll nightdress had just enough material to cover her breasts and upper thighs. A thin border of black lace outlined the bottom hem.

"Where's that been hiding?" I asked. I wiped at my mouth

with the back of my hand, worried I might actually be drooling. I felt a little like a cartoon wolf eyeballing its next meal.

Julia looked down at her silk lingerie. "I didn't bring all of my clothes to St. Paul. There wasn't space in the condo," she said. "I left a few things behind."

I licked my lips, not bothering to hide my approval. "You should have consulted me. I think your packing priorities need some adjusting."

A pleased smile curled onto the edges of Julia's mouth. "More nightgowns and less practical clothes, perhaps?"

"Yes, please," I eagerly agreed. I pulled back the duvet to invite Julia into the space beside me.

"Mmm, clean sheets," she approved as she climbed into bed. She wiggled closer until she could reach me. "Thank you again for cleaning the house, Cassidy. It was very thoughtful of you."

"I told you I was good at something besides the bedroom." I turned on my side to face her. "Speaking of which ... did you know this is only the second time I've slept in this bed?"

Her dark eyebrows slightly furrowed. "That can't be right."

"It is. The only time I slept over was the Fourth of July. I didn't think I'd be able to handle fireworks, so I begged Chief Hart to give me the night off. I drove my bike out here." I softly laughed at the memory. "Shit, I didn't even stay the whole night."

"Because you had a nightmare," Julia recalled.

"I was so scared to let anyone witness my PTSD." I hummed and stared at the ceiling. "And look at us now."

"Indeed," she murmured in return. "No more scampering off in the middle of the night."

"No more secret patrol car sex either."

"You still have access to a police car," she pointed out.

I sat up on one elbow. "Oh, really?" My voice lilted in surprise and amusement. "You'd still go slumming with me in the backseat of a patrol car when we have this big 'ol luxurious bed?"

"Nothing says you have to become boring once you're monogamous, my dear."

"Being in bed *does* have its advantages though," I remarked.

"And what would those be?" Julia questioned.

"We've got all of this space to spread out. And I don't have to rush. I can take my time in bed." I purposefully lowered my voice. "I can strip you bare without worrying that someone will see."

"You've got all the space and all the time right now, Miss Miller," Julia pointed out. The next words came out as a husked whisper. "Whatever shall you do with it?"

If I'd thought the pizza from dinner had made me sluggish, the low burn of Julia's voice jolted me awake.

"You're not too tired?" I double checked. It had been a long day, physically and emotionally.

"Darling, if I ever claim to be too tired for more orgasms, have my head checked." She turned the question on me: "Are *you* too tired? Having a hard time keeping up, Marine?"

"Oh, now you've done it." I pounced on top of her with a quiet growl.

Julia gazed up at me with a look of longing and appreciation. She twirled a loose tendril of my blonde hair around one finger. "I really do love you."

My heart swelled, close to bursting. The words that I'd worked so hard to hear from her came easier and easier. "I love you, too."

Chapter Three

Afghanistan, 2012

I've lost count of how many days we've been in the desert. Each evening of trudging through ankle-high sand has blurred together into one long nightmare from which I cannot awaken. At the safe house—which had turned out to be a death trap—I'd scratched hashmarks on one of the crumbled walls. Out in the middle of bumblefuck nowhere, there's no way to mark the passage of time, unless I start carving up my own flesh.

I knew Pense would be in no condition to travel under his own power, so I'd constructed a makeshift sled from rebar and canvas, which were in ample supply among the remnants of the blown up safe house, in order to drag his ass across the desert. He's a slight guy, so I might have been able to carry him over my shoulder if not for my own injuries.

One of the common arguments against women in combat is that we lack the upper arm strength to carry a wounded buddy out of harm's way. But you don't carry another Marine like he's a baby;

standard military technique is to use a fireman's carry—to sling your fallen friend over your shoulder. My legs were fine, but my back still stung like hell.

I'd taken Amir's shirt before we left. He wasn't going to need it anymore, and the back half of my uniform had been sliced up like Swiss cheese from the dirty bomb. I haven't been able to look at my back yet, and I'm half-scared to ask Pensacola about it, but if my skin looks anything like my tattered uniform, I might not have much more time either. If heat stroke or dehydration doesn't get me, the sepsis will.

I know it's too much to hope running across Camp Leatherneck in our wanderings, but if we can just find a river, maybe a tributary of the Helmand River, I can regain my bearings. Rivers mean fresh water, but the river basins also house poppy fields. The very thing that could replenish our dwindling supplies could also put us more in harm's way.

The Helmand Province is one of the most dangerous of the country's thirty-four provinces, not only because of insurgent activities, but also because of the region's high production of opium. Intel suggests that Helmand is responsible for around forty-two percent of the world's total production. Opium is more profitable than growing wheat.

We travel at night under the watchful gaze of the moon's pale light. It feels like a spotlight shining directly down on two hobbled Marines, but it's the best we can do. Before the sun rises, I try to find us some kind of shelter or covering to shield us from the sun, the heat, and the enemy until the sun sets and the traveling routine begins all over again. If Pense feels emasculated to be dragged across the region by a woman, he's smartly kept those words to himself.

When he's able, Pense and I talk about all of the things we're looking forward to when we get back to the States and are out of this sepia-colored wasteland. He's got his new wife, Claire, back home. I've got my childhood bedroom in St. Cloud, Minnesota.

He tells me about his mom's cooking. They're southern transplants—his parents moved to Detroit from Georgia for his dad's work when he was little.

"Sweet potato pie, Miller," he croons. "You haven't really lived until you've had my mama's pie."

If we'd been back at Camp Leatherneck, I would have never let such an obvious reference to his *mom's pie* go unchecked, but I don't have the energy to pounce on the double entendre.

He asks me what I'm most looking forward to, or at least what's the first thing I'm going to do when we're back in the U S of A.

"Water," I say, stupidly.

We've been rationing our supplies for some time now. The other Marines in our unit had each had their own emergency ration kit in their packs. We salvaged as much as we could before we left—whatever hadn't been obliterated, along with the man to whom it had been originally assigned.

"I'm going to take the world's longest shower," I say. "Not worry about running out of hot water or water pressure. I wanna stand under that shower head and let all of this shit go down the drain."

"I wasn't gonna mention it, but you *do* smell pretty ripe," Pense teases me.

I don't mind the taunting. I actually live for these moments when he's in a good mood. It makes it easier to pretend that I'm not going to die out here.

～

I woke up the next morning to the sound of birds chirping instead of my usual alarm. The sun hadn't fully risen yet, but the world beyond Julia's bedroom windows was already awake. I turned to the woman beside me. Julia slept curled on one side, facing me. Her eyes were closed, but lightly lidded. One hand was hidden beneath her pillows, while the other formed a loose fist, close to her face. Her hair was getting longer, too. I carefully tucked a lock of raven hair behind one ear. Her dark lashes fluttered, but she didn't wake up. I would have been content to remain in bed, watching her sleep, if not for my complaining bladder. I slid out of bed as quietly as I could to avoid waking her up. She could continue to tackle that daunting To Do list soon enough.

After a visit to the *en suite* bathroom, I tiptoed past her still sleeping form and ventured downstairs. After a thorough scrubbing of the kitchen the previous day, I knew where to find the coffeemaker and where Julia stored the coffee filters. I prepared an extra-large, extra-strong pot of coffee and poured myself a cup. I pulled a second cup from the cabinet so it would be waiting for Julia once she came downstairs. I grabbed the local newspaper I'd bought at the grocery store and took it, along with my coffee cup, to the back porch.

It was cold outside, especially since I only wore a t-shirt and sweatpants, but the chill would wake me up better than the contents of my coffee cup. I sat down on the porch's steps and closed my eyes. The scent of dead, decaying leaves filled my nostrils. A rough wind disturbed the final, stubborn leaves that resiliently clung to their branches, refusing to give up the good fight, refusing to surrender to the coming winter.

It was so quiet; the silence was appealing. It was a reminder to breathe. To slow down. I'd been running for so long, jumping from one mission to the next, one career path to the next, all in a futile attempt to keep my brain busy. I'd stubbornly believed that if I just kept busy, just kept moving, that the nightmares wouldn't be able to catch me.

I wasn't alone with my thoughts for very long; I heard the sound of the kitchen slider opening and closing behind me, followed by Julia's soft steps on the wooden porch.

"I thought you'd run off until I saw the coffee in the kitchen."

I took a drink of my coffee and spoke into the mug. "Can't get rid of me that easily."

Julia sat down beside me. She'd covered her flimsy nightgown with a more substantial robe, but her legs were still exposed to the elements.

"What are you doing out here?" she asked. She set down her coffee cup and began to rub at her bare legs.

"I don't know," came my honest reply.

My response was far from satisfactory, but she didn't interrogate me for more. Instead, she rested her head against my shoulder, and I basked in the gentle press of her body leaning against mine.

I heard her take a long breath and exhale. "Do you want to come to the assisted living facility with me today?"

I remembered her mother from our one brief meeting. Julia and her father looked nothing alike; she was her mother's daughter. Delicately built. Black hair streaked with white. Long hair, pulled back into a tight bun.

"Do you want me to come?" I asked carefully.

"Mmhmm," she confirmed.

"Then, yes. I will absolutely come with you."

Her body sagged a little heavier against me. "What do I even say to her?"

I set my coffee cup down so I could wrap my arms around her midsection. I pressed my lips against her perfumed hair. "The truth, I suppose."

~

With the exception of the VA hospital where I infrequently met for group therapy with other vets, and the maternity ward where Pensacola's wife, Claire, had given birth, I'd successfully avoided being in a hospital since leaving the military. It had taken time for the wounds on my back to heal sufficiently before the doctors were ready to discharge me. Multiple surgeries had been necessary to remove the debris and shrapnel imbedded in my flesh, but even then they hadn't gotten it all. I still beeped going through security screenings.

Olivia Desjardin wasn't in a hospital, but the assisted living facility still smelled strongly of disinfectants and other sterile scents that brought me back to my own hospital bed and the idle days spent watching talk shows, game shows, and soap operas with Terrance Pensacola.

Julia looked timid and unsure of herself. She normally strode into a room, head held erect, back straight, and made eye contact with everyone she confronted. Her body seemed to fold in on herself, as though she was trying to take up as little space as possible. I gripped her hand a little tighter in encouragement, but she still looked scared.

I recognized Joy, the woman who looked after Mrs. Desjardin. Joy was a small, Asian woman—Hmong, if I'd had to guess. Minnesota had been a popular relocation spot for Hmong refugees during the 1970s when their home country of Laos had been ravaged by war. Her jet black hair was pulled back in a long ponytail, and her salmon-colored scrubs set her apart from the other staff members milling around the building who primarily wore blues and dark purples.

Having a full-time caregiver for her mother was a sensitive topic for Julia. I knew she felt guilty that she'd passed off her care to a stranger, but as Mrs. Desjardin's disease had progressed, it had become a full-time job.

"Good morning, Ms. Desjardin," she smiled.

Joy's eyes flicked from Julia's face to mine and then down to our joined hands.

Julia seemed to have forgotten me, even though we continued to hold hands. When she didn't introduce me, I took over the task myself.

"I'm Cassidy. Hi."

"Hi, Cassidy," Joy responded. "It's good to meet you." She turned back to Julia. "Are you ready for this?"

"As ready as I'll ever be," Julia said with a sigh. "Thank you for insisting I be the one to tell her, Joy. This will probably be the hardest thing I've ever had to do, but I know it should be me who tells her about my father."

"Of course," Joy replied. "And as hard as this is going to be for the both of you, remember that your mother is stronger than she looks—just like you." She smiled encouragingly. "Your mother has experienced a lot of little deaths since being diagnosed. The loss of her ability to drive a car, the loss of her independence."

"The loss of Jonathan," Julia somberly added.

I remembered from the first time I'd unofficially met Mrs. Desjardin that she'd asked her nurse about Jonathan. At the time, however, the name hadn't meant anything to me.

"She asks about your brother from time to time," Joy observed. "And I gently remind her that he's been dead for a while. And we might look at photographs together of him, and I ask her about him and what she misses most about him to reaffirm that he's no longer with us. It will be the same with your father's death."

Julia audibly exhaled. "Any advice on how to do this?"

"Be kind," Joy said, "but don't tiptoe around the issue. Use words like 'death' or 'dead' – not 'passing away' or that your father has gone to a better place. Be concrete."

"Okay." Julia nodded curtly. "Wish me luck."

"Do you want me to go in with you?" Joy offered.

"Or me?" I piped up.

"No. Thank you both," Julia said. "But this is something I've got to do on my own."

Julia tugged at the sleeves of her cardigan and straightened the front buttons. She flicked at her hair before knocking softly on the closed door to her mother's room.

"Come in!" came a slightly muffled reply.

Julia cracked the door open and stuck her head inside. I could hear the quiet melody of a piano song filter into the hallway. "Hey, Mom," Julia gently greeted. "How are you doing today?"

Julia stepped into the room and shut the door behind her.

I exhaled a breath I hadn't realized I'd been holding.

"Can I get you something to drink while you wait?" Joy offered.

My eyes stayed on the closed wooden door. "Don't suppose you've got any beer?" I asked, only half joking.

"I'm afraid coffee is the best I can do."

I turned to Joy and gave her a thankful smile. "Coffee would be great, thanks."

I sat in a stiff chair in the hallway just outside of Mrs. Desjardin's room while I waited for Joy to return. The chair was cushioned, but cracks in the fake leather upholstery revealed the white foam padding underneath. Julia had probably been too nervous, too preoccupied about the conversation she was about to have with her mother to comment on the condition of the assisted living facility. The staff seemed kind and capable, but I was sure Julia was counting down the days until she could move her mom to more upscale accommodations in the Twin Cities.

39

It wasn't long before Joy returned with coffee. She handed me the cardboard cup and sat in the vacant seat beside me. I thanked her for the errand and took a tentative sip of the scalding, hot liquid.

"It's not very good," she warned as I brought the cup to my lips.

"I'm not picky," I returned.

We sat side-by-side, unspeaking. I passed the cardboard cup from one hand to the other and stared at the closed door that separated me from Julia and her mother. It would be a lie to say I wasn't tempted to press my ear against the door to hear their conversation. I'd tagged along that day to help Julia, but so far I wasn't feeling very helpful.

I cleared my throat. "You don't have to babysit me if you have rounds or other patients to check on."

"Residents," Joy gently corrected me. "We're not a hospital."

"Right. Sorry." I took another sip of the hot coffee. "Have you lived here long?"

"In Embarrass?"

I had meant the United States, but I was too ashamed to admit that to her.

"Five years," she said. "Time flies."

"How do you like it?"

"I like it fine," she said noncommittally. "The cost of living is much lower than in the Twin Cities, which is nice."

"How about family?"

I didn't want Joy to feel like I was interrogating her, but it was a nice distraction from the conversation happening on the other side of the door.

"They're all in Minneapolis. Before that we were in refugee camps all over—Laos. Vietnam. Thailand," she listed, "but I was too young to remember any of it."

40

"That's got to be tough to be away from them," I observed.

"I get back for birthdays and holidays. I have a lot of cousins," she smiled, "so it ends up being pretty frequent."

"Are you an only child?"

"No. I have four older brothers. They weren't too excited about me taking this job and moving up here. As the only daughter I should be in Minneapolis to care for my parents—not other peoples' parents. They remind me of that every chance they get," she said, making a face. "But my parents moved us here so we kids could have a better life; what kind of life would it be if I never got to experience it?"

"That's pretty brave to leave everything and everyone you know to move to a place like Embarrass," I observed.

She cocked her head. "You think so?"

"I don't know," I shrugged. "Maybe you had a different experience than me. But this place ... these people ...." I struggled to find the right words. "They tend to keep to themselves."

"You did alright; you met Ms. Desjardin."

I felt a blush creep onto my cheeks.

"I'm sorry," Joy apologized. "Maybe I misread the situation. You're together, aren't you?"

My throat tightened at the question. When I'd first moved to Embarrass, Julia had been very deliberate in her desire that we be discreet. She was fiercely private, but you also never knew how the residents of a small, remote midwestern town might respond to the news that the city prosecutor was sleeping with another woman. Living in the Twin Cities, neither of us had felt compelled to hide our relationship. Those who disapproved of two women in a relationship were in the minority.

"I'm here with her, yes," I responded. "We, uh, we're roommates in St. Paul."

"Roommates who hold hands," Joy evenly observed.

"We're together, yes," I finally relented. "We're dating."

"There isn't a word for being gay in Hmong," Joy noted. "It's pretty frowned upon. Not that *I* care," she was quick to qualify. "My cousin Dao Came Out to her parents, but they totally ignored it. They didn't kick her out or disown her or anything, but they just don't acknowledge it. She stopped bringing girlfriends around the family, and the family has stopped bugging her about when she's going to get a boyfriend."

"Wow. That's really rough," I frowned.

"What did your parents say when you told them?" she asked me.

My mouth opened, but nothing came out.

Nothing. My parents had said nothing. Because I still hadn't told them.

Miraculously, the door to Mrs. Desjardin's room opened at that moment, saving me the embarrassment of having to admit to Joy that I still wasn't Out to my parents.

The door opened and Julia reappeared. I scrambled to my feet, nearly spilling my cup of coffee in the process. Julia took my awkwardness in stride.

"My mother would like to go for a walk—to get some fresh air. Would that be okay, Joy?"

Joy remained in her chair. "Of course. But bring a sweater. It looks like it might rain."

Julia flicked her eyes towards me. "Would you like to join us, Cassidy?"

I hadn't expected the invitation, and I found myself tripping over my words. "Yeah. Okay. I can do that."

Julia turned her head and spoke over her shoulder, back into her mother's room. "Grab a cardigan, dear. It's cold outside."

While I continued to wait in the hallway, I searched Julia's features for some sign of how their conversation had gone. Had she actually told her mother? How was she taking the news? But Julia's face told me little; I would have to wait and broach the topic later.

A small woman, thin boned with shoulders beginning to hunch forward, shuffled into the hallway. Her hair was pulled back in a low bun. It reminded me of a stereotypical librarian hairstyle, but I knew that Julia's mother had been a teacher's aide at the elementary school in Embarrass in her younger days. Mrs. Desjardin let her daughter help her into a navy blue cardigan and waited while Julia buttoned up the front.

"Mom," Julia started, "I'd like to introduce you to someone very special. This is my friend, Cassidy."

Mrs. Desjardin leveled her gaze on me. "Have we met before?"

"Not officially, ma'am, no." I fell back into the comfortable routine of using honorifics.

Mrs. Desjardin offered me her hand. "I'm sorry. I have to ask that." Her eyes flicked in Joy's direction. "I'm a bit forgetful these days."

I gently shook her hand in greeting. Her bones felt fragile beneath the skin. Mrs. Desjardin couldn't have been much older than my own mom, but her mental disease had taken its toll physically as well.

"It's nice to officially meet you, too, ma'am," I offered.

Outside, the day had turned damp; it was the kind of chill that settles into your bones and refuses to leave without a hot bath or at least chicken noodle soup. It was less than ideal walking conditions, but if both Joy and Julia thought it was okay for Mrs. Desjardin to be outside, I wasn't going to throw a fit. The facility's grounds were sprawling and well-manicured. Because the center was located at the edge of town, it had had room to grow along with its resident population. Julia had invited me on the walk, but the sidewalk that snaked through the park-like grounds was only wide enough for two people. Julia and her mother walked ahead while I lagged behind a few steps. It was hard to not feel like the third wheel; I should have been grateful for the opportunity even if she'd only introduced me as her friend.

Special friend, I silently noted.

The two women walked at a leisurely pace. There was no place to go and no place to be. They stopped periodically to admire the colors of a tree with particularly vibrant leaves. They didn't speak about Julia's father, however. They didn't address what was going to happen next with Mrs. Desjardin's living situation.

I looked up at the darkening sky when I felt the first drop of rain. Julia noticed the change in weather, too.

"Come, dear," she gently urged her mom. "It's time to bring you back."

The warmth of the assisted living facility was welcomed after the brief visit outside. I stamped my feet on a welcome mat to dislodge any dirt or leaves that might have still clung to the bottoms of my boots.

Julia and her mom shared a long embrace.

"I'll stop by tomorrow," Julia promised. "We can go over the details of Daddy's funeral."

Mrs. Desjardin nodded somberly.

"It was nice to meet you, Mrs. Desjardin," I chimed in.

Julia's mom looked in my direction. "It was nice to see you again, Katie."

"Cassidy," I corrected.

Mrs. Desjardin's features crumbled in concern. "I don't know a Cassidy."

"Come now, Mrs. Desjardin," Joy interjected. She held the older woman by her elbow. "It's almost time for lunch."

Julia and I stood side-by-side and watched as Joy ushered Mrs. Desjardin down the corridor. Mrs. Desjardin turned to her long-time nurse and seemed to chat amicably, without a care, without concern that she didn't know anyone named Cassidy.

"Katie was a friend of mine growing up," Julia said as we watched her mother's retreat. "She was blonde, too, so maybe that's where the mistake came from. I wouldn't take it heart though. In time," she sighed, "she'll forget me, too."

It had started to rain in earnest by the time we left the assisted living facility. The sky continued to darken as we drove beyond the city limits and back to Julia's house. I watched Julia repeatedly glance in her rearview mirror. I didn't think that anyone was following us, but I did worry that Julia was regretting leaving her mom at that place. The staff all seemed kind and capable, but Mrs. Desjardin would be dealing with the dual disorientation of not being in her own home and the news of her husband's death.

I grasped Julia's hand across the center console. "She'll be okay," I promised. "Those people are pros. Joy won't let anything happen to her."

Julia tucked her lower lip into her mouth and tightly nodded.

"You're doing everything you can," I continued. "And once the funeral is over, she can move to the Twin Cities and you can see her whenever you want."

"Whenever *I* want, sure," Julia countered. "But is that what's best for *her*? I've wanted her to be in St. Paul with me since I moved there, but I'm not so sure."

It was a familiar conversation, one we'd had leading up to and after the family court case when Julia and her father had fought over her mother's custody. Would her mother be better off in Embarrass—the only place she'd ever lived—or should she be moved to a facility closer to Julia?

"Nothing needs to be decided today. You've got time to make that decision," I reminded her. "One bite at a time."

Chapter Four

Afghanistan, 2012

Pensacola's playful taunts have been coming less and less frequently. I try to keep him talking so I know he hasn't passed out—or worse. The makeshift sled leaves a trail in the sand, but that can't be helped. I've since lost the fear of being found by insurgents. I haven't seen another person besides Terrance in so long, we might as well be the last people on the planet.

My mind wanders as we travel in the evenings. Lately I've been fixated on the book *The Little Prince*. It was one of my mom's favorite books to read to me when I was little, but most of the deep content hadn't really registered with me at the time. A pilot's plane crash lands him in an African desert. He believes himself stranded and alone until a little blond boy appears, asking him to draw him a sheep. Was he only a mirage? Or was he really a prince from a distant planet who'd fallen in love with a vain and petty flower?

One sees well only with the heart. The essential is invisible to the eyes.

My eyes are in a constant state of fatigue. They burn and ache like I've stared at the steady glow of a bonfire for too long. The dirty bomb had obliterated everything in its path, including my sunglasses. But my eyes should be the least of my worries.

Sometimes I regret the decision to leave the safe house. We'd gambled that no one was coming to look for us, but maybe we were wrong; maybe we should have given it a few more days. Which fate was preferable? Starvation and dehydration or being captured by the enemy? I don't want to think about either, but I can't help the pessimistic thoughts that frequently slip into my brain.

～

A muffled groan vibrated in my throat when I felt movement beside me. The covers were drawn back but then were returned to their original place once Julia slipped out of bed. I didn't open my eyes.

"What time is it?" I hadn't heard an alarm.

"Early," she hushed. "Go back to sleep."

I rolled onto my back and unwillingly opened my heavy eyes. "Why are you up?"

"I have some errands to run. Loose threads to tidy up before the wake tomorrow."

"Can I help?" I wanted to be helpful despite my body's desire for more sleep.

"No, dear," she lightly refused. The floorboards creaked as she rounded the bed to come sit on my side of the mattress. "I can handle it. Just a few tedious tasks like going to the DMV to cancel my father's driver's license."

"When will you be back?"

"I'll text you when I'm on my way home. It might take some time though," she warned. "I need to forward his social security check to my mother, cancel his driver's license, his voter registration, forward and then cancel his mail," she listed. "Notify the credit reporting agencies so someone can't steal his identity. And I promised my mother I'd stop by for a visit."

Her voice became tighter with each recited task.

"One bite at a time, remember?"

Julia blew out a long breath and pinched the bridge of her nose. "I know. Just keep reminding me of that, okay?"

"Every hour, on the hour," I vowed.

Julia bent over me and pressed her lips against my forehead. Her fingers brushed at a few errant strands that had worked their way free from my ponytail during the night. "Try to stay out of trouble while I'm gone."

"Well that's no fun," I teasingly complained.

A small smile worked its way to Julia's lips. "At least wait for me to get home before the trouble begins."

I watched Julia retreat to the bathroom. The door shut behind her, and I heard the shower turn on. I could have tried going back to sleep, but that probably meant a return to the Afghanistan desert.

I reached for my phone on the end table closest to me and shot off a text: *You free for lunch today?*

My old coworker, David Addams, was already seated at a booth when I walked through the front door of Stan's diner later that day. His light blue eyes swung in the direction of the glass-plated door when my entrance triggered the tiny bell above the front door. He sat facing the open layout of the diner, an ingrained habit

I had also picked up from being in the military and then as a police officer. I never voluntarily sat with my back turned to an entrance, but he'd already claimed the preferred bench and the space beside him was occupied with his gun belt.

The uniform was uncomfortable to sit in. All of the gadgets that hung from the thick leather utility belt needed room to spread out or else the gun holster, baton, handcuffs, and mace or taser dug into your thighs and waist. David had taken his belt off altogether and it sat on the empty space beside him on the vinyl upholstery.

"You on the clock?" I asked, in lieu of a proper hello.

David grunted and stabbed a French fry into a pile of ketchup on his plate. "Chief has me back working swing shift."

I slid across the bench seat and plucked a laminated menu from the table. David hadn't waited for me to place his order, but I wasn't offended. When you're on duty, you're never guaranteed a lunch break. You eat in the patrol car; you shovel down food in between calls.

"Was the department able to find a replacement for me?" I asked.

"Is that a trick question?"

I arched an eyebrow. "No?"

"I thought maybe you were fishing for a compliment or something. Like, no way, Miller. You're irreplaceable."

I snorted. "God, if I ever get that big of a head, slap me."

David held up a big, meaty palm. "If you insist."

"Real cute, Addams," I smirked.

Even though I hadn't seen David since I'd left Embarrass and we'd only spoken a few times on the phone, we fell back into an easy banter. We had only known each other a handful of months—the same amount of time as I'd known Julia, in fact—but our mutual experiences of being Marines and police made it feel like we'd always been friends. That shared, unique perspective was more unifying than if we'd grown up together in the same *cul de sac*.

"Are you guys handling the William Desjardin case yourself or is another agency helping out?"

"BCA," he revealed, confirming my earlier assumptions about the case. "They sent in a field agent from Grand Rapids."

At just over 10,000 people, Grand Rapids, Minnesota was significantly larger than Embarrass, but it was still a relatively small town.

"And get this," David continued. "It's another chick."

"Hit on her yet?" I asked.

David snorted. "Not my type."

"She shot you down," I guessed. I couldn't help my grin.

"You female cops are all the same," he said sourly. "You take yourselves too seriously. What would a beer with a coworker hurt?"

"It might have to do with the fact that we have to be twice as good as the typical male cop to be taken seriously," I observed with as little bitterness as I could muster.

"Well, whatever," David dismissed. "Special Agent Rachel Andrews is hot on the case. I don't mind the extra help though," he admitted. "It's hard enough keeping this town together with just the Chief and me without a murder case to dig into. With you gone, there's no night car anymore; once I clock out, dispatch forwards calls to the State police."

A waitress came to take my order and my food was promptly delivered. I had a million questions for David about William Desjardin's death, but I waited until my lunch arrived before I dug into him. Small towns ran on gossip. I didn't want to risk our waitress overhearing our conversation and adding fuel to the rumor mill.

I took a bite of my club sandwich before I launched into my first question: "How did he die?"

Julia had been stingy with the details surrounding her father's death, and I'd been too chicken shit to ask.

"Gunshot wound to the stomach," David said around a mouthful of fries. "BCA thinks Desjardin probably interrupted a burglary in progress."

"A burglary?" I said the word with a good amount of skepticism. "You really think someone was bold enough to break into the Mayor's house?"

Julia's words about her father leaving his car keys in his vehicle came to mind.

"*Former* mayor," David reminded me. "After you left us high and dry," he couldn't help the dig, "a squad car was at the Desjardin house nearly every week. Vandalism mostly. Someone painting words like 'thief' and 'liar' on the garage door."

"Geez. He pissed off a lot of people, huh?"

"Understatement," David confirmed.

"Why does BCA think it was an interrupted burglary? Were there broken windows? A shattered doorjamb?"

I tried to think back to when Julia and I had driven to her parents' house to get her dad's car. I hadn't noticed any signs of a break-in, but they might have gone through the back of the house instead.

"You could ask for yourself," David noted, "Andrews is staying at your old digs above the laundromat."

I held my hands up. "I'm not trying to step on anyone's toes. I'm only here to support Julia; I'm not police."

It wouldn't have been legal or ethical for me to do any official police work anyway. As a cold case detective for the city of Minneapolis, I had a slightly longer reach than the typical beat cop, but that jurisdiction certainly didn't stretch all the way to Embarrass.

"It was a sloppy shot," David said, "not a kill shot. He bled out over time instead of it being a clean kill."

"So not premeditated," I guessed.

If the intruder had broken in for the primary purpose of killing the former mayor, it probably would have been a shot to the back of the head—execution style. Reliable. Efficient.

Unexpectedly, the memory of a pair of dark, piercing eyes floated in my thoughts. I set down my sandwich and attempted to swallow the bile that threatened to climb up my throat. I should have made Amir turn around so I didn't have to see the look in his eyes when I finally pulled the trigger. I should have had Pensacola do it instead of me. But I'd never killed anyone before—how could I have known how unshakable that moment would be?

David continued to talk about the case and hadn't noticed any change on my part. I was adept at hiding my mini-PTSD attacks from most people, but Addams had always been a little thick.

"So definitely not self-inflicted?" I asked past the rising panic.

David shook his head. "Wrong entry angle, distance, blood spatter, all that. Plus, no weapon was found. You're not gonna be able to hide a gun when you've just shot yourself and you're bleeding out of your stomach. The blood spatter would have been like a treasure map to the hiding spot."

"Any suspects?" I pressed.

"If not for the gun, I would have said some punk ass teenagers trying to show off—like when they steal Chief Hart's lawn gnome. We did a thorough search of the home and surrounding property, but more than likely the perp kept the gun just long enough to toss it into the first body of water he found."

Minneapolis was known as the Land of 10,000 Lakes. The

state actually had about 12,000 lakes over 10 acres in size, but that slogan didn't quite have the same poetry to it.

A missing murder weapon made the crime exponentially harder to solve. We'd gotten lucky in the Kennedy Petersik case that the gun had been discovered in the car with her—because she'd committed suicide. We'd gotten even luckier that the National Tracing Center in Martinsburg, Virginia had been able to match the weapon's serial number with a registration, although in hindsight, connecting the gun to Landon Tauer's father had thrown us off the right trail for some time.

"Have you contacted any neighboring departments? Maybe it's bigger than the Mayor's house," I posed. "Maybe there's been a string of home burglaries in the area."

David stroked his square jaw. "That's a good idea, Miller. I hope you don't mind me suggesting that to the BCA agent and pretending the idea was mine."

A good-natured chuckle escaped my lips. "I wouldn't expect anything else."

~

My cellphone rang on my walk back to Julia's car. I hoped it might be her calling, telling me she'd finished her errands for the day, but a different name flashed across the screen. In the not-so-distant past, it was a name that had unearthed unsettling memories. I tended to ignore his calls; I would send them straight to voicemail. But now our relationship was healthier, more stable, largely because I'd stopped trying to run from the nightmares and had asked for help dealing with my PTSD.

Instead of rejecting the call, I pressed the green button and I brought the phone to my ear. "Terrance Pensacola: how the hell are you?"

"Hey, Miller," he returned the greeting. "What are you guys doing tonight? We're in your neck of the woods. Do you and your lady want to grab dinner with Claire and me?"

"Damn, I wish we could," I said in earnest. "But we're up north right now."

I felt fairly confident that Julia wouldn't mind me sharing with Pense the reason for our trip, but it still didn't feel like it was my news to share.

"What are you doing in the Twin Cities?" I asked.

"Doctor's appointment. They're fitting me with new legs."

"Those robot ones from the clinical trial?"

"Those are still being tested," he said, "but in the meantime our insurance company is letting me get running blades."

"Shit, man—running blades?" I laughed. "Are you training for the Olympics?"

"Nah, I'm no Oscar Pistorius. But I'll be happy to get out of my chair once in a while. Maybe I'll even be able to push Baby Miller in his stroller instead of Claire having to push us both. Although you should see the pipes on my wife these days," he seemed to brag. "Between carrying around a baby and pushing her husband in a chair, she could beat any Marine in an arm-wrestling competition."

"Even you?" I posed with a smile.

I heard him huff into the phone. "Let's not get carried away."

"So what else is new?" I had reached Julia's parked car and I hadn't expected the phone call, but hearing Pense's distinct drawl was a nice distraction.

"Nothing besides diaper blowouts and projectile vomiting."

"You or Baby Miller?" I teased.

"Why do I even bother to call?" he mock complained. "So much abuse."

"Oh, you love it."

"Hey, this is totally random, but have you kept in touch with Brent Boyer?" Pense asked.

"Brent Boyer," I breathed. "Damn, I haven't heard that name in a while."

When Pensacola and I had first been hospitalized before we were sent back to the States to fully recover, we'd been laid up in a giant triage unit on a base in Afghanistan. Brent Boyer had been in a nearby cot. He and his team had also been ambushed by a dirty bomb; metal fragments had sliced through his gut so badly they'd had to remove half of his internal organs: part of his stomach, his gallbladder, and his pancreas. We had joked at the time that between the three of us, we made up one full Marine. It was the kind of coarse bullshitting that happens to distract yourself from the seriousness of it all. My physical wounds were only minor, but at the time neither Pensacola or Boyer knew how they'd fare.

"To be honest, Pense, you're the only one from that time in my life that I'm still in contact with. And even then, half of the time I don't even wanna talk to you." I tried to keep my tone light and teasing, but the words were terribly true.

Pensacola didn't give me a hard time. "Yeah, I get that."

"Why were you thinking about Boyer?" I asked.

"I don't know. Just talking about people from the old days. Claire has me going to group therapy at the VA."

"Are you having nightmares?" I worried. "Flashbacks?"

"No, nothing like that. She thinks I don't have enough friends."

I couldn't help my laugh. I covered my mouth with my hand to muffle the obvious sound. "Shit. I'm sorry, man. But just wait until some of those grizzled vets show up at your next backyard barbeque," I chuckled. "Claire might regret her decision."

Pensacola sighed. "What we do for love, am I right?"

"I didn't think it possible, but you're getting more whipped as the days go by," I teased.

"Go to hell, Miller," Pense laughed. "Like Julia doesn't have you wrapped around her little finger. Besides, I'm all contemplative and thoughtful these days. Parenthood changes a person—you'll see."

"*I'll see?*" I repeated. My voice sounded like a squeak.

"Sure. Why not?"

"You might not be an anatomy major, but there's something biologically missing from the equation if Julia and I ever wanted kids."

"Bullshit," Pense called me out. "If I can walk with robot legs, you can have kids."

"I, uh, it was really nice hearing from you, but I've got to get going," I deflected. "Let me know next time you're in town. We'd love to see you guys."

"Will do," Pense approved. "Give Julia a kiss from me."

"Only if you kiss Claire for me," I playfully countered.

Pense laughed. "Okay, forget I said anything."

Chapter Five

I took my time driving back to Julia's house. She hadn't texted me with any updates on when she anticipated being home, but she had warned me that it might be another long day. There were so many details to finalize; her father's wake was the following morning and the funeral would be the next day. The more efficient and productive Julia was, the sooner we could go back to the Twin Cities.

I was mindful, however, to enjoy the unexpected break from work. I wasn't on vacation, but it was nice to be able to escape the basement of the Fourth Precinct for a few days. As a beat cop I'd spent the majority of my days behind the wheel of a patrol car. I was at the mercy of dispatch and my in-car radio, but when I wasn't responding to calls, I could move about my assigned territory freely. Sitting behind a metal desk all day was still something I was getting used to.

When I reached Julia's house, I turned into the long driveway, but stopped the car short of where she typically parked. Another vehicle was in the driveway—one I didn't recognize. A short-haired woman stood on Julia's front stoop. I got out of the car and shut the driver's side door with extra energy. The sound of the slamming car door caused the woman on the concrete steps to jump.

I squinted into the afternoon sun. "Grace Kelly?" I hadn't recognized my friend from a distance. "What are you doing out here?"

My friend held up a flower-patterned casserole dish. "I brought lasagna. It's frozen, but when you're ready to eat it, just pop it into the oven at 350 degrees for 45 minutes."

I was struck by the kind gesture. "Wow. Thank you. That's really thoughtful."

I didn't bother asking how she knew we were in town or that we were staying at Julia's house. As Grace herself had once told me, secrets didn't stay secrets for very long in a place like Embarrass.

"Do you want to come in?" I offered.

Grace looked unprepared for the invitation, like she'd been expecting to ding-dong-ditch the hot dish and scamper away.

"Oh! Uh, sure! If I'm not imposing."

"Julia's in town running errands and making funeral preparations," I explained, unlocking the front door. "I'd love the company."

Grace followed me inside and waited, frozen casserole dish in hand, while I shut the door. She lifted her head and looked around the generous foyer. "Gosh, I've actually never been inside this house before. It's massive."

The comment was a surprise at first until I remembered that Julia had only been living in the house since Jonathan's death. If Grace had ever been to a birthday party in elementary school it would have been at the home of William and Olivia Desjardin, not the country estate that had once belonged to Julia's grandparents.

"Do you want the grand tour?" I offered, half joking.

Grace seemed to remember the purpose of her visit and shrank back in embarrassment. "Sorry. Investigative instincts are hard to shut off sometimes."

I nodded in understanding. As a police officer and former military, I was the same way. I'd always found it difficult to turn off being a cop and just enjoy being a civilian. My eyes were always scanning my surroundings, on the lookout for something or someone suspicious. Even walking by an illegally parked vehicle made my skin itch.

"Can I get you something to drink?" I offered. "There's not much in the refrigerator, but there's water in the tap."

"Water would be great," Grace smiled.

She followed me, casserole in tow, to the kitchen at the back of the house. If the size of the rooms or the furnishings continued to impress, she'd successfully dampened her wonderment. Nothing could prepare her for the kitchen, however.

She stood in the threshold, eyes wide and mouth agape. "This is bigger than my entire apartment."

"It's a little excessive, right?" I chuckled.

Grace shook her head emphatically. "It's perfect. I'm never leaving."

I pulled two glasses from a cabinet and filled them with water from the faucet. "I'll relay your approval to Julia. She loves this kitchen."

Grace settled onto a stool at the oversized island. "How is she doing?" she asked.

I sighed. "That's a good question."

I trusted Grace not to run off and publish a front page story about all of this, but it also wasn't my place to be telling anyone Julia's business. She was a fiercely private person.

"She's holding up, all things considered. Right now she's busy with all the details, so I don't think she's had a real opportunity to process yet."

Grace nodded sagely.

"So, what's the town gossip saying about the Mayor's death?" I asked.

Grace Kelly visibly blushed. "Oh, I don't know about that."

I quirked a skeptical eyebrow.

"Oh, okay," she quickly caved. I couldn't tell if her hesitancy had been authentic or just for show. "No one seems particularly torn up about it. People are naturally worried about our little idyllic town not being as safe as it once was, but as far as Mayor Desjardin being dead?" She winced with the weight of her next words. "There's not a lot of upset people. Life goes on, as they say."

Her words seemed to validate my earlier conversation with David.

"I saw David Addams today. He said the Mayor's house had been vandalized over the last few months."

"Bored teenagers," Grace guessed. "I don't think anyone had a real vendetta against the man, especially once he returned all that money. But," she sighed, "I doubt people will be lining up to give his eulogy."

"Are you coming to the funeral?"

Grace seemed to hesitate. "Should I? Am I supposed to?"

"I mean, if you're busy or have to work, I totally understand. But it would mean a lot to me—and Julia," I was mindful to add.

"I was honestly kind of surprised that there would be a public wake or funeral at all," Grace admitted.

"Because Julia and her dad were fighting?" I questioned.

"That," Grace agreed. "But the family—they're so ... so private. Even though Mr. Desjardin was the mayor, he wasn't a very open or welcoming man."

"The apple doesn't fall far from the tree," I frowned.

"I didn't mean that as a slam against Julia," Grace quickly clarified. "I just don't think many people were allowed into their inner circle. And when Jonathan died, their circle got even smaller and harder to penetrate."

"If people didn't like the mayor, how come he kept getting elected?" I wondered.

"He wasn't *disliked*. He just wasn't, like, people's favorite person. But he was good at his job. I suppose if it's not broken, why fix it?" Grace frowned and shook her dead. "I shouldn't be speaking ill of the dead."

"I don't think you are," I defended my friend from herself. "You're being straightforward and real. And from what very little I knew about the Mayor, I feel like he would have appreciated that."

Grace blew out a deep breath that ruffled the bangs of her pixie cut. "Just don't be asking me to speak at the funeral."

"So that means you're coming?" I asked. My voice lilted hopefully.

Grace made a face. "Fine. Yes. I'll be there."

I hadn't realized until then how important it would be to me that my friend show up. "You're such a selfless person, Grace," I admired. "No wonder Rich adores you."

Grace Kelly's pale cheeks darkened. "The L-word has yet to be exchanged."

"Are you kidding me?" I exclaimed. "What are you guys waiting for?"

Grace's blush deepened even more. "It's all on me. I can tell he's ready, but I've actually never said 'I love you' before. To family members, sure. But not to someone I was dating."

My jaw hung open. Grace Kelly Donovan was the sweetest, bubbliest, and most optimistic person I'd ever met. I would have thought she said "I love you" as often as saying her name.

"But do you?" I asked. "Love him? I mean, it's totally fine if you don't. He's one of my best friends, but he's also a chauvinistic, cocky prick sometimes."

"I ... maybe. Probably," Grace conceded. "I don't know what I'm waiting for." She sighed into her hands. "I'm like a girl waiting until prom night to have sex for the first time because it's supposed to be special and perfect. But the first time is never special or perfect, so I don't know what my hang up is."

I cocked my head to the side. "Wait. You're not a virgin, are you?"

Grace gasped and slapped my shoulder. "No! I'm not *that* bad."

"Just a Love Virgin," I grinned.

"Don't tell Rich," Grace pled. "He doesn't know I've never said it before. I don't want him to think I'm some frigid weirdo."

"You're not weird," I told her. "Everyone has their own timetable for these kinds of things."

"What about you and Julia?"

I took a quick drink of my water. "What about us?" I asked, playing dumb.

"Have you two exchanged the L-word?"

"Only on DVD."

Grace blinked once. "What?"

"Nothing," I dismissed. "It was a dumb lesbian joke."

I took the moment to drink the rest of the water in my glass. I felt Grace's eager eyes on me. It was obvious I wasn't going to be able to dodge her question forever.

It was old news, but confiding in a female friend was new territory to me. I'd never been in a meaningful romantic relationship before, but I'd also never really had close female friends growing up. Sleepover parties, makeovers, and gossiping about crushes had never been my scene.

I licked my lips. "We've said the L-word to each other."

I didn't reveal anything else. Grace probably knew we lived together, but I wasn't comfortable sharing that I'd also kind of casually proposed marriage, too. It had felt right at the moment, but now the memory was embarrassing.

Predictably, my admission caused Grace to squeal and clap her hands. "Oh, I'm so happy for you two!"

"Thanks, Grace." I found myself smiling at her enthusiasm. "We're pretty damn happy about it, too."

~

I was reading an old magazine in the front den when Julia returned later that night. I heard the key in the front door and her heels on the marble in the foyer. I didn't immediately rush to the front door like an anxious puppy even though I was excited she was finally home.

"Cassidy?"

"In here."

Julia stepped into the den and leaned against the doorframe. "This looks cozy," she observed with a smile. "I'm glad you've made yourself at home."

I'd changed into sweatpants and a long-sleeved t-shirt after Grace Kelly had left. I'd also made a fire in the wood-burning fireplace in the den and had helped myself to some of Julia's bourbon.

I didn't allow her comment to make me feel self-conscious or like I'd overstepped boundaries. I'd cleaned this house from top to bottom; I deserved to get cozy.

I patted at the empty couch cushion next to me. "Why don't you get cozy, too?" I suggested.

Julia joined me on the couch. She sat with her back against the arm of the couch with her feet on my lap. I handed her my drink and she took a generous sip before closing her eyes.

"How was today?" I asked. I pulled down the zippers of her ankle boots and tossed the shoes to the ground. I pressed my thumbs into the arches of her feet.

Julia made a quiet approving sound at my touch. "It was a good day. A little faith about my father was restored."

I arched a curious eyebrow. "Oh yeah?"

"I went to the bank to take care of my father's finances, but I also looked in on my mother's—and all of her money was still there."

My brow furrowed. "Did you not expect it to be?"

Julia raised her shoulders and let them fall. "Honestly? No," she admitted. "When my father was granted custody of my mother instead of me, he also gained control of her assets. Her bank accounts. Stock portfolios. Real estate. Everything. I've heard horror stories of people whose family members steal or spend all of their money once they've been assigned guardianship. I really worried he might rob her blind like he tried to do with the city. But it was all there. He didn't touch any of it." She ran a hand through her hair. "Honestly, I might have been dreading this day more than having to tell my mother that he was dead."

"Wow. Really?"

"I may not have been close with my father anymore, but I never thought him purposefully malicious. Greedy, yes. Selfish, of course," she admitted. "But not truly evil. It's a small thing, maybe, but the fact that he left her money intact ..." She trailed off. "Maybe he still loved her."

It was a unique way of assessing the situation. My smile felt crooked on my face. "I'm glad that you're glad," I said in earnest.

Julia shut her eyes and shook her head. "Anyway. Sorry. How was your day?"

"I had lunch with David Addams."

"And how is Cowboy doing?" she asked with a smile.

Her attention shifted from me to the back of the house when the oven timer went off in the kitchen. The chime was subdued, but persistent.

Julia tilted her head. "Did you make dinner?"

"I *heated up* dinner," I clarified.

Julia stood from the couch in one fluid motion. I would have been content to remain on the couch, massaging her feet, but I didn't want Grace's hard work to go to waste by burning the lasagna. I also didn't want my attempt at cooking dinner to burn down Julia's house.

I followed Julia to the back of the house. She shut off the oven timer and peered through the illuminated window. "This doesn't look like a microwave dinner. Where did the lasagna come from?"

I didn't take offense to her assumption that I hadn't been the meal's *chef de cuisine*. She knew better. My culinary prowess had expanded in our time together, but this was still above my abilities.

"Grace Kelly dropped it off."

"Busybodies," Julia reflexively mumbled.

I arched an eyebrow in my girlfriend's direction.

Julia immediately dropped her head. "I'm sorry. That was unkind of me. This place. It's poison." She made a frustrated sigh. "I can already feel myself reverting. De-evolving. Becoming Julia B.C."

"B.C.?" I questioned.

"Before Cassidy."

Even though she looked so despondent, I couldn't help the grin that sprawled across my face. "I love that. You should use it more often."

"Don't get a big head, Miss Miller," Julia sternly chastised. "You've improved my disposition somewhat, but nothing says it's permanent."

I batted my eyelashes. "Then I guess I'd better stick around to make sure you don't revert to Old Julia."

Julia snorted. "Old. Flattering."

"You know what I mean."

After a dinner of Grace Kelly's lasagna and a quick garden salad we tossed together, Julia and I spent the rest of the evening watching movies in her den on her laptop. Next to the kitchen, the formal, yet cozy space was quickly becoming my favorite place in the house. Even though her father's wake was the next day, it was a nice, ordinary evening, and I was thankful for the opportunity to bring some normality to the situation.

It was still relatively early when we made the trip upstairs to go to bed, but the sky was already dark. I laid in the king-sized bed, feeling Julia's body heat radiate beside me. Absent the noxious city sounds of traffic or emergency sirens, I concentrated on the wind and the rustle of dead leaves.

Julia's voice cut through the night. "I can't sleep."

I'd been close to falling asleep myself—one of the rare occasions since we'd arrived in Embarrass that I didn't find myself tossing and turning—but Julia's late-night proclamation pulled me back to consciousness.

"What's wrong?" I asked.

"My brain is going a hundred miles an hour," she complained. "I can't get it to shut off."

I rolled onto my side to face her. "Do you want to talk about it?"

She reached across the mattress and toyed with the v-neck cut of my t-shirt. "I'd rather you took my mind off of it."

I allowed myself a quiet chuckle. "I think I can do that."

I shifted closer on the mattress. Underneath the sheets, blankets, and duvet, I rested my hand on her hip. Another nightgown I'd never seen before had made its debut that night. I ran my palm across the thin silk material. My hand traveled to the bottom hem of the nightgown and I inched the garment up her thighs. I continued to blindly explore until I no longer felt silk—only skin.

I arched an eyebrow. "No underwear?"

She shrugged with nonchalance.

I pulled the heavy covers back to expose her body. I didn't worry about her becoming cold without the bedsheets; I had every intention of keeping her warm.

I took my time to just feel her body. I stroked my hands along her slight curves, enjoying the sensation of her expensive night-gown beneath my hands. Her body was lean and femininely muscled from a regimented diet of barre and spin classes. She enjoyed my gentle and tender touch. Her eyes fluttered shut and her body swayed, rising and falling slightly to meet my hands.

Her nipples had become hard beneath the sheer nightgown. The room was only illuminated by the moon and the stars, but I could still see their distinct profile. I dropped kisses on her exposed collarbone before tonguing the hardened buds through the silk shift. I sucked on her breasts through the refined material. I had no idea if you were supposed to get silk wet, but Julia voiced no complaints. Quiet sounds vibrated in her throat and encouraging fingers twisted the curls at the nape of my neck.

I held her hips as I worked my way down her tantalizing figure. I pressed firm kisses to her abdomen, to the space above her bellybutton, and lower still. I inched the nightgown up her smooth thighs to expose her naked sex. I settled on my stomach between her legs and hooked my arms beneath the backside of her knees.

I pressed more deliberate, soft kisses to her inner thighs. I looked to her face in between each flutter of my mouth and touch of my tongue. Julia's eyes were open. She watched me with intense anticipation. She'd trapped her lower lip beneath her top row of teeth. Her noises were restrained even though there was no one for miles. It was habit though; we shared common walls in St. Paul, and Julia tried to be a considerate neighbor.

I nipped at the tender flesh of her upper thighs. The change in pressure and intensity pulled more muted noises from Julia. I positioned my fingers on either side of her pussy lips and spread her apart. I ran my tongue the length of her hairless slit. I continued my penetrating eye contact, which seemed to make Julia whimper and squirm even more. I flicked the tip of my tongue against her clit with a light yet rapid touch. Her upper thighs twitched around my ears and her fingers sank more deeply into my curls.

I sucked her clit into my mouth and hummed. I drew myself up on my knees for better leverage and slid my fingers up and down her weeping slit. I collected her arousal on my fingertips and spread her juices around. I pressed the tips of two fingers against her opening and slid inside to the first knuckle. I continued to suckle her clit while I gave her a moment to adjust to my fingers.

Julia whimpered when I pressed forward another inch. No matter how many times we were intimate like this, I would never get used to the delicious way she stretched around my fingers. I rolled my tongue across her hooded clit.

I heard Julia sigh above me. "I don't think it's going to work. Not tonight."

I pulled away from her addictive sex, but only slightly. "What do you need? What do you want me to do?"

"I'm sorry, darling," she sighed again. She lovingly stroked her fingers through my chaotic hair. "Everything you're doing feels good, but my brain is getting in the way."

I licked my lips, still tasting her on them. I wasn't ready to throw in the towel or wave the white flag just yet. "I guess it's time to call for backup."

"Backup?" she echoed.

"I've only got two hands," I noted. "If your brain is so busy, we might need a little more assistance tonight."

Julia's tone took on a hint of impatience. "Whatever are you talking about?"

I sat up on my knees. "Give me your hands."

Julia looked skeptical, but she presented me with both hands, palms up.

I took control of her left hand first. I slid it down the top of her camisole nightgown. "Play with your tits," I said, purposefully being a little crude.

Julia bristled. "I'm not going to—."

"Yes, you are," I said more sternly. "You're going to pinch and pull on your nipples, and you're not going to stop until I give you permission. Is that understood?"

I heard her sharp intake of air. "Fine."

I licked my lips. I hadn't topped Julia in some time. She usually reserved those moments when she needed to be fucked to forget or to distract her from something. It wasn't the most healthy coping mechanism, but who was I to judge?

"You can begin," I told her.

Julia hesitated only momentarily before I saw her hand moving beneath the fabric of her pajamas. I would have preferred her entirely naked, but there was something erotic about the suggestion of what was happening beneath that silk barrier. It forced me to image her long, feminine fingers taking purchase of a hardened nipple and the way her short, manicured nails might scratch across the sensitive bud.

I wasn't done just yet though; she had another idle hand.

I dipped my head briefly to her core and placed wet, sloppy kisses to her pussy. I flattened my tongue and ran the length of her slit. I swirled my tongue around her clit to make sure she was ready.

I wordlessly reached up to her. Without having to be told, she knew what I wanted. I took her right hand in mine and drew it between her thighs. She let me manipulate her fingers so her middle and forefinger pointed to her sex. I flicked my eyes to her upper body to be sure she hadn't forgotten her other assignment; if anything, her left hand only moved more vigorously beneath the top of her nightgown.

I pressed Julia's fingertips against her wet and ready opening and pushed. I worked the muscles in my throat as I watched the tips of her fingers disappear. I involuntarily clenched my thighs together at the erotic sight. She hadn't touched me, but it didn't matter; there was a high probability that I would cum just from watching her get off.

I grabbed onto Julia's forearm and thrust upward, forcing her barely-embedded fingers to penetrate her deeper.

"Jesus," she growled.

I guided her right hand with my own until she took over the task without my encouragement. I pressed my tongue hard against her clit while she worked her fingers in and out of her sex. Satisfied she wouldn't stop, I leaned back to admire the view.

I wasn't a casual viewer for long; Julia yanked on my shoulder, and I allowed her to pull me in for a deep kiss. She moaned into my open mouth as I stroked my tongue—coated in her cum—against her own.

Her left hand—the hand that had been mauling her covered breasts—worked its way between my own thighs. She shoved her hand beneath the elastic band of my sweatpants and she forced her fingers between my thighs. I, similarly, hadn't been wearing underwear, and the evidence of my arousal had collected on my inner thighs. Normally, Julia would have taunted me to discover me so wet and aching for her, but she only groaned.

"Come here." Her voice flirted with desperation.

There was little I could do to get closer to her, but she found a way. She slid one finger and then two into my eager sex.

"Oh shit," I moaned.

Julia simultaneously fingered herself along with me. The movements of her hands were erratic, frenzied, and lacking in her usual elegance. But it didn't matter.

"Julia!" I gasped. I clung to her flexing bicep.

Her eyes narrowed in determination. I couldn't tell if she was more focused on getting me or herself off, but both results seemed inevitable.

I grabbed her face in both hands and crushed our mouths together. We swallowed each other's noises as formerly subdued noises turned into ragged, desperate cries.

"Cum for me," she pled.

Her mouth dropped to my shoulder and she bit me through my t-shirt. A strangled cry tumbled past my lips, torn between the shock of pain in my shoulder and the mounting pleasure tightening my core. The night was supposed to be about her, but I'd somehow gotten distracted. Her thumb swiping at my clit and her deep, unrelenting fingers might have had something to do with it.

I rolled my hips and met her rhythmic thrusts. "There, right there," I encouraged her.

I was momentarily taken aback when I realized her right arm was wrapped around my torso and her right hand was stabilizing my back. She'd abandoned her orgasm for my own.

"That's not ..." I panted. "That's not the plan."

"Fuck your plan," she rumbled.

She leaned forward and the momentum had me toppling onto my back. Her fingers remained inside me. She tugged my sweatpants down my thighs, but not completely off. She worked her hand up the front of my t-shirt and she pinched my nipples. Everything I had instructed she do to herself, she now did to me.

"That's-that's not fair," I weakly protested.

A smug smile appeared on her lips. "You've successfully distracted me, darling. Well done. Now let me finish the job."

I closed my eyes only to feel a warm mouth cover my clit. Julia lashed her talented tongue against the jumbled nerves, and I screamed. Julia had been too distracted for an orgasm, but I didn't suffer the same problem. I felt it first between my thighs—a warm, intense pulse. The feeling expanded like a pebble disturbing a puddle as the orgasm rippled through the rest of my body.

Julia suckled my clit until the attention became too much.

I flexed my toes; I could feel the aftershocks in every extremity. "Not fair," I feebly mumbled.

Julia pulled the covers up to blanket us both. She snuggled close and nuzzled her head between my shoulder and my neck. "Deal with it."

Chapter Six

Afghanistan, 2012

I should be sleeping. I'll need my energy when the sun has set and it's time to resume dragging Pensacola behind me on his makeshift sled. I should be sleeping, but instead I'm trying to figure out if the small dustup I see in the distance is an incoming sandstorm or a vehicle.

Either way, we could be in trouble.

I continue to squint into the distance while simultaneously trying to remain hidden. Pensacola's sled doubles as a makeshift tent to keep us out of view during the day and helps to shield us from the worst of the sun's unforgiving heat. The dust cloud gets bigger and closer over time, but it appears contained instead of expanding to a thick wall of wind-guided sand.

My gut says it's an oncoming vehicle, but there's no way to know if it's friend or foe from this distance.

The vehicle slows on the side of the road, and my body tightens with worry that we've been spotted. I try to flatten myself even more against the cracked, arid ground. I self-consciously touch the Beretta M9 at my hip and the seven-inch Ka-Bar knife I keep sheathed on my belt.

The sand-colored Jeep comes to a full stop about 50 meters away and two figures hop out of the vehicle. Both individuals wear long white robes and head coverings that stand in contrast to their deeply tanned skin and full, dark beards. Some make of assault rifle is slung across each man's chest.

The two men exchange a few muffled words before they separate, one standing in front of the parked vehicle and the other to the rear. It takes me a second to realize why they've stopped.

They're pissing on the side of the road.

With no elevated topography or physical structures between us—just miles and miles of flat, dusty earth—their voices carry as if they were standing next to us. The men don't speak Farsi, one of Afghanistan's official languages, and the one with which I have the most experience. I still recognize a few words in their conversation, but it only deepens my apprehension.

"Pashto," I mumble to myself. The two languages share the same alphabet and some of the same words. But they're definitely not NATO friendlies.

"Give me my gun." Pensacola's rough voice surprises me. He should be sleeping, too.

In addition to my Beretta, we'd decided to bring along an M16 on our makeshift caravan. We left behind an arsenal of weapons at the safe house, but most had been damaged during the explosion, plus the guns are heavy and would have only added to my burden.

The M16 is Pensacola's. It's a familiar weapon and was also the gun most likely to still work, but neither of us knows for certain. Hell, it might shoot crooked for all we know.

"Miller. The gun," he rasps.

"They don't know we're out here," I quietly protest, not

wanting to draw attention to our location. "Just wait for them to leave."

"They have a vehicle. This is our best chance at survival."

"Stop talking," I hiss. "They'll hear you."

"They're gonna hear my gun in a second. Now, give it to me before it's too late."

My brain floods with doubt. What if he misses? On a good day, the M16 is accurate, but it's not a sniper rifle that's intended to cleanly pick off two bodies at this distance. If they're not immediate kill shots, we're as good as dead. We're sitting ducks. Was it worth the risk?

I stare at Pensacola to gauge his level of confidence. I expect to see wild desperation in his surprisingly blue eyes, but I only see dogged determination.

My limbs feel stiff as I gingerly reach around to detach the M16 from my torso.

"Roll me onto my stomach," Pense grimly instructs.

I help him move with as much speed as we dare. This bathroom break isn't going to last forever, and if they zip up before Pensacola can get into position, we'll have wasted the opportunity to take their vehicle.

From his stomach, Pense aims his weapon and exhales.

My heart is lodged in my throat. I don't want to look, but I also can't pull my eyes away.

Pop, pop, pop.

One figure drops on the sandy terrain. His body falls straight down like a heavy sack of potatoes.

Pop, pop, pop.

The second figure is still standing.

"Fuck," I hear Pensacola lamely grumble.

The cheerless, formal tone of the mansion's doorbell echoed through the house.

"Oh no," I heard Julia's quiet complaint.

"What is it?" I mumbled. Half of my brain was still in a ditch by the side of an Afghan road.

Julia exhaled. "I forgot to tell you—Reggie called me yesterday to see if he could stay here until after the funeral. Embarrass doesn't exactly have any motels, except for those religious nuts who run the bed and breakfast off the highway."

"Reggie's here?" My brain and my tongue were disconnected.

The mattress moved beneath me, and I felt the press of Julia's lips against my sweaty temple. "Come down when you're ready."

I heard the creak of wooden floorboards and the quiet tread of Julia's bare feet. My eyes opened just in time to see her pull on a robe and exit the room.

I rolled onto my back and shut my eyes. My eyelids felt heavy, and the bedsheets were tangled around my limbs after another restless night. I hadn't been sleeping well since our arrival to Embarrass. The quiet of Julia's rural mansion provided too much room for my memories from war to stretch their metaphorical legs.

I would have preferred to hide out upstairs for the rest of the day or at least until the noises coming from downstairs had silenced, but I would have to face the music—or rather, Julia's cousin—eventually. My fatigue was swiftly replaced with a nervous knot in the pit of my stomach. Despite my twenty-eight years, I hadn't really had a proper significant other. As an adult, I'd never been introduced to someone's family as their girlfriend. I couldn't think of a more high-pressure situation than this—the morning of Julia's father's wake—for my first time.

I ran a brush through my sleep-chaotic hair and put on a bra beneath my t-shirt. My feet were noisy on the grand staircase as I descended. I jerked to a stop at the bottom step when I observed a stack of suitcases of various sizes and colors crowding the entry-way. Did Reggie think he was permanently moving in? My confusion deepened when a blond-haired child no older than four or five years old nearly collided into my legs.

"Careful!" I yelped in surprise.

The boy looked up at me and offered a dimpled grin.

"And who might you be?" I asked.

"We're playing tag!" he squeaked, not answering my question. "You're It!"

The boy slapped his hand against my thigh and scampered away in the opposite direction where he was joined by another blond-haired child. The two raced around a small, raised table in Julia's grand foyer. My body reflexively seized, not only at the sight of unexpected children, but at the recognition than an expensive-looking vase rested unsteadily on top of the table. One of the boys bumped into the lacquered table. The vase wobbled on its base, but didn't fall over.

The little boy and his equally youthful playmate squealed loudly before racing off in the direction of the kitchen. My body moved after them, protectively, following the sound of their laughter and small, frenzied feet.

"Holden!" I heard a female voice yell. "No running in the house!"

The stranger's voice was followed by a second unfamiliar voice, also female. "Boys! Take it outside!"

I heard the distinct sound of the kitchen sliding door opening and slamming closed.

What the hell was going on?

When I finally entered the kitchen, I was unprepared for the explosion of sights and sounds. A gaggle of strangers had flooded the back kitchen. I scanned their unfamiliar faces. Was this a home invasion?

I stood in the doorway and cleared my throat. "Uh, morning?"

Julia, miraculously, appeared in the crowd. "There you are." She separated herself from the throng and swept close to my elbow. "Everyone, this is my partner, Cassidy," she introduced above the chaos. "Cassidy, this is everyone."

She proceeded to provide names for all the strangers in the room, all of whom were aunts and cousins and cousins' children. William Desjardin had been the eldest of four siblings—his three younger sisters had the same pale blue eyes and blonde-turning-silver hair as their brother. When I'd first met Julia's father in his capacity as the city's major it had struck me how dissimilar he and Julia looked.

The kitchen was crowded, but I only recognized Julia's cousin, Reggie. When our eyes met during Julia's introductions, his dark features showed no recognition. To be fair, he had never met me before. I'd only scowled at him from afar at Embarrass' annual Summer Solstice festival when my heart had been twisting in my chest when I spotted Julia hanging off his arm. It had been an unwarranted jealousy, however, and Julia had later cleared up that the dark and handsome man was her cousin and not my competition. Reggie and Julia's dark heads made them stand out from the other Nordic-featured family members. I wondered if that had made them so close.

When the introductions came to a close, a dozen set of expectant eyes continued to train on me. "Uh, nice to meet you all. I hope there's not a pop quiz later on everyone's name," I tried to joke. "Julia, can I see you for a second?"

Julia's bright smile never faltered. She looked maddeningly calm despite the unexpected situation. My girlfriend had a special talent for appearing unflappable. "Of course."

I stalked out of the kitchen and only stopped when I believed we were out of earshot from the others. "I thought you said *Reggie* would be staying with us," I hissed.

"I only extended the invitation to him," she told me, frowning. "But he apparently made the mistake of mentioning he was staying with me, and the rest of the family invited themselves."

"So they're all staying."

"I can't just turn them away, Cassidy," she reasoned. "Where would they go?"

"You introduced me as your partner."

"And?" Julia started to look impatient with our conversation.

"You're a lawyer. They might just think we work together."

There was no way anyone would ever mistake me for being a lawyer, but that was beside the point.

Julia pressed her lips together. "Would you like me to re-introduce you to my family? What would be your preferred moniker? Girlfriend? They might just think you're a friend who's a girl," she pointed out. "How about significant other? Or, perhaps you'd prefer I referred to you as the woman who gives me multiple screaming orgasms? Tell me—what's going to make you happy?"

The longer she spoke, the more embarrassed I became. I could feel my cheeks redden and my gaze sank lower into the floor.

I looked up when I felt her fingers curl around my wrist.

"These people don't matter, Cassidy," she said softly. "They're family, yes. But that's just a category. Believe that everyone who is important to me knows exactly who you are and how much you mean to me."

The soliloquy was exactly the kind of thing I wanted to hear, but my stubborn refusal to let things go and to be happy caused the next idiotic words to bubble up my throat: "What about your mom?"

The fingers that had reassuringly circled my wrist loosened.

The sincere intensity on Julia's features shifted to a sadness that I never wanted to see on her face.

"Cassidy."

The singular way in which she uttered my name held all the explanations I'd ever need. The timing was wrong. Her mother was sick. She was already dealing with the death of her husband and being removed from her home. Too many things were changing all at once. And even if she did introduce me to her mom, there was no guarantee that she'd ever remember me.

I sighed, and with the breath, I tried to release my own frustrations and disappointment. "I know," I conceded.

~

A few hours later, I stood in a corner of the Embarrass funeral home, slowly destroying an empty Styrofoam coffee cup. I dug my short nails into the pliable, non-biodegradable material, branding small crescent moon shapes into the exterior of the cup. My heels sunk into an avocado-colored plush rug as I shifted my weight from one foot to the other. I wished I'd worn more comfortable shoes. They were only kitten heels, nothing compared to the spiked stilettos that Julia routinely wore, but my feet were better suited to black combat boots.

The walls of the funeral home were covered in faux wooden paneling that probably hadn't been updated since the 1970s. Framed pictures of various Christian-themed motifs hung from the walls. Watercolors of Jesus carrying a sheep and of winged angels watching oblivious children play reminded me of Sunday school in the church basement growing up.

The furniture in the room was stiff and unwelcoming. Rows of metal folding chairs faced the closed casket, which had been positioned against one wall. Other, more permanent furniture, lined

the perimeter of the room. The muted colors of the velvet-uphol-
stered chairs were supposed to be comforting, but it only
reminded me of dust and death. People spoke in hushed tones,
filling the room with white noise. The air smelled musty; it made
me itch. I wanted to open all of the windows, to force fresh air and
some vibrancy into the room. But I remained rooted in place
instead.

Julia stood by herself next to the raised wooden casket. The
coffin was stained a pale color, the only lightness in the dark,
somber room. She'd made the decision to have a closed casket. Her
father had been shot in the stomach, so presumably his face would
have been unmarked by the violence of his death, but I knew she
worried about how her mother might react to the very visible
evidence that William Desjardin was dead.

Her mother sat in a folding chair close to the casket. The few
visitors who had showed up to pay their respects tended to greet
Julia first, despite her infamy, before moving on to Olivia. In a
small town like Embarrass, I wouldn't have been surprised if even
people who'd never formally met the Desjardins knew of Olivia's
deteriorating condition. Her dementia wasn't necessarily a family
secret, yet it also wasn't something spoken about openly.

Olivia's nurse sat in another folding chair, not far away. Joy
wore black pants and a dark blazer instead of her usual salmon-
colored scrubs. I didn't know if she was there in an official capacity
or if she was simply there to support the woman whom she'd cared
for over the past several years. Regardless of the reason for her
presence, I was sure it helped put Julia more at ease.

I had hoped to see a familiar face or two at the wake, but
everyone I knew in Embarrass had apparently decided to keep
their distance from the former Mayor's wake. Grace had promised
she'd attend the funeral, but apparently that offer didn't extend to
the wake as well. William Desjardin may have evaded prosecution

from a criminal court, but he had been deemed guilty by the court of public opinion.

When there were no new visitors to greet, Julia alternated between checking on her mother and her aunts. I smiled reassuringly whenever she glanced in my direction to let her know that I was okay on my own—I wasn't, not exactly—but she had enough on her plate without worrying if I was getting bored at her father's wake. I knew I could have tried to strike up a conversation with any of Julia's relatives, but they'd remained closed off and cloistered from the other infrequent visitors throughout the visitation hours. The youngest first and second-cousins had their attention glued to hand-held gaming systems while the aunts and some of the older cousins huddled around the refreshment table.

Julia's generalized introduction of me to her family still sat in my stomach like a heavy stone. Maybe I would have felt more comfortable inserting myself into their family circle if she'd been more forthcoming about our relationship, but even if she had explicitly defined me as her girlfriend, I probably would have still been by myself, sulking in a corner of the room, making myself as small and as unobtrusive as before.

Once the aunts and older cousins had managed to plow through the few refreshments the funeral director had provided—it was a wake after all, not a goddamn buffet—they started to complain about the late hour and hunger pains. Julia gave them her blessing that they go. She and I had been the first ones to arrive, and we would be the last ones to leave.

Alone, without her hawkish family staring at us, Julia melted into my arms. Her body language radiated exhaustion. She'd put on a brave front—a stiff upper lip—with others around, but with me she could let her guard down.

"Are you ready to go?" she asked.

I opened my mouth, but instead of words, a creaky noise came out. I covered my mouth to cough and try again. I hadn't spoken to anyone in several hours.

"Do we need to do anything?" I asked. "Fold up chairs?"

Julia shook her head. "No. The funeral director said that once visitation was over that we could leave."

I couldn't help but glance anxiously in the direction of the closed casket. "We just, uh, we just leave him down here?"

The corner of Julia's mouth twitched. "That's not really him anymore," she stated pragmatically.

Neither of us was very religious, but I knew she was right.

It had felt dark inside of the funeral home, but I hadn't realized that the sun had already set outside while we'd been at the wake. Julia's black Mercedes was the only vehicle left in the small parking lot besides the actual hearse. In the morning, the casket would be loaded into the back of the stretched vehicle and William Desjardin would be buried in the family plot at the Embarrass cemetery.

"The wake was, uh, nice, right?" I said, struggling to make mundane conversation.

"It was uneventful," Julia said, unlocking her car. There was no danger of her car being looted in Embarrass, but the precaution was probably automatic. "And for that I'm thankful."

"Were you expecting big drama?" I honestly didn't know.

"I don't know what I was expecting," she noted, "but I certainly had my fears."

"Like what?"

"The police being there. Nosing around to find his killer."

I frowned, remembering my own attendance at Kennedy Petersik's wake. I hadn't been in uniform, and I hadn't been there in an official capacity—I'd only been accompanying my colleague

Stanley who'd been a friend of the family—but that hadn't kept me from poking around the Petersik's house while they were still actively grieving.

"And no Wendy Clark, thank God," Julia's voice broke into my thoughts. "You might have had to restrain me if she'd been bold enough to show up."

I arched an eyebrow at the admission. "Restrain, eh?"

"I know it takes two to tango," Julia breathed. "I shouldn't place the blame on her for my father's indiscretions. But I quit my job over it. You resigned from yours. I left my hometown. I abandoned my mom."

The final words sounded distressed.

"Hey, it's okay," I hushed. I could sense that the guilt train was about to leave the station. "Everything happens for a reason. It all worked out. And you're here now for your mom."

Julia ran her fingers through her hair. She looked nearly embarrassed by her short outburst. "God, I could use a quiet bath. And an oversized glass of red wine."

"What's stopping you?"

Julia frowned. "My family. They're going to be so bored at the house. I don't have cable. I disconnected the internet. There's not enough food for all of them."

"You're not a hotel, babe." I challenged. "It's not your job to entertain and feed them. Are you worried they'll leave you a bad Yelp review or something?"

My comment drew a small smile from her lips.

"Once we get back to the house, you go straight upstairs and run yourself a bath," I instructed. "Let me take care of your family."

Julia opened her mouth, excuses ready.

"And after I get your family settled," I continued, "I'll be upstairs with your wine."

85

Julia's mouth closed. She drew her lower lip into her mouth and bit down. "Okay."

It was probably painful for her to have conceded so easily. She must have been really exhausted to have not put up more of a fight.

When we returned to the country home, Julia escaped directly upstairs. Her aunts and cousins and cousins' children were scattered around the house, probably raiding the pantry and the liquor cabinet or digging through all of Julia's belongings.

I found Reggie, alone in the formal dining room, reading a paperback novel at the table. I knocked on the open archway to announce my presence. He looked up from the open book and smiled.

"Hey," he greeted.

"Hey," I returned. "If I give you my credit card and a flyer for a local pizza place, can you make sure the relatives get fed tonight?"

"I can do that," he confirmed. "But you don't have to pay, Cassidy. You and Julia have been more than generous with your hospitality."

I rubbed at the back of my neck, uncomfortable with all of the adulting. "It's fine. It's more so Julia doesn't wear herself out trying to please everyone."

Reggie nodded in understanding.

"I think there's boardgames or cards in one of the upstairs guest rooms," I continued, "and there's DVDs in the den if the kids' Gameboys run out of juice."

"I don't think they're called Gameboys anymore," he smiled, showing off deep dimples, "but I'll be sure to relay that information."

Confident that my delegation of tasks to Reggie had been successful, I opened a bottle of cabernet sauvignon that I knew was one of Julia's favorites and grabbed two wine glasses. I silently tiptoed upstairs, careful not to draw attention to myself or to my mission.

The door to the master bedroom was closed. I juggled the open wine bottle and glasses and successfully opened the door without dropping or spilling anything. Julia wasn't in the bedroom, but the clothes she'd worn to the wake were sprawled across the mattress like a disintegrated person.

I knocked quietly on the closed bathroom door.

"Unless that's Cassidy," I heard Julia's voice, "I'm not interested."

I tried the door handle and, finding it unlocked, I entered. The master bathroom in Julia's condo was more upscale and updated, but there was a historic, vintage charm to the checkerboard tile floor, porcelain clawfoot tub, and free-standing pedestal of her bedroom's *en suite* bathroom.

Julia was already in the bathtub. Her eyes were closed and her head was tilted back. She'd rolled up a hand towel as a makeshift pillow between her head and the end of the bathtub. Bath oils had produced a translucent sheen across the top of the elevated water level, obscuring her body from view.

"Reggie is ordering pizza for everyone," I announced, "and I told him where all the games and DVDs are."

"Thank you for taking care of that, darling," she thanked me. She ran a damp hand through her hair. "I didn't realize until I got into the tub how much I didn't want to see them tonight."

"It's no problem," I brushed off. "Operation Distract the Desjardins was a success."

"I'm actually the last of the Desjardins," Julia remarked.

I thought on her statement and realized she was right. William Desjardin was the only male among his sibling group. Unless one of his sisters had decided to keep her maiden when she married, he would have been the only Desjardin from that generation to carry on the family name. Traditionally, Jonathan would have been the next to bear the family name into the next generation. But Julia was the only one left.

"Can I *Pretty Woman* you?" I blurted out.

Julia's eyebrows knit together. "Rescue me from a life of prostitution? Teach me which fork to use at dinner? Refuse to sell me a cocktail dress?"

"No," I huffed. "The bathtub scene. You be Richard Gere, and I'll be Julia Roberts."

"I'm going to pretend you didn't just ask me to be a man."

My description had been ridiculous, which made me feel equally so. "Never mind," I grumbled.

"I'm only teasing, darling," Julia chuckled. "Get in while the water's still warm."

I took the time to pour a generous glass of wine for both Julia and myself. When I delivered Julia hers, she wrapped damp fingers around my wrist.

"Hurry up and strip, soldier," she murmured. "I don't like to be kept waiting."

"Yes, ma'am."

Julia watched me, unblinking, while I undressed. I'd already removed my heels the moment we'd returned to Julia's house. The bottoms of my feet felt sweaty, although it could have been condensation from the cool tile floor and the thick, humid air.

I started with my shirt—a simple black, button-up blouse. I didn't have an expansive wardrobe, but I'd been going to so many funerals and wakes as of late that a portion of my closet was starting to fill up with the somber colors of grief. I unfastened the top buttons and worked my way down, slowly releasing each button to reveal another inch of my pale skin.

I untucked the shirt entirely so it hung open in the front. The top button of my dress pants came next and then the zipper. I looked up at the sound of displaced water as Julia shifted in the bathtub. She seemed to lean forward in anticipation of what was coming next. It wasn't exactly a strip tease, but I took my time with each button, zipper, and clasp.

I shrugged out of my dress shirt and hung it on a hook intended for a towel. I tugged my pants past my hips, and gravity took care of the rest, leaving me in my cotton bra and underwear. I didn't have sexy lingerie—nothing compared to what Julia wore on the regular, but she had never complained or teased me about my functional undergarments. I suspected she was more interested in the body parts they covered and only saw them as a nuisance to be removed. I unfastened my bra and it, along with my underwear, soon joined my pants on the floor.

Julia curled a dripping finger in my direction, beckoning me to come closer. I'd joined in her in the bathtub on one other occasion, although I'd been fully clothed and out of my mind after a particularly challenging session with my therapist, Dr. Susan Warren. This tub was smaller than the one at her condo, but I was confident we could make it work.

Julia scooted to the center of the tub, making room for me behind her. I stepped into the tub, one foot and then the other. The water was hot, but I grit my teeth and willed my flesh to adjust. I had a naked woman who needed a leg hug. I slid down the back of the tub; Julia made herself small so I could wedge my legs between her and the tub's walls.

"Are we making your *Pretty Woman* cosplay dreams come true yet?" she asked.

I brushed Julia's glossy dark hair over one shoulder so I could have better access to her flawless back. I pressed warm, solid kisses against her shoulder blades.

"Getting there."

I was keenly aware that we weren't alone in the house. I didn't worry about anyone barging in on us, but I also doubted that the walls of the old home were well insulated. Making Julia scream my name while I worked my fingers and tongue between her thighs was certainly one way of making the nature of our relationship clear to her aunts and cousins, but I was no exhibitionist. And even with Julia's tailbone pressed snuggly against my clit, the presence of so many extended family members under one roof successfully kept my libido in check.

"What do you think our life would be like if we'd never left our jobs, never left this place?" I found myself asking instead.

"Would we be living Happily Ever After, you mean?" Julia posed. She leaned back onto my naked chest, resting her body weight against me. "Would I still be city prosecutor and you an Embarrass police detective, and would we be sharing a bath right now?"

"Maybe. I don't know," I struggled. I traced invisible patterns on her collarbone with the ends of my fingers. "But do you ever think about the What Ifs?"

"My life is one long list of What Ifs, darling," Julia noted. "What if I'd stayed a classics major? What if I'd never gone to law school? What if Jonathan had never enlisted and was still alive today? Would I have ever left this place?" She dropped her voice to no more than a whisper. "Would I have ever found love?"

"Maybe it's dumb," I started, "but I'd like to think we were always going to meet. It might not have been at a bar in Minneapolis. Maybe I would have still taken the Embarrass job, and maybe I would have seen you at Stan's diner or in City Hall. I wouldn't be able to rest until I knew your name."

"That's a quaint thought," Julia murmured. She paused before continuing. "I'm sorry things are so serious right now."

"Death is pretty serious," I observed.

"I know. But relationships are supposed to be filled with laughter and passion, especially when they're new. We haven't even been together a year."

"Life came at us fast," I agreed. "We didn't really have much of a honeymoon period. One minute we were sneaking sex in the patrol car, and the next I was arresting your dad for fraud."

Julia exhaled. "When you put it that way ..."

"All the more reason we should have an *actual* honeymoon," I said cheekily.

Julia twisted her head to give me a sharp look. "Cassidy. Don't joke."

I held up hands that were starting to prune from the warm water. "You know how I feel, babe. My heart is on my sleeve. My cards are on the table—all of those corny sayings. Say the word, and I'll get down on one knee."

My unapologetic honesty seemed to fluster her. She dropped her head, chin resting on her chest. "It hasn't even been a year," she quietly demurred.

I toyed with damp tendrils that had secured themselves to the back of her neck. I wasn't quite sure how I'd managed to navigate our conversation in this direction. "We've never been convention-al," I said carefully. "Why start now?"

Julia lifted her head and ran damp hands through her hair. "This isn't a serious conversation," she dismissed. "I don't have the bandwidth for this right now."

"That's okay." I wrapped my legs around her a little tighter. "Don't worry about it. I'm persistent; I'm not going anywhere."

Chapter Seven

It was quiet in the house when I woke up the next morning. The caravan of Julia's aunts, cousins, and second-cousins had yet to stir. Julia continued to sleep soundly beside me. Early rays of morning sunshine filtered through the bedroom drapes and shone down on her makeup free face. I was tempted to wake her with progressively intimate kisses, but I decided to let sleep overrule morning sex. The week had been taxing; I wanted her to find rest wherever she could.

I silently slipped out of bed and pulled the disrupted covers back up Julia's body. I couldn't completely ignore my urge to touch her, however. Leaning over her reposed form, I lightly brushed her loose hair away from her face and pressed my lips to her forehead. I heard her heavy sigh, but her eyes remained closed in sleep. I tiptoed out of the master bedroom and carefully closed the door behind me.

It was the morning of Julia's father's funeral. Although I had been present at a number of burials, some even very recent, I had never been involved in the planning of the services—not that Julia had let anyone really help her with those decisions. But similar to the responsibilities I'd given myself all week, I turned my attention to my self-appointed role—feeding my girlfriend.

But would she want to eat an actual breakfast on the morning before her father was buried? Could I convince her she needed more than coffee and a stiff upper lip to make it through the day? And what about the rest of her family? I wasn't sure if we had enough remaining food from my one grocery trip to feed them all or what food might still be in Julia's pantry. My thoughts were completely preoccupied with mentally gauging how many eggs were left in the refrigerator that I didn't notice the closed second-floor bathroom door or the increased humidity in the air. The bathroom door swung open, and I collided with a solid, wet body.

The force of the collision pushed the air out of my lungs. My arms flailed in an effort to avoid stumbling down the nearby staircase. My brain similarly struggled to catch up with my physical reaction to assess what had just happened and with whom, and if I was okay.

When I finally managed to steady myself, it took me a second too long to realize I'd nearly run over Julia's cousin, Reggie, and that in the chaos of the moment, the towel he had wrapped around his freshly-showered body was now on the floor.

"Oh shit!" I exclaimed. "I'm so sorry."

I averted my gaze to the floor, to the ceiling, to the pattern of the hallway wallpaper—anything to avoid looking in the direction of Julia's cousin while he struggled to cover himself up again with the damp, fallen towel. I finally settled on clamping my hand over my eyes. I'd seen plenty of naked men in my days in the military and then again in the police academy, but none of those men had been related to the person I was dating.

"It's, uh, it's safe to look now." He sounded vaguely rattled, but I couldn't blame him. He'd been enjoying his solitary morning routine until I'd plowed into him like a linebacker on a quarterback.

"Shit, I'm sorry," I repeated my previous apology. "I didn't think anyone else was awake."

"It's fine. No harm done. No broken bones or bruises."

I still couldn't make eye contact with him. "I was going to get the coffee going. You want some?"

"I'm pretty much wide awake now," he joked, "but coffee would be good."

I wasn't over my embarrassment enough to start joking just yet, so I mumbled another apology before hustling downstairs and away from the scene of the crime.

I busied myself with setting up the coffeemaker while simultaneously listening for other sounds in the house. It appeared, at least for the moment, that our collision hadn't woken up anyone else. I rattled around in the pantry for possible food options knowing it would only be a matter of time, however, before the rest of the house woke up. I could only imagine the kind of chaos that might ensue in the kitchen if I didn't have breakfast ready by then. Julia's stress level was already at its limit, and a houseful of her relatives wasn't helping my blood pressure either. My military training kicked in as I gathered pots and pans of various sizes. Anticipate needs. Coordinate a response. Attack from multiple angles.

I had managed to pull out eggs, milk, and butter from the refrigerator by the time Reggie bounded down the stairs and joined me in the kitchen. He'd thankfully put on real clothes since I'd last seen him. He rolled up the sleeves of a grey sweatshirt with the name Harvard screen printed across the chest.

"What can I help with?" he offered.

I pulled some still-frozen bacon out of the freezer. "I'm still working on the menu," I said. "I've gotten as far as scrambled eggs and bacon." I gestured to his sweatshirt. "Did you go there?"

Reggie looked down at the front of his shirt as if he'd forgotten what he wore. "For my MBA, yeah. I did undergrad at U of M though." His phrasing and tone made his accolades sound more humble than they actually were. "Julia said you were in the Marines?"

"Yeah. Two tours in Afghanistan," I confirmed.

It occurred to me that I had no idea how much or what of my life, past or present, Julia had shared with others, especially with her family.

Reggie shook his head and looked a combination of amazed and thoughtful. "Damn."

I never knew how to respond when people commented about my military career. I was two years removed from that life, but most days felt like I'd only just left. I was thankful when Reggie didn't ask any follow-up questions.

"Scrambled eggs, bacon, and waffles sound good?" I'd managed to find a box of waffle mix in the pantry that wasn't past its expiration date yet.

"Sounds great," he enthused. "Just tell me what you want me to do."

"Uh, I can handle the eggs and bacon if you want to get started on the waffle batter." I was more adept at pouring bowls of cereal than actually cooking, but I figured even I couldn't mess this up as long as I didn't burn anything.

Reggie grabbed the waffle mix box and began reading the directions. I started to crack eggs and gently folded them in an oversized frying pan.

Now that Reggie was wearing actual clothes, I took a moment to appraise the man I'd once mistakenly believed to be my competition. He was broad shouldered with a medium build. His compact physique indicated he was probably comfortable in a weight room or gym. If I didn't know any better, I would have thought he and Julia were brother and sister. They had the same dark hair that was almost iridescent when the light hit it just right, and the same serious, thoughtful eyes. Reggie had a dimpled grin, and it seemed to appear more easily than Julia's hard-earned smiles. The comparison made me reflect on how I'd never seen pictures of Julia's actual brother—Jonathan—before.

"Did you grow up in Embarrass, too?" I asked.

"No. I'm from Duluth. All of the Desjardin siblings except Uncle William left Embarrass after high school."

"But you visited in summers, right?" I partially remembered what Julia had told me about her cousin.

He nodded. "I'm an only child. Julia, Jonathan, and I were close in age—closer than the rest of the cousins—so my parents sent me here when they wanted me out of their hair."

I was impressed that Reggie hadn't stumbled on Jonathan's name. I was hardly bold enough to mention him in Julia's presence, but I also hadn't spent my summers growing up with him.

"What was Julia like, before?" I found myself asking.

Reggie's bushy eyebrows knit together. "Before what?"

"I dunno ...." I gestured uselessly with the spatula in my hand. "Just ... before. She doesn't really talk about the past with me."

A lopsided grin appeared on Reggie's face. "I'm not sure I want to spill company secrets and face her wrath. But I'm sure if there's something you want to know about her, all you need to do is ask."

I curled my upper lip at his practicality. "You make it sound so simple and civilized."

. . .

The scent of bacon eventually lured others from Julia's family out of their respective guest spaces. Barely a good morning or hello was shared before they started piling their plates high with food. I remained at the stovetop, continually cracking more eggs and tending to the sizzling bacon while Reggie kept an eye on the waffle griddle and made small-talk with his relatives. I was more than happy for the task so I didn't feel compelled to join their mundane chatter. I still wasn't sure of everyone's names and how specific people were related to each other.

I had just opened another package of bacon when Julia finally emerged from upstairs. She wasn't wearing makeup, but her hair looked more styled than it typically did when she woke up with me in her St. Paul condo. A more modest robe than the ones I'd gotten used to seeing her in was cinched tight around her waist.

She didn't bother with generalized morning pleasantries with her extended family, but instead circled the kitchen island to stand next to me at the stovetop.

"What's all this?" she asked. She looked a little stunned by all of the kitchen activity—nearly as perplexed as I had been the previous morning.

"Reggie and I thought it would be nice if breakfast was taken care of."

"Is that right?" she musically mused.

"This is all Cassidy," Reggie deflected. "I'm just pouring batter into a waffle maker."

"I saved you some coffee," I said, gesturing to a ceramic cup on the counter. "If you're hungry, this next batch of bacon will be done soon, and I can make you eggs however you want them."

Hands slipped around my waist and Julia pressed her nose against the side of my face. "You didn't have to do all this."

I didn't let her words or her proximity distract me from my

task. "Just trying to make things a little easier for you this morning."

Her hands tightened on my hips and her lips brushed against the outer shell of my ear. "My hero," she whispered for only me to hear.

Julia's affections didn't go unnoticed. The kitchen had become perceptively quieter as Julia had become more demonstrative. I hadn't expected her to be so affectionate and comfortable in front of her extended family. Perhaps the smell of waffles and bacon or her lack of caffeine had her forgetting our surroundings.

Julia didn't bother pulling away or putting any distance between us even though the percolating coffee machine and the sizzle of bacon fat in the cast iron pan had become the only noises in the kitchen.

"Does anyone have a problem with me kissing my girlfriend in my own home?" Julia bit out. "Cassidy made you breakfast. I think that warrants some appreciation."

A chorus of mumbled thank yous followed Julia's censure.

The confrontation seemed to light something from within her, like the small, indignant outburst had revived her. "I'm going upstairs to shower," she said. "You've done enough down here. Make the freeloaders do the dishes."

I jolted upright when her hand connected solidly with my backside.

~

The earth was soggy from the previous days' rain. My dress shoes made a wet sucking noise with each heavy step. I didn't know how Julia managed to traverse the soaking ground in her high heels. Perhaps she was too stubborn to let even the environment ruin her outfit.

Julia had made the decision that there would be no formal church service. Instead, a small, mixed group of onlookers huddled together in folding chairs on uneven ground beneath a canopy at the Embarrass cemetery. In a piece of morbid good news, Julia's father had died just before the temperature changed and the ground would have been too frozen to dig a grave. If that had been the case, William Desjardin's body would have had to be stored somewhere until the ground had thawed in spring. At least this way, Julia and her family would be able to have some ritual of closure despite his murder remaining unsolved.

The day was grey, but Julia still wore her sunglasses. The accessory had been a permanent fixture on her face since arriving in Embarrass despite the sun not having made an appearance all week. I sensed the blackout glasses were part of her body armor. Death was never easy, never comfortable. And she must have felt the opposite of the Prodigal Daughter coming back to her hometown. No one was giving her the key to the city anytime soon.

I'd secured a seat beside Julia in the front row, closest to the casket and open grave, but her body was turned away from mine so that she could comfort her mother. Reggie sat on the other side of Olivia Desjardin. The two sandwiched Mrs. Desjardin with gentle compassion.

My instinct was to grab Julia's hand or at least to rest my hand on her knee, but I didn't feel comfortable doing either. Julia hadn't told her mother who I really was to her. As much as I hated to be in this closeted position, I had no grounds on which to mount a complaint. I hadn't told my own parents about my relationship with Julia and neither of them were in mourning or had been diagnosed with dementia.

I didn't know what to do with my hands. I alternated between clasping them together, as if in silent prayer, and clutching my slightly bouncing knees. I felt a soft touch on my right knee. I looked down and saw a gloved hand attached to Grace Kelly Donovan's arm. We locked eyes and she gave me a small, reassuring smile. Grace was one of the very few people in Embarrass who knew about the former city prosecutor's affair with the former police detective, and despite the story's potential to be front page news in the local paper, she'd been faithful to my request for discretion.

"Please bow your heads. Let us pray." The Catholic priest in town, Father Mike, officiated the brief service from a portable wooden pulpit. He raised his arms in the air. "Dear Heavenly Father, in sure and certain hope of the resurrection to eternal life through Our Lord Jesus Christ, we commend to Almighty God our brother William, and we commit his body to the ground: earth to earth, ashes to ashes, dust to dust. The Lord bless him and keep him, the Lord make His Face to shine upon him and be gracious to him, the Lord lift up His countenance upon him and give him peace. Amen."

A murmuring of voices around me repeated the blessing: "Amen."

"At this time," Father Mike announced, "I'd like to invite William's daughter, Julia, to say a few words."

Julia stood and flattened the front pleats of her black dress. She walked toward Father Mike, and I stared after her in surprise. It hadn't occurred to me that she would be speaking at her father's funeral and she hadn't mentioned anything about it.

Julia removed her sunglasses before addressing the group. "Thank you for coming today." She stared at a creased piece of paper upon which she'd written her father's eulogy. She shut her eyes and was silent for a long moment—long enough that I considered jumping to the podium myself to save her from the moment. Someone in the small crowd quietly coughed; the noise seemed to awaken Julia from her temporary slumber.

Her eyes fluttered open. She folded the piece of paper and returned it to the pocket of her wool trench coat as if deciding to forego her prepared remarks. "My father was not a perfect man," she said. "He failed the people he should have cared about the most and the hometown he should have treasured. But I'm not perfect either," she stated, "so it's not my place to judge him or his decisions. Instead, I choose to remember and honor the man who wanted the best for me. The father who challenged me to reach higher than I ever thought I could achieve. He might not have been the best at expressing it, but I know I was loved." She took a breath. "I know he was proud of me in his quiet, private way." Julia cast her eyes on the closed casket. "Rest easy, Dad."

~

After the burial, Julia invited the funeral attendees back to her home. We hadn't yet been inside of her parents' home. I wondered if the blood had been cleaned up yet. Typically when a crime scene has been thoroughly inventoried and photographed, the location is released to the owner of the property. Depending on the chaos left behind, you might hire a crime scene or forensics cleaner, someone specially trained to remove human biohazards like blood, brains, or fecal materials. I doubted anyone in Embarrass had those kinds of skills.

The doorbell was getting a workout with a steady stream of townsfolk dropping off casseroles and gelatin salads and sheet pan desserts. Julia busied herself dividing a banquet-level of food between the kitchen island and the formal living room. Disposable plates, utensils, and napkins needed constant replenishing and a giant punch bowl of soda water and juices needed refilling.

The crowd of well-wishers at Julia's home seemed larger than the gathering at the cemetery. Either more people were in attendance at the post-funeral function, or it only seemed so since we were inside. I was impressed so many people had driven out to the Desjardin country home. Julia, however, had a different reaction.

"Buzzards," she muttered with open disdain. "Jostling for a front-row seat to the freak show."

She had paused long enough from hostess activities to open up a bag of ice in the kitchen. Someone had dropped off a plastic container of grocery store shrimp cocktail that needed chilling.

"Why are you doing this if you hate half of the people here?" I asked.

"It's tradition," she said simply. "People would talk."

"When have you ever cared about what people think?"

Julia set her mouth hard. "This is different."

I wanted to press her for more, but the doorbell rang again and she took off for the front of the house, a fake smile plastered to her features.

The post-funeral potluck, like the day's earlier funeral and the casket viewing before that, had been uneventful. No one broke into uncontrollable wailing and no arguments escalated into shouting matches. It was probably the most neutral moment of mourning I'd ever been a part of. There was still a definite divide between Julia's relatives and the people of Embarrass. It reminded me of a middle school dance with the boys along one wall and the girls congregated on the other. No brave souls ventured into No Man's Land, however, to ask for a dance.

While Julia made sure her visitors were well fed and not ashamed to have seconds, I stayed out of the way. I sat in the kitchen, drinking light beers with Reggie. I recognized a few faces as they piled paper plates with hot dish and pasta salads. With the exception of Julia's relatives, most other people were city employees with offices in City Hall. I was keenly aware that the former city clerk, Wendy Clark, had not been in attendance at any of the functions. It was probably for the best though.

I was disappointed that neither Chief Hart nor David Addams had bothered to make an appearance. David was probably working, but as someone who had worked with Mayor Desjardin for decades, I had expected Chief Hart to at least attend his funeral. Maybe I'd underestimated the bad blood between the Embarrass police department and the Desjardin family.

I'd finished off two beers by the time the sounds in the house had started to quiet down. The Embarrass crowds had returned to town and most of Julia's relatives had left earlier in the afternoon with the excuse that they had a long drive home. I was sure Julia would be thankful to get her house back soon.

"Cassidy, would you mind terribly packing up all of this food?" she asked. "I need to drive my mother back to the assisted living facility before it gets too late."

"Of course," I agreed.

Reggie drained the rest of his beer and hopped up from his seat. "I'll help, too," he offered.

Julia looked between the two of us. "You two seem to be getting chummy," she observed with a smile.

"I guess that's what happens when you've seen someone naked," Reggie shrugged.

Julia's mouth fell open. I could feel my face burn up to the top of my ears.

"It's not ... it was ... I mean—I ... accident," I bumbled.

Julia licked her lips. "I'm eager to hear this story when I get home."

Reggie grinned from ear to ear. "And I'll be sure to be gone by then."

Julia left soon afterwards with her mother. The house, which had been so chaotic and noisy before, was now silent. I pulled out all of the Tupperware containers I could find while Reggie transferred leftover food to the plastic containers.

"She likes you," he observed. "And Julia doesn't like anyone."

"Oh yeah?" I tried to not sound too eager to hear more.

"You know how private she is," Reggie noted. "So to bring you around the family is a major deal."

"She didn't exactly introduce me," I protested.

"She did in her own way," Reggie countered.

I rinsed off various serving spoons and loaded them into the dishwasher. "When ... when did you know about me?"

I was unabashedly snooping, but I was curious how early on Julia had told her closest relative about me.

"A little after she moved back to St. Paul," he said. "After she resigned as city prosecutor. I met up with her in the cities at a wine bar. Sometime between the truffle popcorn and the chicken liver pâté, she told me about a woman she'd betrayed in Embarrass. It took a few glasses of wine to coax the full story out of her," he admitted with a sly chuckle, "but she was absolutely devastated. She didn't know if she'd done the right thing in defending Uncle William if it meant hurting you."

I exhaled deeply. "Wow. That's ... wow."

Julia had never divulged that story to me; I had been curious about the time between when she'd left Embarrass and when we'd reconnected in the Twin Cities, but I'd never thought to ask.

"I'm glad you gave her a second chance," he said.

"Yeah," I said wistfully. "Me, too."

Once the smorgasbord of potluck food had been tucked away in storage containers and casserole dishes and serving bowls had been soaked and scrubbed, Reggie packed up his luggage and headed out. He'd been joking about leaving before Julia returned, but the sky was only growing darker while we waited for her return.

I'd assumed Julia was only dropping off her mom at the assisted living facility and not hanging out with her. It made me feel a little abandoned, but I couldn't really nag her about spending more time with her mom on the day they'd buried her father.

I gave the floors a quick cleaning so all signs of interlopers would be erased before Julia's return. I showered and changed into my pajamas and opened a third bottle of beer. I was in the kitchen, scrolling through my cellphone, beer in the other hand, when Julia came home.

She dropped her purse on the kitchen island and sighed. "Can I get one of those?"

I nodded and dutifully retrieved a bottle of beer from the fridge. I twisted the cap open and presented the drink to her. Julia accepted the beer with a smile and took a long pull. She looked unnatural in her funeral dress and heels with the long-neck beer bottle.

I hadn't said anything since her return. I hadn't even said hello. My silence didn't go unnoticed: "Is everything okay, dear?"

"Yes. No. I don't know." I swallowed hard. I couldn't believe I was actually going to say the ridiculous words out loud. "I've been feeling a little neglected since we got here. But it's selfish," I corrected in a rush. "I'm being stupid and juvenile, pouting because you're not paying attention to me when you're dealing with stuff that's way more important."

Julia didn't miss a beat. "Nothing is more important than you, Cassidy. I'm sorry I haven't done a better job of demonstrating that."

"You've been through the gauntlet this week," I couldn't help defend her. "The funeral, your mom, extended family showing up," I listed off. "You've been a real champ."

"Thank you, dear." Julia set her unfinished beer on the kitchen island and wrapped her arms around me. "So," she said neutrally. She pressed her nose against my cheek. "Tell me about being naked with my cousin."

~

Afghanistan, 2012

We're sitting ducks. Pense landed one kill shot, but there'd been two targets. I launch myself off of the hard-packed dirt and start to run. Our tactical trainers at Parris Island debunked the myth that the best way to avoid getting shot is to run in a zig-zag pattern. You weren't trying to evade a crocodile; you were avoiding a bullet to the head. The most efficient way to not get shot is to run in a direct line away from the active shooter. But I'm not running away from imminent danger, I'm running *toward* it.

I think about summers at my family's cabin on Lake Armstrong. A brown bear had stumbled onto the property one day while my parents and I were having lunch outside: hot dogs and my mom's potato salad. My dad jumped up from the picnic table so quickly that the table had nearly toppled over. I remember him yelling and shouting and waving his arms in the air, trying to make himself seem bigger and more threatening than he actually was— and it worked. The bear lost interest in our picnic and crashed back into the surrounding forest.

I don't have any other options. Pense can't move, and there's no way in hell I'm leaving him behind. We've been through too much for it to end like this.

"Over here, mother fucker!" I holler. I raise my arms above my head and start shouting other obscenities. I don't know if they speak English, but some cruder parts of the language are probably universal.

I'm too far away from the remaining hostile to identify the expression on his half-covered face. I can't tell if he's taken aback by my antics, but I'm both terrified and satisfied when he shifts the barrel of his weapon away from Pense's location and trains it on me instead.

Another yell, this one primal and desperate, rips out of my throat. I lower my head and sprint towards the man who intends to kill me.

Pop. Pop. Pop.

I jolted upright in bed. The monochromatic landscape of the Helmand Province faded away and the interior of Julia's bedroom came into focus. Outside, crickets composed their nighttime symphony. I touched my fingers to my throat. It felt raw and used. Had I screamed in real life?

Even if I hadn't cried out in my sleep, my flailing about in bed was enough to wake up Julia.

"That hasn't happened in a while," she stated quietly.

I reached for the glass of water I'd put on the bedside table and feverishly gulped down its contents. I swallowed it down with the sand in my throat. I drank deeply until water dribbled down my chin. The time it took me to drain the glass helped me reorient myself. I was no longer in Afghanistan. I was in Julia's bedroom in Embarrass, Minnesota.

I tugged my hairband out of my sleep-tussled ponytail and pulled my hair back into a tight bun. "There's no cure," I roughly reminded her. "Just the moments in between the nightmares."

"It was a longer moment this last time," she gently observed.

I grunted noncommittally and flopped back onto my pillow. I had no expectation of falling asleep again, but I went through the pretense for Julia's benefit. At the very least, I hoped she would be able to go back to sleep.

Although the room was dark, illuminated only by moonlight, I could feel her eyes on me. I couldn't take offense to her stare, though. If I'd been woken up by another person's bad dream, I probably would have stared at them, too. It was frustrating and embarrassing. She'd seen me at my most vulnerable on multiple occasions, but that didn't make my most recent gaffe any easier to deal with. You didn't just get used to being a freak show.

"Do you want to talk about it?" she asked. "Or maybe write about it?"

I'd been less diligent as of late about writing in my PTSD dream journal. Work had gotten busy with the Kennedy Petersik suicide and then we'd gotten the news about Julia's dad. I was sure Dr. Warren would have been disappointed with my neglect.

Julia didn't let my silence derail her. "Maybe you could talk to Dr. Warren on the phone," she suggested. "Or even video conference. I could call her office and set something up."

My heart sank in my stomach at the prospect of being yet another thing Julia had to deal with.

"You have enough on your plate," I weakly protested.

I didn't particularly like reaching out to Dr. Warren even though as far as head shrinkers went, she was pretty good. But I also knew Julia's hyper-focus wouldn't let me be until I set something up.

"I'll call her," I said, finally relenting.

"First thing in the morning?" Julia pressed.

I exhaled loudly like an annoyed teenager. "First thing," I promised.

I felt Julia move closer to me beneath the heavy duvet. Her hand slid over my lower abdomen and came to a rest just below my bellybutton. "Good girl."

The room was silent for several long minutes. Julia, apparently satisfied that a plan for my broken brain had been settled on, was able to slip back into a deep sleep. I heard the distinct sound of her slow, even breath. I shut my eyes, but knew the same result wasn't in my immediate future.

Chapter Eight

I stared at the blacked-out screen of Julia's silver laptop. She'd set me up in the front den with her cellphone as a wifi hot spot. She'd also promised me privacy. The heavy wooden door had been shut, but I only had her word that she wasn't standing on the other side with her ear pressed tightly against the divider.

I'd never been very comfortable with technology. I'd missed out on a pivotal near-decade by being abroad. In 2004, when I'd originally enlisted straight out of high school, Facebook was just being rolled out to college students. The first iPhone was still three years away. My clunky, white iPod had been filled with Outcast, Usher, and Alicia Keys to distract me on the flight across the Atlantic Ocean. Skype had recently been introduced, which let me keep in contact with my parents when my geographic location wasn't a matter of national security.

The laptop chimed and blooped before my therapist's kind face filled the 14-inch screen. My sessions had recently been cut back from once a week to once every two weeks. Journaling had been working for me—that and the combination of sleeping next to Julia Desjardin on a nightly basis.

I felt a little ashamed that my given task of rewriting my flashbacks had fallen to the wayside, like a kid who'd fallen behind on their homework. If I wanted to get better, or at least minimize my triggers, I knew I needed to be more diligent about following my treatment.

"Hi, Cassidy. It's nice to see you."

"Hey, Doc," I returned.

"I'm glad we were able to meet, even if it's virtual," she said. "The note from my assistant said you had a flashback?"

"I'm sorry," I quickly apologized. "I haven't been writing in my journal."

"It's okay," she assured me. "I'm glad you reached out instead of ignoring the lapse. Journaling isn't a cure-all, but I've been encouraged by your progress with it."

"Me, too," I said in earnest. "That's why I'm kicking myself for getting lazy."

Dr. Warren cocked her head to one side. "Is that what happened? You got lazy with your journaling?"

"Not lazy," I corrected. "But work got busy, and I didn't make it a priority at the end of the night."

Dr. Warren made a thoughtful hum that could be heard through the laptop's internal speakers.

"Which I guess means I wasn't making me or my health a priority," I continued, thinking out loud.

"That's a pretty powerful observation," Dr. Warren concluded.

I scratched at my head, simultaneously proud of myself and embarrassed. "Balance isn't something I have a lot of practice with," I admitted. "Or self-care, I guess. In the Marines, I wasn't an individual; I was part of a unit. Like one of those Transformers that's just a small part of the bigger robot. If I was taking care of myself, it was for the benefit of the bigger picture, not necessarily because it was good for me."

"That's an interesting analogy."

I didn't know how Dr. Warren had kept a straight face. *Transformers? Where the hell had that come from?*

"What I hear you saying is when you were in the military, you'd taken care of yourself for the good of the team," she observed. "Does that sound about right?"

"Uh huh," I confirmed.

"As a civilian, do you no longer feel like you're part of a team?" she inquired.

Her question gave me pause. At work, I was part of the Cold Case unit. It was a small, intimate team and we worked well together. But I had no visions of grandeur; I was replaceable. Unlike Stanley or Sarah, there was nothing special, no unique skill I contributed to the team, that any other cop wouldn't be able to do.

I thought about my immediate family. Team Miller. Beyond random dinners, I was basically estranged from my parents. There was no sense of belonging or of being necessary when it came to them.

My brain stopped on Julia. No matter how many times I insisted that she let me help her or that she be vulnerable and transparent with me, I knew it wasn't her habit to let people in. She was so maddeningly proud, she didn't know how to ask for help. Even if you tear down a wall, the debris remains.

"Cassidy? Did your screen freeze?"

Dr. Warren's concerned voice rattled through my brain.

"No, I'm fine. I'm still here." I blinked a few times to clear my thoughts of depressing realities. "It's not the same, Doc. It's not a life or death situation over here."

"Isn't it?" she challenged. "I'm sure you're aware that humans are social animals. We depend on others. I know that 'dependence' is like a four-letter word these days, but it's true," she continued. "We strive to be self-sufficient and independent, but that's fighting against two hundred thousand years of evolution."

"So you're saying that even if I'm not ready to prioritize my mental health for myself, I should prioritize it for ... for my civilian team?"

"I see it all the time," she confirmed, "for example, with people who have turned to alcohol or drugs to drown out trauma. They might not be ready to kick their addiction for their own well-being, but they want to get better for someone else—their children, their spouse, their loved ones."

Dr. Warren's words were sobering. I'd been licking my wounds and feeling sorry for myself about Julia not being a good teammate, when I was guilty of the same offense. I'd reluctantly made myself vulnerable to her—kicking and screaming even. And by letting my mental health slide, I was also deprioritizing a future with Julia.

"Shit," I mumbled. I sat a little straighter in my chair, rejuvenated by the prospect of rehabilitation. "You're really good at your job, did you know that?" I posed.

Dr. Warren inclined her head. "I may have heard that a few times."

I logged off with Dr. Warren with the promise to prioritize my journaling and to make an in-person appointment whenever I returned to Minneapolis. I exited the den at the exact moment that the doorbell rang. I normally wouldn't have been so bold as to answer the door for Julia, but I was standing right in the front foyer.

I tugged the door open to find a small, bespectacled man standing on the front stoop. His grey hair was carefully parted on one side. I couldn't see his clothes, but his black wool trench coat and his shiny leather shoes looked expensive. He clutched the handle of a fancy leather satchel in both hands.

"Hi, uh, is Julia home?" He clearly looked confused by my presence along with the rapidity with which I had answered the door.

"Sure. Just a second."

I turned my head and shouted back into the house. "Julia!"

"Darling," I heard her voice come from behind me. "No need to shout. We're not animals." She looked beyond me to the man at her front door. "Hello, Mr. Williams. Please come in."

The well-dressed man stepped across the threshold.

"Hello, Julia," he greeted. "You're looking well. I would have stopped by earlier, but I assumed you'd be busy."

The man looked in my direction, clearly waiting for some kind of introduction or explanation as to who I was and why I was there.

Julia inclined her head. "It's been a busy time, yes. Thank you, by the way, for the flower arrangement at my father's wake. They were lovely."

The man waved a black, gloved hand. "It's no bother. Your family was one of my first clients; it's the least I can do."

"Would you like to come in?" Julia offered. "Can I get you something to drink?"

"No, no," he dismissed. "I know you have better things to do than entertain an old fool like myself. This isn't a social call anyway." He snapped open his leather briefcase and pulled out a legal-sized envelope. "This is for you," he said, "from your father."

Julia accepted the envelope. Her practiced polite veneer faltered briefly. "From my ... uh, thank you."

Mr. Williams fished a single business card out of his work bag and handed it to Julia. "Anyway, I've got to be going. Call my office if you have any questions."

Julia's fingers closed around the crisp, unmarked envelope. "I'll do that. Thank you for coming all this way."

"Who was that?" I asked as the door shut with his departure.

Julia stared down at the envelope in her hands. "Mr. Williams. He's my father's attorney—or at least the man he hired to look after the family trust."

"Family trust? Jesus," I snorted, "you guys really are loaded."

"It's really not that fancy," she assured me. "But we're a family of lawyers, so it's only natural that we make sure these kinds of details are looked after."

I stood up on my tiptoes, even though it wouldn't afford me a better vantage point. "What is it?" I asked.

Julia opened the unsealed envelope and pulled out a thin stack of official-looking papers. Her eyes scanned the first few lines. The edges of her mouth curved down. "My father's will."

"Will? People really do that?" I'd written my parents a just-in-case-letter that I'd kept on my person when I'd been deployed, but I'd never had a proper will. But then again, I hadn't really had anything worth willing to someone else.

Julia licked her lips. "I think I'm going to need a drink."

We relocated from the front foyer to Julia's den. She sat on the red velvet couch while I poured her a tall glass of bourbon. I would have gotten a beer for myself, but I was too impatient to make the trip to the kitchen. I'd never been at a will reading before.

I delivered Julia her drink and sat in the empty space beside her. Julia took a large, inelegant gulp of the expensive liquor before setting the glass down on a coaster on the coffee table.

She carefully unfolded the paper that had been in the unmarked envelope and began to read aloud: "This is my last will and testament. I revoke any and all wills and codicils previously made. I direct my executor to pay my enforceable, unsecured debts and funeral expenses. I, William Joseph Desjardin, being of sound mind, do hereby bequeath my possessions," she recited. "I give all my tangible personal property, nonphysical assets, and all policies and proceeds of insurance covering such property to my ... daughter, Julia Rose Desjardin." She paused and took a long, steadying breath before resuming. "I bequeath my residence, subject to any mortgages or encumbrances thereon to ... my daughter, Julia Rose Desjardin."

Julia turned the paper over as if expecting to discover more instructions on the opposite side. "That's-that's it," she blinked. "That's all it says."

"He gave you everything?"

Her eyes blinked rapidly. She continued to flip the piece of paper back and forth as if it might make the text on the page change. "I don't ... I don't understand. He didn't leave anything to my mother."

I wanted to be sensitive to the situation, but didn't have the language with which to do so. "*Can* she be the beneficiary?"

Julia nodded. "She's been ruled legally incompetent, but she can still inherit assets of an estate. I mean, God, some people leave all their possessions to their cat."

She chewed on her lower lip, her beautiful features twisted in confusion. "I figured I would have been written out of the will after I sued him for custody of my mother."

Her voice was low, no more than a whisper, as if the statement wasn't intended for my benefit, but rather her brain's attempt to work out this new mystery.

"Maybe it's an old will?" I proposed. "Before you guys started fighting."

She re-examined the document and shook her head. "No. It's new. It's actually from the day after I last visited."

My brow furrowed. "I thought you'd said it wasn't a good visit?"

"It wasn't," she affirmed.

I sat back on the couch. "Wow. Why do you think he did that?"

"I can't even pretend to know how that man's mind worked." Julia flicked a lock of hair away from her forehead in annoyance. "But I suppose I should be grateful that he didn't leave anything to that woman, Wendy Clark."

The perplexed look on her features shifted to exhaustion. "Oh no," she breathed.

"What?"

Julia pursed her lips. "The Aunts are *not* going to be happy about this."

∼

Dinner that night consisted of leftover hotdish and other casserole-shaped food that had been dropped off at Julia's house the previous day. Most of the sympathy food had been delivered by people who hadn't bothered to go to William Desjardin's funeral, but even if the people of Embarrass had kept the Desjardin family at arm's length, they still participated in the Minnesota-Nice ritual.

Once Mr. Williams had left and her father's will had been read, Julia had promptly changed into black yoga pants and an oversized sweatshirt. It was another outfit that hadn't made the St. Paul wardrobe cut.

Julia poked at the food on her plate, looking uninterested or at least uninspired by the meal. I couldn't recall ever seeing her eat something so pedestrian as tuna fish noodle casserole with potato chips crumbled over the top for an extra crunch. She'd been quiet and contemplative since the lawyer had left.

"Do you think you'll keep your dad's house and this one? Or will you try to sell something?" I asked.

With her father's death, Julia was now in possession of two mansions in the township of Embarrass plus a far more humble cabin on a small inland lake farther north. She also owned her St. Paul condominium. I didn't have a single square foot on this planet that I could claim as my own. It was these kinds of material gaps that I'd had to work to overcome so I didn't constantly feel unqualified to be Julia's partner. It was definitely a work in progress.

"I haven't given it much thought," she admitted. "Even if I do, I have no grand illusions of getting fair market value. This house was already notorious enough without my father dying here."

My question was probably unfair. She'd only officially gained ownership of the multiple properties with the reading of her father's will a few hours prior. I didn't want to overwhelm her, so I changed the subject.

"Why did your grandparents live way out here instead of in town?" I wondered aloud.

The privacy was certainly appealing, but it was also a bit inconvenient to have to drive so far for a gallon of milk.

"It's where my grandfather grew up," she explained. "He was an only child, so he inherited the land when his parents passed. He made his fortune in the lumber industry, and after they married, he had this house built for my grandmother. Whatever she wanted, he made it happen. Or so the story goes."

"That's kind of romantic," I had to admit.

The admission made me frown after a while. Her grandfather had built a massive mansion for his new bride. What kind of grand gesture could I ever offer Julia?

"When I moved back to Embarrass after Jonathan's death," Julia continued, "my parents wanted me to move back in with them. That was never going to happen," she said with a rueful shake of her head. "This house had been sitting empty since my grandparents died, so there was quite a bit of work that needed to be done to make it livable. I hired contractors for the big projects like updating the kitchen and bathrooms, but I did many of the improvements myself."

"I had no idea you were so handy," I innocently remarked.

Julia arched an eyebrow. "You'd be amazed what you can accomplish when you've got unlimited free time and are actively ignoring the grieving process."

"You're not gonna start knocking down walls in the condo when we get back, are you?" I kept my tone light even though we were tiptoeing around a serious topic.

I couldn't help notice that she hadn't cried yet—not at the wake, not at the funeral—but I didn't know how to bring up the topic without sounding judgmental. People grieved differently; who was I to judge if Julia's process included re-grouting the tile in the master bathroom?

"No, darling. I think the walls will be safe."

I held up my hands. "Not saying I wouldn't give my left arm to see you in a tool belt," I qualified.

Julia tilted her head back and laughed. It was a glorious sound. It was also something I hadn't heard in a while. She might chuckle at my antics, but these moments when her guard was down and she let loose had been rare over the past few weeks.

I stood up and began to stack the dishes at my place setting. Julia continued to sit and sip from her wine glass. I could feel her eyes on me as I consolidated the plates and utensils on the table to make for a more efficient trip to the kitchen.

"You don't have to do that," she remarked.

"I know," I conceded, "but I like to be useful."

"I can think of a better use of your time," she rasped.

I laughed lightly. "Oh yeah?"

Julia wet her lips. "Come here, soldier."

The low burn in her tone sent a shiver of anticipation down my spine. The dining room was dimly lit, but I recognized the sharp glint in those caramel-colored eyes.

The legs of my chair squeaked when I pushed back farther from the table. The wooden floorboards quietly groaned beneath my feet as I rounded the table. Julia remained seated as I stopped to stand beside her. I felt a sliver of trepidation as I considered what she might do to me. But whatever she was concocting, I was sure I'd become a willing participant.

Julia stood up, her movements graceful and silent while my own had been loud and clunky. She took purchase of my hips and maneuvered me ever so slightly until my backside pressed against the edge of the dining room table. I slightly stiffened when she reached past me.

I heard her low chuckle. "Just getting my wine, darling. There's no need to be jumpy."

"I'm not," I said defiantly.

She lifted an elegant eyebrow. "Oh? I don't make you nervous anymore?"

I released a shaky breath. "Still terrified."

My response coaxed a smile to her lips. "I'm glad I haven't lost my touch."

She held her wine glass by its stem, pinching the crystal between her first two fingers and her thumb. She took a long sip of her drink and regarded me over the top of the glass. Her ruby red lipstick had become smudged around the rim over the course of the evening. She seemed to be thinking, considering her next step. I licked at my lips, my backside still lightly resting on the edge of the formal dining table, all too eager for her next command.

"Take off your shirt."

My fingers didn't stumble on the buttons of my flannel shirt. I unfastened each individual button, starting at the top. I kept my eyes locked on Julia's face as I worked my way to the bottom. With the front of my shirt open, I shrugged the garment off one shoulder and then the other before letting the shirt slip soundlessly to the floor.

I stood before Julia, naked from the waist up. We hadn't gone anywhere that day, so after my video call with Dr. Warren and the unexpected arrival of William Desjardin's Last Will and Testament, I'd abandoned my bra.

Julia's features remained impassioned, almost bored, as she observed me. It was a look that might have made another person shrink away, but I had nothing to be self-conscious about from this angle. If anything, I stood a little taller, a little prouder, for her inspection.

Julia stepped close, inserting herself into my personal space. Her eyes never strayed from mine, which is why I loudly gasped in surprise when I felt chilled liquid splash down the valley between my naked breasts.

"Wh-what the hell?" I sputtered. I looked down to see the faint red stain of the contents of her wine glass splattered across my pale skin.

I didn't have time to register additional shock or disbelief before Julia was dipping her head and running the flat of her tongue along my collarbone.

"Mmm," she throatily purred. "I've always loved this vintage," she approved.

The red, translucent liquid dripped between the valley of my naked breasts, down my abdomen, and soaked into the waistband of my grey sweatpants. Julia ran a single finger up the center of my stomach, collecting spilled wine on her fingertip. She sucked the digit between her painted lips and hummed again.

I reached for her with a grunt, but somehow she was anticipating the move and deftly avoided my grasp. She clucked her tongue against the roof of her mouth and waggled a finger—the finger that had just been in her mouth—in my direction.

"You're all sticky, my dear," she admonished with false concern. "We don't want that getting on my clothes."

For once, she was dressed as casually as me in yoga pants and an oversized sweatshirt. This had nothing to do with staining her outfit. This was all about control. But I was willing to play her game.

Her fingers ghosted down my sides and came to rest at the waistband of my sweatpants. The clucking noise continued. "Your pants are wet."

"Yeah, I wonder how that happened," I sardonically returned. Just because I was willing to play her game didn't mean I couldn't push back a little.

"Let's see what else I can make wet."

The dining room held a slight chill; as I stood there in only my sweatpants, the waistband damp from Julia's spilled wine, I should have felt cold. And yet, a fire burned through my veins. If she touched me—really touched me—I might spontaneously combust.

Julia stepped close with one leg lodged between my own slightly parted thighs. My breath hitched in my throat when she slid her hand down the front of my sweatpants. Her fingers immediately sought my clit, which she rubbed in a rough circle. Those elegant fingers reached beyond the sensitive bundle and she drew her fingertips up and down my slit. My body had no choice but to respond.

My hips canted in her direction and a needy whine ripped up

my throat. She'd already warned me about touching her, so I resisted the urge to grab on to her and pull her tight. My fingers curled around the edge of the dining table instead.

"I don't know," she playfully considered. Her fingers continued to lazily travel up and down my shaved sex. She dipped her fingers into my folds, but resisted actual penetration. "It's a good start, but I think we can do better."

"What did you have in mind?" I panted between uneven breaths.

Julia removed her hand from the front of my sweatpants. "Pants off and turn around," she husked.

I tugged my sweatpants down my hips and onto the floor and spun on my heels without hesitation. Like obeying a drill sergeant at boot camp, I'd always been amenable to her commands.

She pressed the full length of her body against mine. One arm wrapped around my waist while the other subtly pressed between my shoulder blades. I knew what she wanted from me without needing to be told. I bent over with my upper torso flush against the dining room table. The beveled corner of the table pressed into the tops of my thighs. I could feel the slight pull of the muscles in my calves and hamstrings. My stomach was tacky from the red wine, and my skin stuck to the lacquered wooden surface. I spread my legs apart and readied myself.

Julia favored this position precisely because it made me vulnerable. Lying on my stomach, the scars on my back were on full display. She slowly stroked her fingers down my spine. Wherever her touch contacted scar tissue was like a blind spot. I'd lost sensation in some of the more damaged spots, which had only made the adjacent skin even more sensitive. The act itself was intimate—almost taboo. Besides doctors, Julia was the only one who had ever touched my physical defects.

"I'm almost disappointed I didn't think to pack the strap-on," she mused aloud.

My eyes shuttered at the suggestion. The words brought to mind vivid, explicit memories of Julia's last birthday present to herself.

"Would you like that, dear?" Julia taunted. "To be fucked from behind? To be thoroughly fucked by my cock?"

"Oh my God. Julia," I groaned. Her coarse words alone had my body overheating. "Please," came my strangled plea.

She pressed against me from behind, pinning me between the table and her lean body. She subtly thrust forward and her pelvic bone struck my naked backside. The dining room table was heavy and sturdy, but the movement caused it to skid against the wooden floorboards.

Julia blanketed my body with her own. "You're lucky I don't feel like having the floors refinished," she rasped into my ear. "I'd make you feel me in the morning."

I audibly swallowed. "Sounds like an excuse to me."

"Is that so?" I could hear the mirth in her tone. A foot nudged the inside of my own. "Well then. Wider," she commanded.

The farther I spread my legs, the less leverage I possessed. I was completely vulnerable, completely spread open for her.

Julia continued to take her time. She lazily stroked her finger-tips across my back. She poured herself another glass of wine. She drank at a leisurely pace and refused to touch me where I needed her the most.

I yelped in surprise when liquid hit the center of my back. Whatever wine had remained in her glass trickled down my spine and dripped down my ass.

"I'm plenty wet already," I sourly complained. "You didn't have to do that."

"I'll be the judge of that, my dear," she coolly replied. She fisted my hair into a makeshift ponytail and pulled my head back. I had no choice but to arch my back. "Are you going to continue to complain, or should I stop right now?"

Despite my instinct to taunt her and resist, I couldn't ignore the dull, persistent ache between my thighs. I needed her.

"I'll be good," I promised.

"Good girl." Julia loosened her grip on my hair and swatted my backside again. The force caused the table to shake. Dishes clattered and wine glasses threatened to topple. She rotated between slapping my ass and rubbing the stinging flesh.

I heard her disappointed sigh. "Think of all the fun we could be having if only I'd been more prepared."

"I'm having fun," I practically panted.

"I suppose my fingers will have to do for now," she said, almost sounding remorseful.

She pressed me into the table with a hand in the small of my back. I hissed when her fingers finally parted my thighs. I felt her cup my overheating sex from behind. Her middle finger pressed against my clit with her surrounding digits resting on my outer lips. The combination of cabernet sauvignon, sweat, and my early arousal had made me uncomfortably tacky and damp.

Julia removed her hand again. I was about to vocalize my annoyance until I heard her sucking on her fingers.

"Delicious," she murmured.

Her hand returned between my legs and she flicked my hooded clit. Shocks, like I'd been electrocuted, buzzed down my legs. The intense sensation was followed by a more gentle touch. She rubbed her fingertips against me in lazy, wide circles.

I shifted my weight from one foot to the other, hoping she might slip a finger inside me. What she was doing felt good, but I'd expected her to fuck me—to use my body as a distraction from the preceding days' events. All of the foreplay leading up to this moment had indicated I should hold onto the edge of the table and brace myself.

A single finger entered me and stilled. I wiggled my backside with impatience. My calves were well toned from swimming and running, but they were starting to ache from maintaining the prone position. Julia withdrew her finger and slid back in. I'd expected more force; I'd expected my breath to be cut short. Instead, she penetrated me with great care.

Her ministrations continued, solid and smooth. I jerked slightly when I felt her lips brush against my backside. She kissed and licked the pale flesh she'd earlier abused.

"You're so beautiful, Cassidy," I heard her words of praise.

I didn't have a ready response, although I didn't think she expected one.

She replaced one finger with two, but I was wet enough to accept the addition. Her knuckles bumped into my ass each time she penetrated me from behind. The two fingers disappeared and I experienced a different sensation when Julia pressed her thumb into my waiting sex. It filled me less than her double digits had, but it allowed her greater access to my clit.

My groans became louder and more pronounced as her slick fingers slipped across my sensitive clit. "Fuck that's good," I encouraged.

The hand at the back of my back pressed me harder into the dining table. My naked breasts were mashed against its surface. Julia quickened her pace.

"Should I let you cum?" she rhetorically asked.

I only moaned in response.

Her fingers disappeared yet again. I bit down on my lower lip to keep from crying. She wanted me to beg.

I struggled with the word: "Please."

A sturdy hand palmed each of my ass cheeks. "So polite."

I felt my ass being pried apart and a wet tongue slipped between my cheeks.

My head jerked off the table, and I nearly threw out my lower back. "Holy fuck!"

Julia thrust her tongue into my pussy. I couldn't help myself; I wedged my arm between my body and the table so I could rub my clit. I fully expected to be censured for touching myself without her permission, but it only seemed to turn her on even more. I heard her quiet grunt; her hands tightened on my hips, and she pulled me harder against her face. When she didn't stop me, I continued the assault on my clit like I was trying to start a goddamn fire.

The combination of her warm, wet tongue and my determined fingers vaulted me over the edge.

"Cumming!" I cried out.

I collapsed onto the table and eventually slid to the scuffed-up floor. My thighs shook from the power of my orgasm and my legs were exhausted from maintaining the commanded position for such an extended period.

I heard, rather than saw, Julia pour herself a new glass of wine.

"Remind me to call a contractor in the morning, dear. These floors are a mess."

Chapter Nine

William and Olivia Desjardin's home was no longer an active crime scene. The yellow police tape had been removed from the front door and all evidence had been processed and photographed. When someone dies, even from a brutal murder like the one Mr. Desjardin suffered, the responsibility to clean up falls to the home owner, not the police department. Julia had hired a hazardous waste cleaning crew from out of town to erase all signs that anyone had died inside the house. I could smell the distinct scent of clean carpet when we first walked in. Morbid as it was, I hadn't thought to ask David in which room they'd found the Mayor's body. The cleaning crew had done a nice job; if there was a missing area rug or panel of carpeting that had needed to be removed, it wasn't obvious.

I observed the layout of the first floor as I stood in the front entryway. The front door opened to a formal living room, which connected to the formal dining room. The furniture was a little old fashioned and the finishes weren't as updated as Julia's country home, but it was still much nicer and significantly larger than the home in which I'd grown up.

I followed Julia into the home, past the formal living and dining room to the back of the house where I discovered a kitchen, sunroom, and sunken rec room. I had only been allowed entry as far as the dining room on my one previous visit. I had been inside the house before, but only briefly, when Julia's mother had wandered off in the middle of the night.

Julia dropped a small cardboard box onto the kitchen counter. The box contained multi-colored circle stickers, markers, and various other items we would need to get the house ready for the estate sale. It had been Julia's idea to sell most of her parents' possessions. Her mother wouldn't need much beyond some photographs, knick-knacks, and other mementos in assisted living. Julia didn't need the money from the sale, but I suspected this was just another step toward coping with her father's death and getting more closure.

I continued to take in my surroundings while Julia began to unpack the box we'd brought. I looked around the kitchen, taking in the refrigerator magnets, shelves of knick-knacks, and a kitschy silver spoon collection. "Is anything missing?" I wondered aloud.

"Missing?"

"Yeah. If BCA thinks it was a burglary, what did they steal?"

Julia frowned. "I'm not sure. I wasn't in this house very often after I came back to Embarrass."

"And I suppose your mom wouldn't be able inventory the home very well either," I noted.

Julia shook her head. "To be honest, I doubt they took anything. My father had a Rolex that he wore every day. When I first visited the funeral director, he asked me if I wanted him buried in it or not. So the thieves didn't even take that off of his wrist."

"What a clusterfuck," I grunted. "You break into a house in broad daylight. You shoot a guy in the stomach, but you get so spooked that you just run off?" I shook my head. "Did any of the neighbors hear the gun shot?"

"You're asking the wrong person, darling."

"I'm sorry," I quickly apologized. "I'll let it go. I'm sure BCA's got this covered."

Julia's cellphone, which she'd set on the kitchen counter, buzzed against the laminate countertop. She frowned when she retrieved her phone and read the new text message. "I have to run to the assisted living facility for a second. Joy just texted that my mother is refusing to eat." She frowned more deeply. "Will you be okay on your own for a little while? I'll be back as soon as I can."

I nodded. I was getting used to being on my own while Julia tended to a million little fires.

"I'm so sorry, darling," she apologized as she hurriedly tossed her phone and keys into her purse. "I know I keep doing this to you."

"It's really okay," I insisted. "Go help your mom. Do you want me to get started on this stuff while you're gone?"

She bit down on her lower lip. "If you don't mind. Maybe start here in the kitchen?" she suggested. "You could start putting price tags on the flatware and table settings."

"I don't know what any of this stuff should cost," I warned.

Julia waved a dismissive hand. "The prices aren't really that important. The people who show up tomorrow will be busybodies who only want to see the inside of this house." Her tone took on a sour bite. "Maybe they'll buy a souvenir to commemorate their voyeurism."

"Wow, babe. How do you really feel?" I tried to lighten what had quickly become a tense moment.

Julia curled her lip. "I've tried to escape this place. Twice," she reminded me tightly. "There's a reason for that."

"I get that," I appeased. "But the elephant is almost eaten. Just a few more loose ends to tie up before we can go home."

My words were meant to comfort Julia, but they were also for my own benefit.

"Thank you, Cassidy." Her voice lost its earlier heat. "You've been so wonderful and patient and accommodating this week. I couldn't have done this without you."

"I think you could have," I smiled, "but I'll take the compliment."

She returned my smile, which let me know I'd successfully diffused the situation. "I'll be back as soon as I can," she promised.

After a quick kiss, Julia rushed out, leaving me alone in her parents' house, and trusting me to put a price on their worldly possessions. She'd promised a swift return, but I anticipated this familial errand might take a while. I had no experience in yard sales since I'd never been in possession of a surplus of items I'd wanted to get rid of. But this was a tangible way I could ease Julia's burden, like grocery shopping or cleaning, so I was committed to doing a good job.

I opened one of the upper kitchen cabinets and wearily sighed at the stacks of plates and bowls and serving dishes. This was going to take forever.

Julia returned under an hour later. In that time I had managed to organize and price out the plates, bowls, and coffee mugs in the upper kitchen cabinets along with an unexpected collection of pint glasses from various Minnesotan breweries. I'd also managed to clutter the kitchen floor with pots and pans, casserole dishes, and cookie sheets. I was sitting in the center of the kitchen floor, planning my next move, when I heard the knock on the rear kitchen door.

Julia's face peered at me through the door's glass cutout. I saw her struggle under the awkward shape and size of two pumpkins, one clasped under each arm.

I hopped up from the floor and opened the door. "What are those for?"

"I stopped at a farm stand on my way back," she explained. She shifted the weight of one of the large pumpkins to her hip. "I robbed you of a proper Halloween a few weeks ago."

I stared incredulously at the two orange orbs. "You want to carve them right now? What about the estate sale?"

"We'll have time for that later," she promised.

She handed me one of the oversized pumpkins, and I dutifully lugged it to the eat-in kitchen table. Julia rummaged around in the drawers until she found markers for designing, oversized spoons to scoop out the pumpkins' innards, and knives of various sizes. I waited while she painstakingly covered every square inch of the kitchen table with newspaper so we wouldn't get pumpkin goo all over the clean kitchen.

Never one for patience or planning, I grabbed a serrated knife and plunged it into the top of my pumpkin. I sawed a circle around the long green stem and pulled off the top. Normally I would have removed the seeds and guts with my bare hands, but I used one of the metal spoons Julia had provided to at least pretend to be civilized.

I watched Julia in my peripheral vision as she drew on her pumpkin with a black marker.

"What are you going for?" I asked. "Funny or spooky?"

"Those are my only choices?" she posed.

I shrugged as I continued to remove the pumpkin's inner goo.

"Can't say I've ever seen a sexy jack-o-lantern, but I'm sure you could pull it off."

A small smile, coy but pleased, tickled at the corners of her mouth. "I had a hunch that you might be into this kind of activity."

"A hunch? What does that mean?"

"I can imagine you getting very excited for Halloween when you were little," she observed. "Carving pumpkins. Getting dressed up. Trick or Treating. Eating too much candy."

"I still eat too much candy," I joked. "Do you want me to take out the seeds for you?" I offered.

Julia rolled up the sleeves of her button-up blouse. "That's very chivalrous of you, dear, but I can manage."

Seeing Julia Desjardin elbow-deep in pumpkin guts bordered on the absurd. She had once described a childhood of climbing trees, fishing off of piers, and grass-stained blue jeans. It hardly seemed possible. She was so particular as an adult, so polished and refined, that I had a hard time imagining her as being different as a child. We'd never really discussed how she'd garnered the reputation as Embarrass' untouchable ice queen, but I supposed that kind of change occurred over time, not overnight.

"How did it go with your mom?" I asked.

Julia wrinkled her nose as she continued to clean out her pumpkin. "I don't blame her for not wanting to eat. The food at that place looks horrendous."

"But you finally got her to eat?" I pressed.

She nodded, but the frown remained fixed to her beautiful face. "I promised her I'd get her out of there soon. I know she'd prefer to come back to her house, but that's really not feasible. I can't afford around-the-clock care, and I'm not selfless enough to give up my life to live with her here."

"She wouldn't want that for you," I jumped in.

I really had no idea what Olivia Desjardin was like, but I

couldn't imagine any loving parent wanting their child to give up their own life and happiness in that way.

"You're probably right," she conceded. "But it *was* my mother who guilt tripped me into coming back to Embarrass after Jonathan's death."

I reflected on her statement. I'd thought my mom had a considerable talent at making me feel guilty. I didn't call enough, I didn't visit enough, I didn't accept her friend requests on social media. But she'd never given me a hard time for not wanting to live in my hometown of St. Cloud. In fact, I imagined it was a point of pride that she could brag to her friends about—her daughter had gotten out of town and was making a good living on her own without her parents' help. I might have had PTSD, but at least I wasn't living in their basement.

It forced me to dwell on a former Marine friend, Geoff Reilly. He hadn't exactly been a friend, but we'd served together. After he left the military, Reilly had been living in his mom's basement. And not much later after that, he'd committed suicide. If I hadn't found the police academy, throwing myself from one mission to another, I might have been in a similar situation.

I shook myself out of darker thoughts and redoubled my efforts on my pumpkin. While I'd been daydreaming, Julia had finished cleaning out the insides of her pumpkin.

"How's it going over there?" I asked.

Julia turned the face of her pumpkin away from me. "No peeking," she chastised.

The tip of Julia's tongue poked out between her top and lower lip as she concentrated on her pumpkin's design. While I aggressively hacked into my pumpkin's face, she was predictably more patient and precise with her carving.

"It looks like I'm not the only one having fun," I lightly teased.

"It's been a while," she admitted. "I'm a little rusty."

"I'm sure it'll be perfect."

I'd had an idea in my head of what I wanted my pumpkin to look like. I'd been going for a scary, jagged-toothed monster. It wasn't *exactly* going to plan, but it wasn't a total disaster.

"Are you ready for the big reveal?" Julia asked.

I cut out a few more spiked teeth into my pumpkin's crooked smile. "Ready," I confirmed.

"On the count of three," Julia prompted. "One...two...three."

At three we turned the carved face of our respective pumpkins so the other person could see our artistry.

"Is that ... is that a scary clown?" I asked.

The carved mouth was similar to my pumpkin's with razor-sharp teeth. But the top of the pumpkin's face was reminiscent of a clown with a large, bulbous nose and wide, expressive eyes.

"You said I could do scary or funny," Julia shrugged, "so I did both."

I smiled and shook my head. "Only you would find a way to overachieve at pumpkin carving."

"Should we put these outside?" she proposed.

I nodded. "Yeah. And I think I saw some candles in one of these drawers."

I explored the drawers closest to me until I found two tealight candles. A little more rummaging produced a lighter.

We carried the carved pumpkins outside and staggered them on the front stoop. I placed a candle in the belly of each pumpkin and lit the tealights. I jogged down the stoop to join Julia on the front lawn. Her arms wrapped around my waist and her chin rested on my shoulder. We admired our work from afar, watching the flickering tealights illuminate the face of each pumpkin.

"Did you do this as a kid?" I asked.

"Mmhmm. My dad was usually too busy to join, but my mom was always good at stuff like this."

"Maybe we can carve pumpkins and put them on the balcony next year," I suggested.

Julia pressed her lips against my cheek. "I'd like that."

A particularly aggressive gust of wind blustered around us. Fallen leaves rustled across the grass and the tealight candles extinguished.

"Well, I guess that's a sign we should go back in," I chuckled.

Julia sighed. "You're probably right."

It was clear neither of us was too excited to resume the daunting task of readying her parents' possessions to be priced and sold. We went back inside, but left the pumpkins on the front stoop.

Julia lingered in the front entrance. "I doubt there's much upstairs worth selling," she observed, "but I'll give you the grand tour if you'd like."

I was eager to glean more about Julia's past and far less ambitious about jumping back into estate sale prep, so I let Julia lead the way up the staircase to the second floor.

Julia wrapped her knuckles against a closed door near the top of the steps. "This is the closet where I had my first kiss."

I arched an eyebrow. "You kissed someone in a closet? That really gives new meaning to closeted lesbian."

Julia made a face. "Funny girl. Didn't you ever play Seven Minutes in Heaven when you were little?"

"Nope. I was a good girl," I grinned.

Julia's mouth twisted. "I doubt that very much."

Another hallway door was closed. Julia caught my stare. "That was Jonathan's room," she said softly. "You can look if you want."

My eyes widened. "I'm not... I wasn't...."

Her smile was gentle. "It's only natural to be curious about my dead brother."

Sensing I wasn't bold enough to open the door myself, Julia stepped across the hallway and opened the bedroom door for me.

I noticed the musty air right away—an indication that windows were rarely opened and that few people regularly went into the space. I stayed in the hallway, but I couldn't help looking just a little. A blue comforter covered a full-sized bed. The walls were painted a lighter shade of blue. The carpet was noticeably older than in the rest of the house. The Desjardins must have gotten new flooring everywhere except in Jonathan's old bedroom. I spied a number of small, faux-gold trophies on a shelf along with various ribbons and medals. A high school varsity jacket had been framed in a shadow box that also hung on the wall. It wasn't exactly a shrine to the young man who'd taken his life; instead, it looked like he might return at any moment.

"He enlisted after he graduated college," Julia spoke beside me. "Jon fought terribly with my father about it. He was expected to go to law school—to follow in my father's footsteps—to be a lawyer, a city prosecutor, and finally a politician. My father had it all planned out. My dad was tough," she said somberly. "Parents want better for their children than they had for themselves."

"Why do you think he enlisted?"

Julia shook her head. "He never told me. But, then again, I never thought to ask. I was too preoccupied with my own life to be concerned about anyone else's."

"Do I get to see your bedroom?" I asked. I was curious to be afforded another window into Julia's past, but I was also in search of a change of topic. Her body seemed to sag with the weight of unpleasant memories.

"That's awfully presumptuous of you, Miss Miller."

I was less hesitant to enter Julia's old bedroom than I had been with Jonathan's. If I had been expecting the same trophies, ribbons, and awards, however, they were absent. In fact, as I entered the room Julia claimed had been hers, I saw nothing in the décor to support that statement. Decorative pillows were piled high on the meticulously made bed. A wooden bureau lined one wall. With the exception of the bed and dresser, the room was empty: no framed photographs, no keepsakes, no mementos of Julia's past.

I turned slowly in the center of the carpeted room. "Where's all your stuff?"

"I live in St. Paul, dear, not Embarrass."

"Didn't your parents keep this room for you?"

"Whatever for?" she posed. "I haven't lived here since I was eighteen."

"Yeah, but Jonathan's room—." I stopped myself. I was comparing apples to oranges.

"Your parents didn't convert your childhood bedroom to something else?" she questioned. "A gym or a craft room perhaps?"

I rubbed at the back of my neck, feeling unwontedly guilty. "It's still my room. Pretty much looks the same as it did a decade ago."

Julia hollowed out her cheeks. "Oh. I guess you'll have to show me some time."

Her words were stiff and empty of feeling. What old wound had I unintentionally opened?

"But, I mean, my parents don't really need the space," I found myself rambling to make amends. "My dad's got a big workshop in the backyard and my mom's already got a space for her crafts, and they don't really get too many guests who stay the night. And it wasn't like I really moved out and had a place of my own."

"Darling. Stop," Julia urged. "You don't need to make me feel better about my parents not keeping my old bedroom."

I curled my lip. "But it sucks," I complained on her behalf.

She gave me a small smile. "Yes," she said in a soft voice. "It does suck. And I'm sure you feel cheated. You wanted to see my old things."

"This isn't about me," I meekly protested. "I'm upset for *you.*"

Julia's lips twisted in a wry smile. "So you weren't hoping to see my old prom photos?"

"Are they black and white?"

Julia's mouth dropped open.

A nervous, nearly hysterical, laugh bubbled up my throat. "I can't believe I just said that."

"I can't believe it either."

I swooped in and wrapped my arms around her body before she could swat me away. "Babe, I'm kidding!"

Her body language remained stubborn and closed off. I squeezed her ribcage tighter and just barely lifted her off the floor. We were built similarly, close to the same height when barefoot, but I had her beat in upper body strength.

Julia started to wiggle and fight back when her feet dangled in the air. "Let me down, you brute!"

She couldn't stay mad at me—pretend anger or otherwise. I could hear the laughter in her words.

"Only if you show me photos of you as a kid," I said, keeping her body in flight.

"We have to get the house ready for the estate sale," she protested.

"Nuh uh," I denied. "I'm not letting you down until you show me those pictures."

Julia tried once more to wiggle free, but she had no leverage. I finally felt her body slump and go limp in defeat.

"Fine," she huffed. "I'll show you. But then we really have to do work or we won't be ready for tomorrow."

I gently lowered Julia to the floor, but I kept my arms around her midsection. "Pictures and then we'll get to work," I vowed.

I sat down on the edge of the crisply made bed while Julia rummaged in the closet. While the room itself was basically empty, the bedroom closet was stacked high with boxes. Julia's youth hadn't been entirely erased, only stored and packed away.

After some searching and rearranging, Julia produced a small box no larger than a shoebox. She sat beside me on the bed and removed the lid. I leaned closer to get a better look at the stack of photographs inside. Julia pulled a handful of prints out of the box. The top photo was slightly sepia in color, a result of not being protected in a photo album, not the age of the photo itself.

I squinted at the individuals in the top photograph. A young girl, maybe six or seven, stood with a smaller boy. Both figures grinned broadly at the unseen photographer.

"Is that you and Jonathan?" I asked.

Julia nodded and handed me the photo for inspection.

She pulled another image from the pile and gave it to me. "You've never experienced an Embarrass winter before. Check out these snow drifts."

"Damn!" I exclaimed. "They're as high as the roof!"

Julia leaned against my shoulder and tapped the photograph. "We don't normally get this much snow, but that winter my father had to shovel out the backyard so we could actually play outside."

I continued to inspect the new photo. A dark-haired little girl grinned at the photographer. She wore a one-piece red snowsuit and matching knit hat. Her smile was so big, her eyes had been forced shut.

"I'm digging the monochromatic look," I teased.

"Please," Julia huffed. "I'm sure you were the pinnacle of fashion at age six."

I looked up suddenly. "Do you ice skate?"

"I'm from Minnesota, aren't I?" she said in lieu of a response.

"Yeah, but do you actually go?" I pressed.

"When's the last time *you* went skating, Marine?" she turned the question on me. "I can't imagine they had ice rinks in Afghanistan."

"It's been a while," I admitted, "but I'm sure it's just like riding a bike." I paused in thought. "Do you know how to ride a bike?"

Julia chuckled. "Just because you haven't seen me do something doesn't mean I don't know how to do it."

"I want to do it all with you," I enthused. "Ice skating. Bike rides. Hiking. Fishing. Camping!"

Julia's dark eyebrows rose higher with each new proposed activity. "Easy there. Take a breath."

I exhaled noisily. "I feel like I wasted so much time being over there. Eight years of my life, and what do I have to show for it? A chest full of medals that are just collecting dust in storage."

"You fought overseas for close to a decade," she unnecessarily reminded me. "I'm sure that provided a lifetime of experiences."

"Experience doing what?" I snorted. "Masturbating, playing cards, and shooting guns at sand."

"Charming."

"I know," I grinned.

I couldn't understand it, but offending Julia's delicate sensibilities was still one of my favorite pastimes. Watching her upper lip curl and her button nose crinkle from something I'd said brought me unexplained joy. I found myself exaggerating or being purposefully crass just to witness that reaction.

"There's no rush," Julia tried to appease me. "We have the rest of our lives to get through your bucket list."

"The rest of our lives, eh?" My voice cracked on the final few syllables. "That sounds like a proposal to me."

"Oh, hush," she dismissed. "Enough of this trip down memory lane. We need to get the house ready for tomorrow."

An unintentional groan rumbled up my body.

Julia arched an eyebrow "Unless you'd rather go home? I can take care of all of this."

With some difficulty, I stood from the mattress. "No, no. I'm here to help. Let's do this."

Julia stared up at me from the bed. "If I'm asking too much of you, Cassidy, just say the word. I don't want to take advantage."

"You can take advantage of me later, woman. Right now we've got a yard sale to get ready for."

Julia's ruby red lips twisted into a smirk. "Help me off this bed, soldier."

I reached down and Julia grasped my hands. With a slight tug, I pulled her to her feet. She released my grip and her hands traveled to the nape of my neck. Her fingers twirled through loose tendrils.

"I never would have been able to do this without you, Cassidy."

"Stand up on your own?" I tried to joke. "You're not that old." My joke came out terse and forced. I'd never been good at accepting compliments or praise. I shifted uncomfortably from one foot to another.

Julia frowned, her lower lip lightly protruding. "I mean it. You know I'm no good at being vulnerable or not having complete control. I never would have made it through this without your support."

Her dark eyes were intense and sincere, causing me to wriggle in place.

I heard her exhale and watched her eyes lift in exasperation. I clearly hadn't responded to her words how she'd intended.

"I love you, you idiot," she sighed.

"I love you, too," I easily returned.

She punctuated her words with a quick, but solid kiss against my lips. I would have trapped her in my embrace and compelled her to linger a little longer, but we were only delaying the inevitable. We really needed to get some work done or we'd be ill prepared for Embarrass' bargain hunters the next morning.

We returned downstairs to the chaos of the kitchen. Our pumpkin carving detour had made the room more messy, but only negligible. It had already been chaotic without the jack-o-lanterns.

"You've done a great job in here," Julia admired. "Can you handle the rest of the kitchen while I check out my father's den?"

I nodded. "Divide and conquer. Sounds like a plan."

I rubbed my hands together when Julia left me in the kitchen. I felt good about my progress in the room, but we had much more square footage to tackle before we were through. I had only just begun putting stickers on casserole dishes and bread loaf pans when I heard the distinct sound of glass breaking come from the next room over, followed by Julia's mumbled curse words.

"You okay?" I called out.

"I'm fine," she returned. "I broke an old ashtray."

Despite her assurances, I abandoned my kitchen-packing tasks to check on her. When I entered her father's study, a dark wood paneled room filled with books, I found Julia on her hands and knees. She gingerly picked up large ceramic shards from the floor and dumped them unceremoniously in a small trash can beside her.

I stooped down to help her pick up the pieces. "I hope it wasn't a family heirloom," I joked.

Julia's head was bent forward, which had caused her loose hair to fall in front of her face. "No," came her dull reply. "Just something I made for him in grade school. I hadn't realized he'd kept it. He didn't even smoke."

"Where's the broom?" I asked. There was no way we would be able to pick up the smallest pieces by hand.

Julia didn't immediately respond. I initially wondered if she'd heard my question until I noticed that her movements had stilled. She was still on her hands and knees, but she was no longer picking up the ceramic fragments. Her face was still hidden from my view, but when she inhaled through her nose, the heavy breath made a telltale rattling sound.

"Julia?"

I said her voice with as much concern and emotion as I could muster. Layers of questions existed in the single, uttered name.

What are you feeling?

Are you okay?

What do you need?

What can I do to make this better?

Her narrow shoulders shook with silent grief. The sorrow traveled down her spine until her shoulder blades and midsection had no choice but to participate. She leaned back on her heels and her hair fell back into place. I could see the twin narrow paths her tears had taken down her cheeks.

"How am I going to do this, Cassidy?"

Chapter Ten

A round-faced woman with thick glasses and a deep frown walked in a slow circle around William and Olivia Desjardin's living room. The crease between her eyebrows deepened. She gestured to a brass light fixture with an off-white canvas lamp shade. "How much for this lamp?"

It had taken us all night and into the early morning hours, but Julia and I had eventually gotten her parents' house ready for the estate sale. We'd advertised that the sale would begin at 9:00 a.m., but when we'd shown up that morning half an hour early, people were already parked on either side of the residential street, hoping to be the first to rummage through the household goods. I'd heard of people camping out for concert tickets, new phones, and limited edition sneakers, but not for a yard sale.

"Whatever the sticker says," I told the woman.

The potential customer's frown deepened even more. "I'll give you five dollars."

I hadn't memorized the price for each item Julia had decided to sell, but I was pretty sure the lamp was at least double what the woman was offering.

My cellphone chirped in my back pocket before I could counter the woman's initial offer. I'd forgotten to silence the ringer after my morning alarm. I glanced quickly at the screen to discover I had a text message from my girlfriend: *I need you upstairs.*

Julia had begged a short break a few minutes earlier. We'd only been open for business for a little over an hour, but the sight of so many people picking over her parents' belongings had proven too much for her.

"I'm sorry. I'll be right back," I told the woman. "Let me know if you have any other questions."

With one fleeting glance at the few individuals milling around the Desjardins' living room, I bounded up the stairs, two at a time.

I'd been on the second floor the previous night, but that didn't mean I felt completely at ease wandering around Julia's parents' home. I was also keenly aware that I'd left potential customers to police themselves downstairs, although I doubted anyone would be so bold as to walk away with a random knick-knack without paying for it.

"Julia?" I called out.

In response, hands darted out of the hallway closet and tugged me inside. The closet door slammed shut behind me, cloaking me in darkness. The storage closet had recently been cleaned out; we'd boxed up the clothes and spare linens the previous night. Only the stale scent of mothballs and a few miscellaneous wire hangers remained.

"Kiss me," I heard Julia's command.

I couldn't see her with any definition in the darkened closet. Only a thin line of light shone in the gap between the hallway carpet and the bottom of the closet door.

"What?"

The hands fisted in the front of my Henley top tightened their grip. "I underestimated how difficult this would be," Julia said roughly. "I'm feeling out of control. I need to take control of something to feel normal again."

"Like-like me?" I couldn't help my stammer.

The hands clutching my shirt pulled me closer. "Lose the pants, lover," Julia husked into my ear.

A wave of arousal traveled up my spine.

Although she'd given me the command, Julia didn't wait for me to comply. She popped the top button of my jeans and pulled down the zipper.

Despite how her simple demand had my body overheating, I resisted. "What about all those people downstairs? What if someone wants to buy something?"

"They can loot the place for all I care," she practically snarled.

She teased her fingertips across the lace at the top of my underwear. Her mouth was hot against my neck. "But I suppose if you'd rather be haggling prices with Embarrass' bargain-basement shoppers, I should let you get back to it."

Her words said one thing, but it was clear she had no intention of letting me leave that closet until she had had her way with me.

I swallowed hard. She peeled open the front of my jeans wider and gave a sharp tug so my pants slipped a few inches farther down my hips. Her hand found its way between my jeans and my underwear. When she stroked my clit through my underwear, my knees, miraculously, only buckled slightly.

"Well, darling?" she posed. Her warm breath tickled my ear. "What are you going to do?"

My hands joined hers at my hips. I rested my palms on top of her hands and I curled my fingers around her hands so we could—together—pull my jeans lower still.

"That's my girl," she purred. I could hear the smugness in her tone.

The waistline of my jeans clung precariously across my upper thighs. I felt the carpet shift slightly beneath my feet as Julia lowered herself to her knees. She pulled on the legs of my jeans; they gave up their remaining resistance and fell to pool around my ankles.

Julia helped me step out of my pants. It was pitch black, the confined closet restricted my movement, and I didn't want to ruin the moment by accidentally kneeing Julia in the face. There was nothing sexy about a bloody nose.

Once she'd successfully stripped me of my pants, Julia trailed her fingertips up and down my bare legs. Her touch was light and teasing, almost contemplative, as if she hadn't quite made up her mind about what to do to me. She stroked her fingers up and down my muscled calves. She swirled her fingertips across my kneecaps and inched her way higher. I inhaled a sharp breath when she lightly scratched her short nails up my inner thighs.

I mourned the loss of the visual of Julia on her knees in front of me, but in many ways, the encounter was even more erotic like this. I couldn't see her, which meant I also couldn't anticipate her next move. I might as well have been blindfolded.

She shifted again on her knees while her fingers curled around the backs of my knees. She pulled me closer with a commanding tug. I stumbled a few footsteps closer until Julia's mouth connected with my panty-covered sex. I reached for anything to hold onto in the dark, but my hands only struck against the scattered wire hangers. They clanged together like a chaotic wind chime.

Julia's stiffened tongue rolled against the front of my underwear. I quietly groaned in satisfaction when her tongue connected with my clit despite the cotton barrier between us.

"Please," I whimpered.

She pushed the center panel of my underwear to the side and ran her tongue along my slit. She stopped short of my clit before returning the underwear's material to its original location. Her patience surprised me. I had been expecting a quick closet fuck, but Julia apparently had had other plans. I similarly marveled at her stamina. My knees would have been screaming in protest by now.

Julia curled her fingers under the elastic waistband of my underwear and tugged them down my thighs. Hands snuck up the bottom hem of my cotton top and rounded the cups of my bra. Long, feminine fingers worked their way beneath the underwire to pluck and scratch my nipples. The recognition that strangers were shuffling around the first floor and that the walls in this house weren't soundproof might have been a turn-on to some people, but I was no exhibitionist. Despite those thoughts crawling around in my brain, Julia's fingers on my nipples and her mouth on my clit were all the convincing I needed to temporarily shelve those worries.

"Oh God," I panted.

I reached again for something to hold on to. My flailing hands found the wooden coat rod above me, and I held on tight.

Julia dug her fingers into my hip bones and buried herself deeper into my folds. She licked me at a feverish pace without penetrating me. I felt consumed. Devoured. Revered. Cherished.

My fingers flexed around the smooth wooden coat rod. I could feel the miniature grooves in the wood that years of shouldering the weight of hangers laden with winter jackets, snowpants, and other heavy clothes had created. The pole wasn't connected to anything, and when I shifted my grip, it fell off its track. The empty wire hangers promptly slid the length of the closet rod and crashed to the floor. The noise was akin to what I imagined a piano might sound being thrown from a tall building.

"I broke your parents' house," I wheezed.

I stupidly continued to hold onto the closet rod that I'd unintentionally pulled from the wall. But in my defense, the closet wasn't large enough for me to cast it to the side without giving my girlfriend a concussion.

I expected my clumsiness might warrant some kind of reprimand, but I only heard Julia's laughter.

"Thank you, darling."

"For making us both deaf?" I proposed.

I could feel my underwear being returned to its proper place. The carpet shifted beneath my shoes as Julia stood from her knees. I heard a distinct click and the closet was bathed in light from a solitary naked lightbulb hanging above us. I blinked into the unexpected illumination as Julia's smiling features came into focus.

"Thank you," she repeated. She placed a small, but warm kiss against my confused mouth. I could taste myself on her lips. "That was exactly the kind of distraction I needed."

"Glad I could help?" I still wasn't quite sure what had happened. One moment I was dripping with arousal and her saliva and the next, the world was crashing around our ears.

The intimate moment was obviously over, so I reassembled my outfit. The wire hanger avalanche had been jarring, but I was still wildly aware of the sticky ache between my thighs. I couldn't wait for the damn estate sale to be over so I could have my Seven Minutes in Heaven with her.

Julia grabbed my hands. "Come on," she urged. "Before they run off with the good china."

. . .

Julia and I descended the rear staircase that connected to the kitchen, still hand in hand. We both paused on the final steps when we spotted someone in the back of the house. A middle-aged man with thinning hair and a visible beer belly beneath his polo shirt and flat-front khakis looked around the kitchen. He was a large man, both tall and broad. He lightly slapped a beige file folder against his meaty palms.

Julia spoke up when the man stuck his head through the doorway that led to Mr. Desjardin's den: "Excuse me. This part of the house isn't included in the estate sale." Her words for the uninvited tourist were icy.

The man jumped, previously unaware of our presence. He spun on the heels of his tan loafers. "Julia! Hey! I was just looking for you."

"And apparently you've found me." Julia's eyes narrowed shrewdly as she descended the final steps. "Tony? Tony Pond? Is that you?"

The man chuckled sheepishly and tugged on his leather belt. "Yeah. With a little less hair and a little more weight."

Julia turned to me. "Tony and I went to high school together," she explained. "I didn't know you lived in Embarrass."

"It's a relatively new development," he admitted. "I left town after graduation, went to college at St. Cloud State. Got married shortly after. I was working at an insurance company in St. Cloud, but got transferred here about a year ago. I didn't know where you were staying in town or how to contact you, but my wife saw the advertisement in the paper for the estate sale. I figured it was worth a shot," he shrugged.

"What is this about?" Julia asked.

"Your dad's life insurance policy."

Julia shook her head and continued to look perplexed. "I filed all the proper paperwork with Sally Hansen at City Hall just the other day," she said. "I have the same policy through the city from when I was prosecutor."

"Your dad took out an extra policy with my company about two months ago," Tony revealed. "Typically we wait until the beneficiary files a death certificate with the company before we release the funds, but I realized you might not have even known the policy existed."

"You're right. I didn't," Julia confirmed. "And I'm a beneficiary?"

"Yep. The only one," Tony noted.

I shared a quick look with my girlfriend. First the will and now this?

"How much is it for?" Julia asked.

Tony studied the file folder in his hands and read aloud: "One million, four hundred ninety-nine thousand, nine hundred and ninety-eight dollars. And zero cents. Two dollars shy of $1.5 million dollars."

Julia blinked. "That's ... that's absurd."

"I don't do the underwriting—I'm just the messenger," Tony seemed to apologize.

"So what do you need me to do?" My typically unflappable girlfriend looked uncharacteristically rattled.

"I'll need a copy of your father's death certificate and the bank account you want the payout deposited to." He laughed awkwardly. "Unless you want a check for 1.5 million dollars. We could do it Publishers Clearing House style."

"No. Direct deposit will be fine, Tony. Thank you."

"A policy this size will take some time," he warned. "Our office will go through our own investigation into the circumstances surrounding your father's death. This type of thing is usually a red flag. If the insured dies within the first two years of the life of the policy, we hold the right to delay the death benefit payout until the full two years have elapsed."

"What kinds of things do you look into?" I was curious.

"Evidence of fraud. Application fraud, death fraud, forgery, and phony policy fraud," he listed.

"Death fraud?" I questioned. The other three categories were more self-explanatory.

"If you kill yourself or someone else to collect the insurance money," he explained. He grinned and turned to Julia. "You didn't kill your dad, did you?"

Julia stiffened at the unsavory suggestion. "No, Tony. I didn't."

"Great! I can check that off my list. Only three more kinds of fraud to go," he laughed again. "You wouldn't believe the lengths some people go to get their hands on this money. A few years back this married couple in Michigan faked the husband's death in a car accident. They dug up a body from the cemetery and set their car on fire to fake his death."

"How'd they get caught?" I wondered.

Tony's grin grew. "The dead body they used had female DNA. And forensics discovered the fire had been started in the front seat, not the engine."

"Wow," I marveled. "After all of that plotting and planning, you'd think they'd at least dig up a dude's body. What a bunch of idiots."

Julia delicately coughed. "We should probably be getting back to the estate sale. I appreciate you taking the time to track me down, Tony."

"Of course! Do you, uh, do you mind if I do a little shopping before I go?" His sheepish grin returned. "My wife asked me to look around while I'm here."

"Please, look around all you want," Julia allowed. "In fact, whatever has a sticker on it is all yours, free of charge."

Tony's eyes lit up. "Cool!"

The three of us left the kitchen and returned to the unattended living room. Given *carte blanche* over the estate sale, Tony Pond eagerly swooped around the room in search of his next future possessions. As I scanned the room of its bargain-hunter occupants and the various stickered items for sale, I was half surprised we hadn't returned to a completely ransacked room. We'd been gone for at least half an hour.

In fact, in our absence, consumers had taken it upon themselves to complete their purchases. A tidy pile of cash sat on the folding table we'd been using as a checkout counter. A stack of handmade notes and Post-its identified who had bought what and how much money they'd left behind. I marveled at their honesty and efficiency.

Julia silently fingered the stack of dollar bills. "I suppose we can stop selling things," she thoughtfully remarked. "I'm apparently a very rich woman."

Chapter Eleven

Two suitcases, various grocery bags, and a cooler filled with the food we hadn't managed to eat were packed into the trunk of Julia's black Mercedes. White drop cloths had been draped over most of the furniture in the house and the thermostat had been set to an appropriate temperature so the pipes wouldn't freeze when winter's brutal weather settled across northern Minnesota. The state was prone to sub-freezing temperatures, but Embarrass' unique climate had earned the town's reputation as The Cold Spot.

Julia twisted the key in the car's ignition. Her sunglasses sat in the center cup holder along with her cellphone. I saw her eyes had locked on the rearview mirror rather than the stretch of road in front of her. What I would have given to be privy to her thoughts in that moment. Did she really want to go back to the Twin Cities? Had she achieved enough closure to be able to move forward?

Julia had said her goodbyes to her mother the previous day. Olivia Desjardin would remain in assisted living in Embarrass until Julia could get a judge to transfer guardianship over to her. We hadn't spoken about how our lives in the Twin Cities would necessarily change once that happened. I only knew I would continue to feel uncomfortable and unimportant until I'd been properly introduced to her mom. But to be fair, that also meant Coming Out to my own parents. I couldn't expect to be brought into Julia's mother's inner circle if I wasn't brave enough to do the same for Julia with my family. I anticipated a number of tough conversations in my immediate future.

"Do you mind if we make a quick stop at my family's cabin before we head back?" she asked. "I want to be sure the water was turned off and the pipes are clear so they don't freeze and burst this winter."

I nodded my head. "Yeah. That's fine."

Julia's cabin was farther north in the opposite direction of our return trip to the cities, and more remote than even her rural mansion. In truth, I wasn't in any hurry to get back to Minneapolis. There would be suitcases to unpack and laundry to do, and then I'd be back in the basement of the Fourth Precinct like I'd never really left. I really needed to take a proper vacation soon.

We drove in silence out to Julia's cabin. Talk radio played quietly in the background, more like white noise rather than anything worth listening to. Beyond the car windows, the sky was clear and blue, and yet I couldn't shake this funk—this melancholy —that had settled on my skin. There'd been flashes, brief moments of laughter and normalcy, but ever since Julia had received word about her father's death, things had felt ... off. I didn't want to over-think it, but I'd had a lot of free time during our time in Embarrass to do just that.

The wheels of Julia's Mercedes crunched against loose gravel as she pulled onto the shoulder of the road. The cabin didn't have a proper driveway, so Julia had to park her car on the side of the little-traveled county highway. We exited the vehicle and I followed Julia's familiar steps down a narrow path through dense forest, which led to a grassy clearing and the modest, rustic dwelling. I'd been struck the first time I'd seen the seasonal cabin; it was a true up-north cottage—a far cry from the level of luxury with which I had associated Julia Desjardin.

"I think the water shutoff valve is by the meter," Julia announced. They were the first words she'd spoken to me since leaving her house. "It will just take a minute."

"Sure thing," I said.

Julia disappeared around one corner of the cabin, while I stood in the lawn with my hands shoved into the pockets of my leather jacket. The normally manicured grass had sprouted into a field after months of neglect. I scanned the immediate vicinity for a shed that might contain a lawnmower. The long grass would need to be taken care of before winter so it didn't attract small pests that might make it their home.

When I didn't see any smaller buildings close to the cabin, I wandered a little deeper into the property. I didn't feel completely at ease poking around, but I was also eager to have a task while Julia dealt with the underground pipes. I didn't find a shed, but I did walk down a narrow, well-traveled path that ended at a series of wooden steps and a floating pier. Julia's cabin was the only visible dwelling around the lake, which made me wonder if her family might have owned the entire body of water.

I walked out to the edge of the dock, my hands still jammed in my jacket pockets. The surface of the water rippled from a gentle breeze. The sun was high in the cloudless sky. The sunshine made the clear lake look almost like a pool of sapphires, dotted with the emerald green of scattered lily pads.

The sound of Julia's steps behind me on the wooden pier preceded her words.

"Water is shut off, but I'll still need to pour anti-freeze down the sinks and in the toilet. I can do that when I come back to pick up my mother in a few weeks though. It should be fine until then," she seemed to think aloud.

I unzipped my leather jacket and felt the cool, November air against my throat.

"Cassidy?" Julia spoke when I didn't respond.

I continued to stare, unblinking, at the surface of the lake. With one seamless move, I shrugged out of my jacket and let it drop to the wooden dock. I grabbed the bottom hem of my sweater and pulled it over my head. The wool garment joined my jacket at the end of the pier.

"What are you doing?"

I stated the obvious. "Taking off my clothes."

"I can see that, dear, but why?" Julia's voice teetered on the fine line between agitated and annoyed.

My hands were at the top button of my jeans. I popped it open and pulled down the zipper.

I finally looked at her over my shoulder. "I can't very well go swimming in this outfit."

The skinny jeans typically clung to me like a second skin. I'd worn this particular pair a few times without washing them, so they hung a little looser on my frame than usual. I shimmied the denim material down my hips and thighs and hopped from one foot to the other to remove my pants entirely.

I stood in only my bra and underwear. A particularly icy wind rustled the dense forest that surrounded the cabin and I roughly rubbed my hands up and down my forearms to generate some heat.

"Cassidy, it's November!"

"What's your point?" I posed.

I'd done polar bear plunges—in a bathing suit, not naked—on a number of New Years' Day mornings. It was an odd way to celebrate the coming of another calendar year, but that's what people did up north. After a few cheap beers, you didn't feel a thing.

I slipped out of my underwear and unfastened my bra. The undergarments completed the untidy pile of clothes. I didn't linger. The moment my bra hit the ground, I dove off the end of the dock. I had no idea how deep the water was, but I leapt in without a second-thought.

I was a strong swimmer—I'd been on the swim team in high school—but I still internally gasped when the icy water struck my naked skin. The air seemed to evacuate my lungs as I plunged beneath the water's surface. I sucked in a sharp breath when I resurfaced. I wiped my hand across my eyes to clear my vision. My ponytail already felt like a frozen rope against the back of my neck.

Julia did not appear amused. She all but stamped her foot on the wooden pier. "Have you lost your mind?"

The lake was cold and, thankfully, deep. I tread in place while Julia glared at me from the shore. Seaweed brushed against the bottoms of my feet.

"Are you coming in?" I called to her.

"Absolutely not," she snipped. "I'm not in the mood for hypothermia."

"It's not that bad," I defended. "Lake Superior in July is probably still colder."

Julia hugged her arms around her torso. Nothing in her body language indicated she was going to join me, but that didn't surprise me. I'd been spontaneous and not a little bit foolish. Julia didn't do either of those things very well.

"Fine," I huffed. "I'll get out." I moved my arms around me in a simple freestyle stroke and began to swim back towards the pier.

"Wait." Julia's one worded plea had me stopping short of the dock's edge.

My breath hitched in my throat, no longer from the cold water but from the movement of Julia beginning to pull off her jacket. Beneath the long wool trench coat she wore a knitted sweater and black skinny jeans.

She tugged off her ankle-high boots and socks and grimaced when her feet touched the ground. My smile grew exponentially when she slipped out of her sweater and wiggled out of her tight jeans. Unlike my own rumpled pile of discarded clothes, Julia carefully folded her sweater, jeans, and jacket and stacked them in a tidy pile away from the water's edge.

I hooted like a college frat boy. "You gotta take it all off, baby."

I could see her pursed lips and the roll of her eyes, but eventually her black bra and matching underwear joined the rest of her clothes.

Her body slightly huddled in modesty and from cold, Julia tiptoed to the end of the short pier. Her steps were quick and light against the wooden boards. When she reached the end of the dock, she dipped her right foot into the lake and grimaced. "This is insane," she muttered.

"Don't think about," I coached from the water. "You've got to jump right in."

I heard her make another displeased noise.

"Hurry up, Julia," I sing-songed. "I'm gonna be a popsicle pretty soon."

I'd actually gotten used to the water's icy temperature. Either that, or my body had grown completely numb. Maybe she'd been right about hypothermia.

Julia raised her arms above her head. I heard the sharp intake of air before she dove, headfirst, into the lake. I turned my face away only briefly to avoid the small splash her dive had produced.

Julia's head popped out of the water. Her eyes were wide and her mouth was open. "You could have warned me!" she loudly gasped.

"About what?"

"The water," she sputtered. "It's *freezing!*"

"It's November, babe."

"That's what *I* said," she grit out.

I lazily tread in the water to keep afloat. "I guess I'm just a heartier Minnesotan than you."

Julia's eyes perceptibly narrowed. "Is that so?"

"What can I say?" I continued to tease. "Some people can't handle the cold."

I knew I was playing with metaphorical fire. My girlfriend had proven herself to be wildly competitive, regardless of the sport or task. Julia floated closer; she bobbed only an arm's length away. I felt like a swimmer eyeballing an approaching shark. She was probably going to drown me.

"What are you doing?" I worried aloud.

"Just swimming, darling," she feigned innocence.

I kicked my feet under the water and started to paddle away.

Julia immediately noticed the new distance between us and stuck out her lower lip to pout. "Don't you trust me?"

"I trust you to dunk me," I declared.

A playful grin slowly spread across her features. She sank lower in the water until only her eyes, nose, and forehead appeared above the water's surface. The action reminded me of a predator stalking its prey, like a crocodile about to spring on an unsuspecting water buffalo.

"No splashing!" My voice sounded tight in my throat. I

blamed the cold water for its high pitch and not my childish anxiety.

Julia's body emerged from the lake just enough for her mouth to reappear. The toothy grin remained. Crocodile, indeed.

"We should probably head back up," she said. "I wasn't kidding about hypothermia."

I nodded, knowing she was probably right. The impulsive decision to go skinny dipping in November hadn't been my smartest moment, but it had been a needed moment of levity in an all-too serious trip.

Neither of us spoke as we swam the short distance back to shore. I hefted myself out of the water first and reached down to help Julia climb back onto the pier. The water had seemed warmer than the chill in the air. I was too frozen to appreciate the view of her naked body and how drops of water clung to her olive-toned skin. Well, mostly.

We grabbed our piles of clothes and rushed up the narrow, matted path that led back to the cabin. Julia deviated from the trail and started to jog toward the cabin instead of back towards her parked car.

I stopped in my tracks, clutching my clothes against my damp body, while I watched her hop onto the cabin's wrap-around porch. "Where are you going?" I called.

Julia pulled a busy keyring out of the pocket of her wool trench coat and unlocked the cabin's front door. "You're soaking wet. You're not getting into my car."

I didn't bother arguing. My teeth were starting to chatter together and my wet feet were going to freeze against the long grass if I stood still for much longer. I changed direction and hustled through the cabin's open door.

It was several degrees warmer inside the cabin, but the moderate heat did nothing for my goosebumps. I performed a cursory scan of the inside of Julia's family cabin. I'd been inside once, but only briefly. The cabin was modest, but clean.

Julia set her tidy pile of clothes onto a blue futon and opened the door of a nearby closet. She pulled two multicolored beach towels from the closet and tossed one in my direction.

I dutifully began to towel off my body while Julia did the same from the other side of the room. I pulled my hair free from its elastic band and dried my damp hair as best as I could before pulling it back into a semi-wet bun. I eyeballed my clothes and leather jacket, which I'd unceremoniously dumped onto the bare wooden floors. My skin was chilled, but I defiantly didn't want to put my clothes back on. It would only mean going back to real life. I wasn't ready for that.

"What if we stayed here for a few more days?" I thought aloud.

Julia was still naked, toweling off her body more thoroughly than I had done. "Here? At the cabin?"

"We've got everything we need," I reasoned. "Running water, a bed, we could make a fire in the woodstove for heat. We've got all that food in the back of your car," I listed. "It's perfect."

Julia bit down on her lower lip as she considered my words. I was half amazed she hadn't immediately rejected the idea outright.

"Think of it as a mental health break," I proposed. "You've been like a candle burning at both ends this past week. Take a few more days to recharge the batteries. Your clients will be better served by a rejuvenated Julia Desjardin."

Julia's lips pursed and her eyes narrowed. "You certainly know which buttons to push, dear."

I wiggled my eyebrows playfully. "We can push each other's buttons, too."

She continued to contemplate my proposal in silence.

I clasped my hands together as if in prayer. "C'mon, Julia." I tried not to whine. "Play hooky with me for a few more days."

Finally, she sighed and shut her eyes. "Okay," she relented. "We can stay a little longer."

"Really?" I felt giddy.

"Yes," she allowed. "But only if you promise me you won't try to get me to stay just a few more days once the weekend is over."

I grinned deeply. "Don't worry. Once we run out of beer, I'll be begging you to leave."

Julia regarded me with a careful look, and I watched her pink tongue flick at the center of her lower lip. "Oh, I'd much rather have you beg me for other things, dear."

If I'd felt chilled before, Julia's gaze had my body heating up in very specific places.

"I suppose I should make a fire so we don't get hypothermia," Julia announced, breaking the spell she'd placed over me.

"I'll grab food and stuff out of the car," I offered. I finished my hasty toweling off and pulled on my sweater and jeans. I had some difficulty with the jeans; the denim stubbornly stuck to my still-damp legs.

The trunk of Julia's Mercedes was packed tight with bags of groceries that we hadn't gotten around to eating and a cooler of leftover hot dish from William Desjardin's funeral. I only had two hands to carry things in, so I prioritized the food over the clothes. As long as Julia could start a fire or continued giving me those smoldering, suggestive looks, I didn't envision us needing the latter.

I dropped the grocery bags and cooler just inside the cabin's front door. I could already feel the heat from the woodstove; Julia had managed to build and start a fire in my short absence. I grinned when I spied her on the futon, which she'd converted into a bed and had half covered in quilts and knit afghans. Even though her body was draped in blankets, I could tell that she hadn't bothered to put her clothes back on. The tidy pile of clothes she'd worn that day on a nearby chair gave her away.

She pulled back the top cover and patted at the empty space beside her. "Hurry up, Marine. Your services are required to warm me up."

"Yes, ma'am," I eagerly agreed, already tugging off my boots.

I yanked off my sweater and tugged down my jeans, which turned out to be much easier to take off than to pull on. I didn't bother folding my clothes like Julia had done. It was just one more step getting in the way of me being naked in bed with Julia.

The futon creaked as I climbed under the covers. I stiffened and stilled my movements with the furniture's initial complaint.

"Are you sure this thing can handle both of us?" I wondered aloud.

"It may not be a proper bed, but I'm sure it will get the job done," Julia assured me.

I continued to wiggle in place on the thin mattress as I tried to find a more comfortable position. The metal frame seemed to poke me in tender places regardless of where I moved.

"No offense, babe, but the floor might be more comfortable," I grunted.

"Getting soft on me, soldier?" she lightly teased. "I've spoiled you so much you can't handle a perfectly serviceable futon?"

"How are *you* okay?" I marveled. I continued to twist and turn, but with each new position, I only managed to discover a new level of discomfort.

"I'm naked in bed with a gorgeous woman; who am I to complain?" she posed.

Her compliment fell on deaf ears. "Yeah, but there's a metal rod digging into my ass."

Julia huffed with growing impatience. This had been *my* idea, after all. "Stop wiggling and come here."

I didn't have time to vocalize a new complaint. Hands seized my naked flesh and long legs draped over me until we were a tangle of naked body parts.

Julia tugged the blankets higher until they covered the tops of my bare shoulders. "Is that better?"

The quilts had a musty smell to them. I briefly considered when they'd last been laundered, but quickly shut down the question. God. Maybe Julia was right. Maybe I *had* gotten soft.

"It's perfect," I lied through my teeth.

Julia pressed her forehead against the side of my face and shook with silent laughter. "It's pretty terrible," she mumbled against me. "You might be right about the sleeping on the floor thing."

"It's not so bad," I tried to appease. I shifted again on the makeshift bed. My movement caused another massive creak, but at least the futon hadn't collapsed under our joint weight.

I played with her delicate fingers under the light thrown off by the woodstove. The orange glow made her normally olive complexion more of a warm peach color.

"What were you like when you were little?"

I admittedly didn't know much about Julia's past. She had shared bits and pieces along the way—brief fragments that I was forced to knit together like an incomplete puzzle. Too many pieces continued to allude me, however.

She didn't pull away or withdraw her hands from mine, which spoke volumes about her willingness to be cross-examined in that moment.

"I always tried to be very good," she started. "If not for my parents' instructions, I think I would have been very wild. I'm sure I was the quickest child to climb a tree. I reveled in going higher than anyone else. I was the first to log roll down a steep hill. The most curious to pick up a frog. But there comes a time in every young woman's life when it's no longer appropriate to have grass stains on your jeans or sticks and leaves in your hair."

"There is?" I rhetorically asked.

"According to my father," she hummed. "He had very high expectations for both Jonathan and myself, but even at a young age I could recognize that my father had a different set of rules for the two of us. He looked the other way if Jonathan did poorly on a test or came home after curfew, reeking of alcohol. Boys will be boys," she sighed.

"And what do girls do?" I wondered.

"They sit up straight. They don't get dirty. They keep their bedroom tidy. They don't make mistakes."

"That settles it; I'm not a girl," I mused.

Julia rolled over on the futon to face me. Her hands stroked along my cheekbones. "You're a lifesaver. That's what you are. Before we met, I was like a caged bird. It was a cage my father had constructed so long ago, but one in which I'd become a complicit prisoner. I'd opened the cage during college, but I slammed that door shut again after Jonathan's death. It's probably why I resisted you so much in the beginning. You'd pried that door open, but I was too afraid—maybe too comfortable—to come out and stretch my wings. Like I'd forgotten how to fly." She dropped her eyes and suddenly looked very embarrassed. "Wow. I really ran with that metaphor, didn't I?"

It was a self-deprecating remark, meant to divert my attention from her revealing omission.

"Keep going," I urged. "I want to hear more about Julia B.C."

"Only if you tell me more about Cassidy B.J." She blinked once. "Please forget I just said B-J."

I chewed on my lips to control my juvenile smirk.

"What was your first kiss?" she asked.

"Spin the bottle."

"First *real* kiss," she countered.

"Spin the bottle," I stubbornly maintained.

She raised an eyebrow, suspecting there was a longer story that accompanied my proclamation.

"I was on the swim team." I couldn't remember if she already knew that, but it didn't really matter. "That was kind of my main friend group—both girls and boys—we were always hanging out after practice or partying at somebody's parents' house after a swim meet. Most of the time we just raided people's liquor cabinets or had a giant bonfire, but this one night someone had the bright idea to play Spin the Bottle."

"$100 dollars it was a boy's idea," she remarked.

I laughed. "You're probably right. I was buzzed on cheap beer, but not so drunk that I wasn't nervous about playing. I hadn't really kissed anyone before, and I didn't want to make a fool of myself in front of all of my friends."

"This was in high school?" Julia interjected. She wasn't judging me, but I couldn't help bristling, if only a little.

"Yeah. I was a late bloomer. Whatever," I scoffed before continuing. "It was an empty tequila bottle. Real cheap shit. But we probably felt fancy because it wasn't apple pucker. Everyone was taking turns, spinning the bottle, laughing about whoever it landed on, and then hooting and hollering when the kissing actually happened. Boys kissing girls, boys kissing boys, girls kissing girls—it didn't really matter; it was just a game. I was trying to have fun," I recalled, "but I got more nervous as each person went."

Julia's hand wandered beneath the quilt. Her hand settled on my knee, and she gave it a reassuring squeeze.

"Anyway. It was my turn, and I spun that sucker so fast—like if I spun it hard enough it might take off like a helicopter. But it didn't. And it stopped on this one dude."

I heard Julia sigh. "I was hoping for a girl."

I held up a hand. "Story's not over yet," I promised. "So anyway, we both get up on our knees, and I can hear everyone making a big deal like they did for everyone's turn. And I was just planning on a quick peck, but the guy shoves his tongue in my mouth, and it was just about the grossest thing I'd ever felt. I jerked back, kind of gagging, and the laughing got louder. But then it was the next person's turn and the game continued."

"I'm liking this story less and less," Julia quietly seethed.

This time I reached for her knee for a reassuring squeeze. "Story's not done yet. People got bored of the game, so it ended soon after that. Turns out it's hard to binge drink if you're playing Spin the Bottle. I was still kind of traumatized, so I went outside to get some air. I wasn't the only person out there though."

"This time it had better be a girl," Julia chirped, almost as a warning.

I allowed a small, sly grin. "Her name was Anna. I didn't really know her that well. She was older, probably a senior, and I was a freshman."

"Ah, and so began your attraction to older women," Julia mused.

"Honestly, I couldn't even describe her to you. It feels like a lifetime ago."

"I'm assuming this was a better experience than Spin the Bottle?" she smirked.

"Fuck yeah," I enthused. "I actually *liked* her tongue."

"Now you're just trying to make me jealous," Julia remarked.

"Your turn again," I decided. "I want to know everything about you. Your first kiss, your first pet, what scared you when you were little."

She flicked at the damp hair that surrounded her face as if brushing away my suggestion. "I'm terrible at being vulnerable."

"Practice makes perfect," I smiled. "You've seen all my scars—physical and mental."

She breathed in a shaky breath. "I suppose you're right."

I grinned a little wider. "I love hearing those words."

Her eyes narrowed in the flickering darkness. "Don't get used to it, dear."

Chapter Twelve

I sat in an Adirondack chair on the slightly unlevel porch of Julia's family cabin. The coffee from the French press I'd found in a kitchen cabinets was strong, and its residual heat in the ceramic mug warmed my hands. On the horizon, a dense fog hovered over the small, private lake, giving the morning a haunted feeling. The fall colors of the forest that surrounded the cleared property appeared muted as if even the foliage wasn't quite awake yet.

I looked over my shoulder when I heard the simultaneous squeak and creak of the cabin's screen door. I took a too-aggressive sip of my coffee when I saw Julia. The hot liquid burned my tongue and the roof of my mouth. I sputtered slightly before setting down my coffee cup on the porch boards. I had expected to see Julia in the doorway, but I hadn't expected for her to be completely naked.

Manicured feet stepped onto the weathered wooden boards. Strong, muscled calves flexed with each step. My eyes raked up the smooth expanse of her stomach and the shallow dip of her belly button. Her bare breasts seemed to defy age and gravity.

Julia raised her arms above her head and inhaled. "I love that smell," she sighed contentedly. "The lake water. The slight tang of algae in the air."

"Did you run out of clean clothes?" I gaped.

Julia dropped her arms to her sides and her eyes narrowed slightly. "Are you complaining about the view?"

"Fuck no," I emphatically swore even though I knew she disapproved of cursing.

She hummed, seemingly allowing the coarse outburst. "Save any coffee for me?"

I scrambled to retrieve the cup I'd set down on the porch's wide-planked boards. I offered her the half-filled mug and she accepted it with a small, pleased smile.

She inhaled the scent of the hot coffee before taking an experimental sip. "Ooh, it's hot," she observed.

I fanned myself in exaggeration. "You can say that again."

Julia smiled above the coffee cup. "You're sweet."

"And you're gorgeous," I countered. I opened the quilt I had wrapped around my shoulders like a superhero's cape. "Get in here."

"Oh, I'm perfectly fine out here," she coyly refused.

"*You* might be fine like that, but I'm not. Get your body on my body," I all but growled.

Julia took pity on me and settled down on my lap. Once she was seated on the tops of my thighs, I pulled the blanket tight around our bodies.

She pressed her cool mouth against my cheek. "Who's the heartier Minnesotan now?" she playfully mused.

"You win all the prizes, baby," I allowed.

I rearranged the quilt so it could envelope Julia's body as well as my own. In my shuffling, my palms unintentionally brushed against her nipples, but I certainly wasn't mad about it. Her nipples were hard. It wasn't surprising; it was probably 40 degrees outside of the blanket.

My hands continued to explore under the blanket. What else was I supposed to do with a gorgeous, naked woman sitting on my lap? I stroked her naked form with neither urgency nor intentions. I was content to just feel her skin beneath my hands and feel the reassuring weight of her body against me.

I was used to Julia in refined, elevated settings where she typically controlled the pace and if sex was even going to happen. But since arriving in Embarrass we'd had sex on her kitchen island, in a closet during an estate sale, and she'd fucked me on her dining room table. She'd had sex with me on my apartment floor in Embarrass the day I'd arrested her father for embezzlement. And when she'd found out that her father had been killed, she'd tried to have sex with me on a pool table in a Minneapolis dive bar.

I wasn't complaining or judging; people coped with grief and stress in a variety of ways. I knew Julia had a tendency to use sex as a distraction from confrontation and trauma. I was guilty of the same troubling habit though—seeking physical intimacy to distract from things that might trigger my PTSD. But I hoped we would soon be able to settle into the routine of regular, boring lives where sex was a compliment to the day and not a coping mechanism.

I brushed her nearly black hair over her shoulder so I could press my lips against the nape of her neck. Neither of us had showered, unless you counted the impromptu polar bear plunge, yet she still smelled and tasted delicious. Spicy sandalwood and earthy rosemary.

"Mm, that's nice," she sighed.

My lips remained on the back of her neck while my fingers continued to explore. I flattened my palms and stroked my hands down her breasts and up and down her torso. I ran my fingertips across her stiffened nipples.

Julia exhaled again—a deeper, lustier breath.

I let my touch linger at her breasts. I pushed and pulled the bundled flesh back and forth. My touch became progressively more aggressive; I pinched the hardened buds between my fingers until I heard her make another noise.

With one hand still lazily flicking at her nipple, I moved my other hand to her naked sex. I slid my hand across the space where upper thigh meets pelvic bone, and I cupped her sex in my palm.

Beneath the blanket, Julia spread her legs wider for me. She reached one arm above and behind her head to reach me. Her fingers tangled in my hair: "Cassidy."

Julia used a lot of nicknames for me during sex: Miss Miller, soldier, Marine, and Detective were just a few examples. But when she breathed my actual name—when she called me Cassidy —I could hear the love and reverence in each syllable. I thoroughly enjoyed the games we played—that tug-of-war for control as we pushed each other beyond our comfort zones—but I cherished these moments the most.

I couldn't see what I was doing, but I knew her body nearly as well as I knew my own. I slid my fingers up and down her shaved lips. Up and down. Again and again. I mashed her clit beneath my flattened fingers and rubbed it as roughly as I had her nipples.

The top of her thighs and the small of her back had become slick with sweat. It was humid, wet, and sticky beneath the blanket, but I wanted more. I wanted her dripping. I wanted her sweat and her cum to coat her inner thighs. I wanted to feel the evidence of her arousal drip between her shaved folds and on to me. I wanted the front of my sweatpants saturated in her juices.

"Fuck me," she whispered. Julia squirmed on my lap. "Please, Cassidy. Fuck me."

I sliced my fingers through her swollen folds and dipped the tip of one finger and then two into her. My arms were long, relative to the rest of my frame, but from this angle, I couldn't penetrate her as deeply as I wanted. That didn't seem to bother Julia though. She continued to buck her hips and grind down on my lap.

An idea popped into my brain, but I wasn't sure how Julia might receive the suggestion.

"Sit on my fingers."

Julia's movements slowed. "Sit on your ..." I could tell she was mentally trying to work out the mechanics.

I withdrew my right arm and wedged it between our bodies. The sweat that had accumulated made it easier for me to slide my hand down her back and wiggle beneath her backside. Julia lifted herself up to make more room. I held my middle and forefinger rigid and felt for her entrance.

Julia held on to the arms of the Adirondack chair as she lowered herself onto my waiting fingers. I steadied my foundation by gripping my right wrist with my left hand. I bit down on my bottom lip as she swallowed me.

"Oh fuck," Julia groaned. "You're in so deep."

I let my head drop forward, and I rested my forehead against her bare back. She was so warm and wet and tight, I thought I might explode.

Julia began to lift her body and then let it fall back onto my fingers. She stretched around my two digits as she dropped lower and lower.

"Oh my God," she gasped. She almost sounded surprised.

She elevated again and slid back down my wet fingers. I could feel her arousal collect between my fingers and drip onto my knuckles. Julia repeated the action again and again while I did my best to keep my wrist steady. She probably hadn't been expecting an upper body workout when she'd rolled out of bed that morning, but I didn't hear any complaints. Instead, only unintelligible sounds hit my ears.

Her movements became more erratic the longer she bounced up and down on my lap. Eventually, she gave up on the up and down in favor of a front to back grinding motion. Her breathing quickened and became more shallow.

"I'm close," she panted. "So close."

"Rub your clit," I ordered.

Julia feigned no modesty or resistance. Her hand immediately disappeared beneath the blanket which had nearly fallen off our bodies. I could feel her hand bump against mine as she helped push herself over the edge. Her head fell forward, and I wrapped my free arm around her midsection to make sure she didn't fall off my lap entirely.

"Cassidy! I'm cumming!" she gasped. "Oh fuck, I'm cumming!" Her body jerked and spasmed and she continued to rub her clit. I flexed my fingers inside of her until her lower body eventually stopped moving.

When her body finally came to rest, I gingerly withdrew my fingers from her sex.

"Fuck," I heard her final whimper.

I retrieved the quilt as best as I could and rearranged it around her body. She might have been overheating, but it wouldn't be long until the early winter air cooled her down again.

Julia leaned back and rested her head on my shoulder. "Thank you," she quietly breathed.

I craned my neck so I could better see her face. "For the orgasm?"

Julia's mouth curved up at its edges. "For that," she smiled serenely. "But I more meant for this moment—this opportunity to reset. I didn't realize how much I needed it. I can only imagine what a mess I'd have been if we'd gone straight back to the cities."

"I wasn't ready to go back just yet," I admitted. "But I know we can't stay here forever. We'd both be running away again."

"As long as we're running away together," she said.

I tightened my arms around her waist and pressed my lips against her temple. "It's you and me, babe," I murmured into her hair. "Always."

~

We stayed on at the lake cabin for another two days. Eventually, however, we'd run out of beer, and I was admittedly starting to feel a little ripe. The cabin had no proper shower, so any bathing took place with a bar of soap and a washcloth at the kitchen sink. It was the kind of scenario to which I'd become accustomed in the military, but those days had since past. Yep. I *was* getting soft.

I repacked the trunk of Julia's Mercedes while she closed up the cabin for winter for a second time. I leaned against the trunk while I waited for her to complete her tasks. I inhaled the fresh, unadulterated northern Minnesotan air. I wanted to commit its scent and taste to memory; I wasn't sure when we'd be back.

Julia made her way up the slightly matted path from the cabin to the car. "You ready?" she asked.

"No," I admitted.

Being cooped up in the rustic cabin with Julia with no worries, no responsibilities, and even no cellphone reception had been a dream—so much so that I hadn't experienced any night terrors of my own.

Julia smiled knowingly. "Get in the car, Marine."

I fiddled with the car radio, searching for a signal, while Julia pulled the car onto the county highway. We'd only driven a few miles closer to civilization when Julia's phone, which she'd left in the cupholder in the center console, started the buzz and jingle. With cellphone coverage restored, the outside world barged its way back into our lives.

"Damn, girl. You're popular," I teased.

When my own phone started to tweet, chime, and buzz, Julia returned the compliment. "It seems I'm not the only one in high demand."

The reminder that the world had continued to spin while Julia and I had pressed the pause button wasn't enough to diminish my good mood. But when I picked up my phone and saw that all of the missed phone calls and text messages were from David Addams, I started to grow concerned.

The text messages all delivered the same sentiment: *Where the hell are you?*

My eyebrows knit together as I scrolled through the one-sided text thread.

Call me back when you get this.

I need to talk to you.

Why the hell aren't you answering your phone??

Did you run off to Canada with her?

Miller! This is serious!

God damn it—listen to your voicemail. It's important.

My stomach dropped when I reached the final unread text message: *Did Julia kill you, too?*

"What the..." I mumbled.

"What is it, dear?" Julia asked.

I glanced in her direction. She'd left her own phone, untouched, in the cupholder in the car's center console.

"I don't know," I told her. "David Addams is freaking out about something."

There was only one voicemail. The bulk of the alerts on my

phone had been for missed calls and texts. I hit play and pressed the phone to my ear.

"Miller." David sounded breathless. "I don't know where you are or why you keep sending my calls to voicemail, but we just got a tip on the William Desjardin homicide. The insurance guy, Tony Pond, turned over Julia's financial records to us. It won't be admissible in court because he really shouldn't have done that, in fact it's probably against the law now that I think about it," he started to ramble, "but anyway, Julia took out a shit ton of money—$10,000—the day before we found her dad. $10,000!" he emphasized. His normally low register tightened in agitation. "The whole family is a bunch of crooks. I sure as shit hope you didn't know anything about it because the Chief is ready to slap the cuffs on your girlfriend." He paused and seemed to gather his breath. "Fuck, Miller. Where are you? Call me back!"

The phone clicked in my ear as the message came to an end.

"Pull over." The phone was still pressed to my ear.

"What?" Julia voiced her confusion.

"Pull the car over, Julia."

All of the energy had been drained from my words. My voice sounded flat. Robotic. The bubble we'd been hiding in had been broken. Exploded.

Julia followed my emotionless command and pulled the black Mercedes to the side of the country highway. The engine continued to run and she turned on the vehicle's hazard lights.

"What's wrong?" she asked.

I swallowed thickly. "I think you should look at your phone."

"Cassidy, what is this about?"

"Your phone, Julia." My words were now strained. "You have some missed messages."

Julia pushed her sunglasses up to her forehead, and I heard her frustrated sigh. I could have just told her what I'd heard from

David, but I didn't know what to say or even how to frame the star-tling accusation.

I watched Julia from the passenger side seat. Her caramel eyes narrowed in scrutiny as she inspected her missed messages and texts. I wondered who had called her and what they'd said. I couldn't imagine David had called her with the same information as what he'd provided me; that had been more of a professional courtesy call for my benefit.

Julia pressed her fingertip to the phone's screen and brought the device to her ear. My throat tightened and a nauseous feeling overwhelmed all other senses.

I didn't know how much time had actually passed—no more than a few minutes—but it felt like an eternity to me. Even though we were in close proximity, I couldn't make out the exact words of the recorded message Julia was listening to. The voice was low and male, however—possibly Chief Hart.

I watched Julia's face for some sign of recognition or some indication of what she knew and what she'd been told. I watched her cheeks hollow as her features become more pinched and tense. Finally, she pressed another finger to her phone's screen and returned the cellphone to its original cupholder.

She wet and pursed her lipstick-less lips. "Well. It seems I'm a wanted woman."

Her tone and words were too nonchalant for me. "What the hell, Julia!" I burst out.

Julia twisted in her seat. "I'd ask you to watch your tone and volume, dear."

"They think you had something to do with your father's death!" I all but hollered.

Julia slipped her oversized sunglasses back to their perch at the bridge of her nose. Even over the gentle hum of the car's engine and the rhythmic click of the hazard lights I could hear her labored breath as she tried to gain control of her emotions.

"Julia."

I knew she required time and space to process this new information, but I wasn't going to give her either. This was too important.

I watched her work the muscles in her jaw and the way her throat moved as she swallowed down complicated emotions. "I suppose I should turn myself in."

I let out a frustrated noise. "This is the most ridiculous conversation I've ever had."

Julia raked her fingers through her raven hair. "I'd like to stay off the local news. We don't need to have a manhunt or a white Bronco situation."

"Tony Pond shouldn't have been able to turn over your bank records to the police, right?"

"A judge would never allow it in court," she confirmed. "In fact, whomever he obtained my records from will be getting into quite a bit of trouble. He was only supposed to get my bank account information in order to deposit the life insurance policy once he completed his investigation." She licked her lips like an agitated cat. "But life in a small town works differently. People bend rules and look the other way. If the people of Embarrass already think I had something to do with my father's death, they'll look for any bit of circumstantial evidence that helps that narrative."

"So what do we do now?" I asked.

"Now I call my lawyer."

"You have a lawyer? Don't you just represent yourself?"

Julia sighed. "If I've learned anything from my trial to get custody of my mother, I'm not very adept at keeping my cool in court. This will go much more smoothly if representation speaks on my behalf rather than me losing my temper over the incompetence of the Embarrass police force." She glanced in my direction. "No offense, dear."

I shook my head. "None taken."

Julia pinched the bridge of her nose. "You should go back to Minneapolis."

"What?" Her words were a surprise. "Why?"

"I have no idea how long this will take, and you can't be gone from your job. You've already taken off enough time because of me."

We'd already spent over a week in Embarrass to arrange Julia's father's burial and to settle the details of his estate. My insistence that we take a few more days to ourselves at Julia's cabin had tacked on additional time away from our respective jobs. I hadn't checked in with Stanley and Sarah, but I assumed they were surviving without me.

"I'll take another leave of absence if it comes to that."

My supervisor Inspector Garnett might not have been able to allow me to be a beat cop again for technical reasons, but with the cold case assignment he'd demonstrated that he didn't want to lose my police skills altogether. I was fairly confident that he'd make allowances for an emergency. And this was definitely an emergency. -

Julia flexed gloved fingers around the steering wheel. I heard the creaky complaint of leather against leather. "This place is never going to let me escape; this town is going to swallow me whole," she murmured. -

I reached across the car and placed a hand on top of hers. "We'll make sure it chokes first."

Chapter Thirteen

Familiar scents had the ability to transport me to an earlier time and place. Charcoal and roasting meats reminded me of tailgating before a Twin's game. Chlorine brought me back to the high school where I'd been on the swim team. Fresh cut grass sent me to my family's cabin on Lake Armstrong. So it was no surprise that the musty air inside of City Hall triggered memories of my short time of employment with the Embarrass police department. I considered a quick trip to the basement to say hi to Chief Hart and Lori, but this wasn't the moment for pleasantries. Until they realized how ridiculous their suspicion of Julia was, I had no reason to visit.

I glanced at the woman to my right, wondering how she felt about being back in the building. Julia's memories of the place would have run much deeper than mine, first as a place where her father's mayor office had been located and then her own as city prosecutor.

She'd dressed up for her meeting with the Special Agent for the BCA. With the exception of her father's wake and funeral, she'd been dressing more casually than what was typical for her. But her armor had returned for this interview. Makeup had been carefully applied. Her slate grey Oxford blouse was crisply pressed and unbuttoned to the third button. A pearl necklace draped across her collarbone. Her steps were light and sure as she ascended the marble staircase to the second floor of City Hall. She lightly touched the wooden banister for balance, although she always looked steady in her red-bottomed stilettos. On any other day I might have been tempted to lag behind a few stairs to admire her backside beneath her pencil skirt, but this wasn't a typical day.

The signage outside of Mayor Desjardin's old office no longer bore his name. Once he had resigned as mayor—at Julia's prompting—the city had held a special election to replace the disgraced politician. Grace Kelly had once told me who'd been on the ballot, but neither name had meant anything to me, and I hadn't bothered to follow up with her about the election's results.

The nameplate on Julia's old office, however, still identified her as city prosecutor.

The door to her former office opened to reveal the BCA agent overseeing William Desjardin's presumed homicide.

"Ms. Desjardin," she greeted. "Detective Miller. Thank you for coming in."

"I didn't really think I had a choice," Julia said icily.

Special Agent Andrews forced a smile to her lips. "Please, have a seat. Can I get you anything to drink? Coffee? Water?"

"That won't be necessary, thank you," Julia answered for both of us.

Special Agent Andrews ushered us into the office where she'd been set up. The police department was technically in the basement, but resources and space were limited. Chief Hart had his own private office, but the rest of the officers shared a common desk space. The department didn't even have a proper interrogation room. Under different circumstances, I would have felt sorry for her. Not only was she an outsider to the small, insular town; she also didn't benefit from the eventual collegiality that formed between police officers forced to share the same spaces—whether that be a squad car or a metal desk.

Agent Andrews helped herself to a small coffeemaker that sat atop of filing cabinet. Julia settled into one of the wooden chairs positioned on the opposite side of her old desk.

Special Agent Rachel Andrews was a striking woman. Despite the early November month, her skin was visibly bronzed. She wore her jet black hair parted down the center. The ends touched just beyond her rounded shoulders. A long, elegant nose split elevated cheekbones. Thin, dark eyebrows framed wide hazel eyes. She sat erect in her office chair. I wondered how she felt, interviewing the woman whose former office she occupied—a name she would see every time she entered the room.

It was surreal to be sitting in a vacant chair across from her old desk. I couldn't even imagine how Julia might have felt about it.

Julia tensed beside me. "That's mahogany." Her eyes shifted from the pedestrian coffee cup on the desktop to Special Agent Andrew's face. "I believe you'll find a coaster in the top right desk drawer."

Agent Andrews ignored Julia's not-too-subtle request. "Your bank records show—."

"My bank records were illegally obtained, Agent Andrews, and you of course know this," Julia cut in hotly. "No judge in this country would allow you to admit them as evidence, so I'd ask that we not continue with this charade."

Agent Andrews folded her hands on the desk and looked quietly contemplative, like someone meditating, or at least someone taking a moment to still her breathing. "If you're innocent, Ms. Desjardin, you should have nothing to hide."

"My *privacy* has been unduly violated by this investigation," Julia snapped. "You're lucky I don't sue both the Embarrass police department and the BCA for these transgressions."

"Don't you *want* us to find out who did this to your father?" Agent Andrews questioned.

"Of course I do—which is why I think it's *asinine* that you'd ever suspect me," Julia huffed. "You're wasting your time. Why would I make such an obvious withdrawal? If I'd wanted to hire a contract killer, I'd use untraceable funds like Bitcoin."

"It sounds like you've put some thought into this," Special Agent Andrews observed.

Julia rolled her eyes. "I'm not an amateur; I'm a criminal defense attorney."

"What was the $10,000 for?" Agent Andrews asked. She leaned forward in her chair. "Tell me and we can put this to bed right now."

Julia ignored the question. "Who else is a person of interest? Who else have you investigated besides myself?" she demanded. "If you're so keen on actually solving this case instead of lazily pinning the crime on the most convenient person, I can't be the only person under your microscope."

Agent Andrews sat back in her chair again. "You know that I can't divulge those kinds of details in an on-going investigation."

"And *you* also know that I have no obligation to be sitting here, answering your uninspired questions," Julia remarked. "So unless you're going to read me my Miranda rights and formally charge me with conspiracy to kill my father, I think we're done here."

Julia stood up abruptly. I scrambled to my feet as well.

Special Agent Andrews remained in her office chair—Julia's old chair. Her features remained impassive. "I'll be in touch," she said. Her words were neutral, but it felt like a warning. "You're not being charged with anything at this juncture, but I would strongly encourage you not to leave town."

Julia expertly navigated the marble staircase in her stilettos while I struggled to keep up. She rushed down the stairs as if fleeing a natural disaster. To be fair, however, the meeting with BCA had been a mess.

"I'm sorry I wasn't more of a help in there," I apologized.

"It's no matter, dear," she dismissed. "Having you in the room with me was enough."

"But I should be able to do something!" I exclaimed. "What's the point of dating a cop if it doesn't come with some legal perks?"

"I don't know; the handcuffs come in handy," she absently quipped.

I looked back in the direction from where we had just come. Agent Andrews hadn't bothered to see us out; we knew the way. "You were, uh, kind of hard on her. She's only doing her job."

Julia slipped on her sunglasses when we stepped outside. "That *was* me being nice."

~

Back at Julia's house, I sat on a stool at the oversized kitchen island while Julia chopped up vegetables for dinner. We'd made another trip to the grocery store on our way back from City Hall, once again unsure of how much food to get to last us for an indeterminate amount of time. The fact that Agent Andrews had told Julia not to leave the area had me worried. She obviously didn't think she had enough evidence against Julia to obtain an arrest warrant, but it was only a matter of time before a search warrant was issued and Julia—who prized her privacy above all—would be scrutinized and studied with a fine-tooth comb.

"Why are your bank accounts still in Embarrass?"

Julia shrugged. "It's the bank account my parents opened for me when I got my first piggy bank. Even though I don't live here anymore, everything nowadays is direct deposit or mobile. I didn't see the need to change it. Where's your money?"

"St. Cloud," I said. "I never saw the need to move my money to a different bank. Don't have all that much money to move anyway."

"Didn't the military pay well?" she questioned.

"It wasn't so bad. I didn't have any real expenses, so I was able to bank most of it. Uncle Sam paid for my meals, lodging, and uniform. I just spent my money on candy and porn."

Julia raised a fine eyebrow. "I'm half surprised you didn't come back with diabetes and a sex addiction."

"Nope. Just PTSD. They should put that in the recruitment brochure."

I could joke about my condition. I was good at that as a deflection tactic. I didn't know how to approach the topic without upsetting her. It wasn't every day you were accused of conspiring to kill your own father. But I also knew I needed the truth from her.

"What was the money for, Julia?"

I knew I didn't have to be more specific than that.

Julia didn't look up. She continued to slice red and orange peppers into thin strips. "Do you think I had something to do with my father's death?"

I'd been thinking so hard on my own question that I wasn't ready for hers.

Julia carefully set the knife down on the butcher block and wiped her hands on a tea towel. She regarded me from the other side of the island. "Do you really think me capable of such a thing?"

"Do I think you did it?" I repeated. "No. Absolutely not. Do I think you're capable?" I took a breath. "Yes."

Her jaw loosened, and I instantly regretted my honesty.

"I don't think you had anything to do with this," I was quick to clarify. "I *know* you didn't. That's not even a consideration."

Julia pursed her lips. "But you think I'm capable of plotting to murder my own father."

The word *murder* made me wince. God, I was an idiot.

"I only meant that you're very smart and resourceful." I pointed at myself. "I'm a blunt object. I'd never get away with that kind of thing. You're brilliant. You know loopholes and backdoor channels and you read the fine print. Fuck," I cursed, realizing I was only digging myself into a deeper grave. "Forget I said anything."

She blinked at me in rapid succession. "That's not the kind of thing that a person forgets, dear."

"Listen—the police are really focused on this $10,000. It's the only reason they're even looking at you. If you could just tell them what it was for, this whole thing would be settled."

"It's nobody's business," she sniffed, returning to slicing vegetables. "It's my money, and I can do with it as I please."

I knew I was stepping on uneven ground; landmines were all around me.

"Well, yeah—except use it to hire a hit man."

Julia slammed her fist against the island, causing the cutting board to rattle. "Is that even a serious statement?" she snapped.

I hopped to my feet. "Julia—this is serious!" Why couldn't she understand that? "You're under investigation for killing, or at least conspiring to kill your dad."

"Ridiculous. This is all ridiculous," she muttered.

"I know it is," I tried to pacify, "but you've got to give the police something." I lowered my volume to try to talk some sense into her. "I know how these investigations go. They'll be obsessed with closing this case. They've got no other suspects, so until you give them a reason to look at somebody else, they'll keep hounding you. The sooner you tell them what the money was for," I reasoned, "the sooner they'll drop you as a person of interest."

My words of wisdom did nothing to chip away at the defensive walls she'd constructed. If anything, she seemed to bristle even more.

"I will not have David Addams gossiping about me around town."

I threw up my hands in frustration. "You'd rather people believe you hired someone to kill your dad?"

"At least that's a conversation I can control," she said bitterly. "It's better to be feared than pitied."

"*Pitied?*" I couldn't understand the word choice. "What was the money for, Julia?"

She continued to hesitate.

I purposefully rounded the kitchen island. "Tell me."

"It's too embarrassing."

"Too embarrassing? What does that mean?" I grabbed onto her shoulders. "*Tell me.*"

"Fine!" Her eyes lost some of their previous fire. She cast her gaze to the floor and bit down on her lower lip. It was a gesture of vulnerability that had my heart aching. "The money was for a doctor."

I dropped her arms as if I'd been burned. "Are you sick?" I blurted out in worry.

"No, darling. Nothing like that." She exhaled deeply. "But I'm not getting any younger, so I decided to have my eggs frozen."

I should have felt relieved that there was a traceable purpose for the large sum of money. But rather than it calming my nerves, I felt injured. We'd had a brief conversation about children in the previous weeks, but how could she have made this decision without at least telling me?

"It costs $10,000 to have your eggs frozen?"

"That's just the down payment."

I nearly choked on my tongue.

"There's injections and retrieval and storage costs as well," she explained. "And if it doesn't work the first time, you pay all over again for a second round of treatment."

I swallowed. "Did you—did they already do it?"

"I had to postpone the procedure because of the funeral."

"But you're really going to go through with it."

"It's precautionary," she said. "It's planning for something that might not ever happen. It's safe. It's so when the time comes—*if* the time comes," she qualified, "I—*we*—have options."

"Options."

Julia rubbed at her face in frustration. "Can we not do this right now?"

"Then when?" I challenged.

"Maybe after the police stop harassing me about if I connived to have my father killed."

I let the rest of my questions die on my lips. She was right; there was too much going on at the moment for us to have a serious conversation about babies and egg storage and fertility treatments.

Julia straightened her shoulders, a signal that she was ready to change subjects. "I never asked how your call with Dr. Warren went the other day. I'm sorry. I was so preoccupied with the funeral, and then it was the will, and then it was the life insurance claim."

"It's fine," I cut in. "The nightmares were my fault. I got lazy about my treatment, and the dreams caught up with me. That'll teach me for neglecting my homework," I stated ruefully.

"Do you have another appointment soon?" she asked.

"I didn't make a follow-up. I didn't know how long we'd be in Embarrass."

Julia frowned. "Cassidy: you can't press the pause button on your treatment. If I'd known you'd done that I would have insisted we go back sooner."

"Which is why I didn't say anything," I tried to defend. "I'm sorry. I'll be better."

I thought about Dr. Warren's words to me during our most recent session. Deprioritizing my therapy didn't just injure me; it hurt all of my relationships, too.

I reached for a slice of red pepper and popped it into my mouth. "I'll call Dr. Warren's office and schedule my next appointment—virtual or otherwise."

"Good."

"But you've got to come clean to Chief Hart about what that ten grand was for," I challenged.

Julia narrowed her eyes. "This isn't a negotiation, Cassidy."

Chapter Fourteen

Afghanistan, 2012

Pop. *Pop. Pop.*

The sound in my ears is a symphony of surprise and pain. The body of the man who intends to kill me twists and contorts where he stands. His hands loosen on his assault rifle and it slips from his fingers. Only the strap slung over his shoulder keeps it from falling to the ground, but eventually it strikes against dusty earth when the man's body tumbles as well.

My hands search my own body. I haven't been shot. I'm whole. I'm still alive. I know better than to celebrate, however; I've seen enough horror films to know that Michael Meyers is never really dead.

I charge upon the two fallen bodies. As I approach, I can tell that Pensacola's first shot hit its mark. A bloody entrance wound dots one of the men's forehead just below his head covering. Crimson seeps into the linen fabric to form a bloody spiderweb.

The second figure, the man who intends to kill me, scratches at his throat. Pense's second shot missed its target entirely, but the third bullet struck him in the lungs. Foamy saliva and specks of blood collect in the corners of his mouth. His lungs are filling with liquid; he's drowning in his own blood.

Before Amir, I'd never killed a living thing before. My dad had never taken me hunting, and I always released the fish I'd caught in Lake Armstrong. Hell, I couldn't even kill a bug; I'd always found a cup to scoop up the spiders and beetles and found a nice plant outside to transfer them to.

As I watch the man who intends to kill me writhe on the desert floor, blood bursting from his lips, I'm reminded of the time my dad hit a deer with his truck. He'd been coming home from work when a young buck had darted onto the highway. There'd been no time to swerve or hit the brakes. In fact, I'd been instructed in driver's ed that the best strategy in that situation was to hit the deer straight on. If you tried to brake or maneuver your vehicle to miss the animal, you might strike another car or the guardrail and do even more damage. My dad kept a shotgun in the back of his truck. It wasn't for protection; it's just what you did in rural Minnesota. After he'd hit the deer and had assessed the damage to the front of his pickup, he'd retrieved the shotgun from the back of his truck and had followed the bloody trail into the neighboring woods to find where the injured buck had limped off to.

My dad's voice sounds loud in my ears as I gaze upon the man who intends to kill me and his struggle for air: "Put him out of his misery, Cass."

I bend down to one knee and try to make my voice soothing. "Shh," I hush. "It's going to be okay." I place my hand over his mouth. "Everything is going to be okay."

The man's eyes bulge and he tries to jerk away. But my adrenalin is pumping too hard and I won't let him go. I press down harder on his mouth and pinch his nose closed. "It's going to be okay," I repeat. "Everything is going to be okay now."

~

Julia was awake beside me. The sun was already up, but it couldn't have been for very long.

"You have to go back." Her voice sounded rough. "You can't be here anymore."

"What?" I struggled to reorient myself from a dusty Afghan road to a king-sized bed in northern Minnesota.

"Your nightmares. I've never seen them this bad or this frequent before."

"I'm-I'm fine," I stuttered.

Julia's voice was low and serious. "No. You're not."

I sat up in bed. "I'm fine, Julia."

Julia sat up as well to challenge me. "Why are you being so stubborn about this? Something about this place or this situation is triggering you."

"It's ... it's ... I don't know what or why it's happening. It's just my dumb brain." I smacked my forehead with the palm of my hand. "I'm messed up."

"You're not messed up," Julia rejected. "But you can't ignore the fact that you're getting worse."

"I'm not leaving you to deal with this on your own."

"And I'm not going to let you stay here," she shot back, emotions growing. "All of the progress you've made these past few month—I love you too much to let you throw it all away."

"I'm fine!" My voice rose to meet hers.

195

"No, you're not."

I felt out of breath. My heart raced, and I could feel the beginnings of a headache creeping into my brain. I pressed my fingers into my temples.

"Take the Mercedes back to the cities and go see Dr. Warren," Julia instructed.

I licked my lips. "Nope. I'm not leaving you."

Julia made a frustrated noise. She threw the covers off her body, half uncovering myself in the process.

I looked after her as she vaulted out of bed with purpose. "Where are you going?"

Julia aggressively opened several dresser drawers and threw clothes onto the bed. "If you insisted on being a stubborn ass, then you've left me no choice."

Her tone, her body movements, and her words had me regretting my own. "What's-what's happening?"

"If you won't go back to the cities without me, then we'll have to solve this case ourselves. No more waiting on the Embarrass police to decide who killed my father."

～

It was the second time using Julia's den to video conference in the short amount of time that I'd been in Embarrass. Prior to that I hadn't used the technology since being back in the States. Stanley Harris's bearded face filled the screen of Julia's laptop. The computers in the basement of the Fourth Precinct office weren't equipped with webcams, so he answered the videocall on his cellphone.

"I need your help," I said.

"What can I do?" he immediately asked.

I was glad Stanley wasn't the type to require small-talk or routine pleasantries to get things started. This wasn't a social call.

"Embarrass police think Julia had something to do with her father's death. And I know how cops work; their desire to close this case will blind them to alternative theories, which is why we have to find out what really happened ourselves."

I heard a feminine voice come through the laptop's speakers: "Are you talking to yourself again?"

"It's Cassidy," Stanley called out.

The screen shook like a scene from *The Blair Witch Project* before Stanley's face was replaced with a different, but familiar face—Sarah Conrad, another of my cold case colleagues.

"Miller! Are you ever coming back?!" she demanded.

"Eventually," I sighed.

I heard Stanley's annoyed tone off-screen. "I need my phone back. We're talking police business."

"What are you working on?" Sarah demanded. "And why aren't you back yet?"

I hesitated. I wasn't sure just how many people I wanted knowing the details of my extended absence.

"I'm at an impasse," I said. "I'm friends with one of the local cops working the case, but I really can't ask him to share files with me. It could get him in a lot of trouble."

I honestly wasn't convinced David would be open to the idea anyway. It was clear there was still bad blood between him and Julia.

"I don't know anyone in the BCA who could help either," I lamented. The BCA didn't only include on-scene field agents. It also included a forensics team whose headquarters were in St. Paul.

Stanley successfully wrestled his phone back from Sarah. There was some grunting and complaining until his bearded face came back into focus. "What about Celeste?" he proposed. "She doesn't work for BCA directly, but she might know some people over there."

Celeste Rivers, the pretty forensic scientist who worked for the Minneapolis Crime Unit, had proven herself to be a trustworthy ally on the last cold case we'd worked. She also happened to have a massive crush on Stanley. Too bad the poor guy didn't have a clue.

"Stanley, you're a genius," I gushed.

"That hasn't been officially documented."

"Hey, while I've got you—do you mind running a name for me to get an address?"

Stanley nodded. "Sure thing. What's the name?"

"Wendy Clark."

~

David had once shared with me the gossip that Wendy Clark had taken an early retirement and had moved away from Embarrass. After word got out that she'd been having an affair with William Desjardin—a married man with a vulnerable, ailing wife—she would have become a social pariah. The people of Embarrass may have been able to forgive her involvement in William Desjardin's embezzlement scheme, but not marital infidelity.

I found the former City Clerk in the front yard of her new house, raking leaves. Her permed, dishwater blonde hair was pulled away from her face in a low-hanging ponytail. I remembered her from our few interactions in City Hall. Early fifties. Fading tan. Not very pleasant to deal with.

I'd driven Julia's Mercedes. I didn't feel comfortable driving her father's car. It still felt a little morbid to be walking around his house or even ride in his car, like he might show up at any moment and scold my boldness. I hadn't told Julia where I was going, knowing that she would have wanted to tag along. It would be hard enough to get Wendy Clark to talk to me without Julia glaring at her the entire time.

I parked on the side of the residential street and walked up the paved driveway. "Ms. Clark?" I announced. "I'm Cassidy Miller. I don't know if you remember me."

I didn't show her my badge, and I dropped my title of detective. I had no official capacity or jurisdiction for being there beyond my own personal interests.

Wendy Clark leaned on the wood and plastic rake. Her eyes narrowed as she considered me. If she recognized me, her features didn't let on. I'd never officially worn an Embarrass police uniform, so it wasn't that she'd only seen me with a badge and in the dark brown cottons and polyester. I'd spoken to her once—briefly—when I'd requested the police department's bank information and she'd told me I needed a warrant. I couldn't be sure if she'd been in the court room when Julia had cross-examined me during her father's criminal trial.

"I've already spoken to the police, Ms. Miller."

I had assumed someone from the department had already questioned and cleared Wendy Clark of any involvement in William Desjardin's death. I wasn't there on official police business, however, but I did have a curiosity that only she could satisfy.

"Were you in love with him?"

I watched Wendy Clark's features shuffle through a variety of emotions. Defensive anger, stubborn pride, and eventually a kind of sad exhaustion. She leaned her weight against the rake.

"Are you hungry, Detective?"

Her question surprised me. My body responded with a reflexive shrug. "I can always eat."

Wendy Clark's home was modest and clean. She had few knick-knacks or other personal keepsakes to collect dust. The property didn't really look lived in, but I supposed she'd only been in the house for a few months at most—not enough time to really get settled.

I sat at a small wooden table in the eat-in kitchen. The sides of the table could fold up and extend like the wings of a bird, but it was only the two of us, so the extra space wasn't needed. She set a sandwich in front of me. Ham and cheese on white bread and a handful of greasy potato chips served on a paper plate.

"You don't work for the Embarrass police anymore," she observed.

I could read between the lines: *What are you doing out here? What do you want?*

"No, ma'am," I confirmed. "This is a personal call—not police business. I know the Embarrass police have probably questioned you about this, but do you know who might have wanted William Desjardin dead?"

She barked out a humorless laugh. "Besides me?"

Again, I shrugged.

"I was an accessory to the crime. William got off scot-free, but I wasn't so lucky. Larry Hart was embarrassed and they needed *someone* to pay for William's crimes. I only avoided prison because my lawyer arranged a deal for me. I had to resign, give up my pension, and leave town. William dumped me quicker than a hot potato when his daughter got him acquitted. I lost everything because of that man. My job. My reputation. Any connections I'd made in Embarrass."

Her admission made me wince. "Seems like any animosity you'd have towards him would be justified."

"Too bad I was in love with him."

"You didn't come to the funeral," I couldn't help observing. I didn't blame her though. She'd been the mistress of a notorious figure; I would have kept my distance, too.

"I didn't want to make a scene. I have too much respect for Olivia. But apparently not enough to not get involved with her husband," she wistfully added.

"Why did you?" I found myself asking.

Wendy looked down at her hands, almost as if she was too embarrassed to face my question. "William was a force of nature. So confident. So charming. So ambitious," she recalled. "I wasn't born in Embarrass. I got married young and had a messy divorce. The opportunity to be city clerk in another town in another state was too good to pass on. It was supposed to be a way to reinvent myself. But even though I lived in Embarrass for a good fifteen years, I was still an outsider. It's almost incestuous how that place is," she seemed to scowl. "If you can't trace your ancestors back three generations, then you don't belong."

I nodded in understanding. I had felt that way too when I'd first arrived in town.

"William promised me the world. We were going to travel. Escape Embarrass and live out the best years of retirement together. He was going to step down as mayor. He was going to leave his wife." She shut her eyes and her head sagged forward. "What a sad cliché."

I didn't think it was my place to be consoling this woman, so I shoved a handful of salty potato chips into my mouth instead.

"I was actually happy when our affair was exposed," she admitted. "But rather than see it as an opportunity to escape, William doubled down. Fought his daughter for custody of Olivia. He was never going to leave Embarrass and certainly not for me. So I took the plea deal."

"You didn't go completely away," I couldn't help observing. Her current home wasn't a long drive from the city center.

Wendy's lips twisted. "Pathetic, right? Keeping hope alive that there would still be a chance for us once the scandal died down."

"And now he's dead."

"And now he's dead," she soberly repeated.

"The police think Julia had something to do with it." I laid out my cards for her.

"Really?" Wendy's voice lilted in surprise. "I guess I don't know how she felt about him, but William admired her so much. He was such a proud papa when it came to her. I don't want to speak ill of the dead, but Jonathan was a bit of a mama's boy. It was Julia whom William truly admired. She was the one who was going to pass on the Desjardin name."

I swallowed hard.

"I didn't really get to know Julia all that well," Wendy continued. "We both worked in City Hall, but we might as well have existed on different planets." She shook her head. "I honestly can't remember us ever having a conversation."

None of Wendy Clark's observations came as a surprise to me. If not for my dogged efforts to charm my way into Julia's life, she probably wouldn't have given me the time of day.

"Did he mention anything to you—maybe he owed someone money or he'd made a new enemy?"

Wendy snorted. "You just described the entire population of Embarrass, Minnesota."

I sighed deeply, realizing how true her statement was. And yet I couldn't imagine someone being so slighted, so furious at what William Desjardin had done that they'd try to have him killed. The more digging I did, the more it appeared the simplest motive —that he'd interrupted a burglary—had been his cause of death. But short of finding the thieves, I didn't know how I could prove Julia's innocence. And my stubborn girlfriend was doing absolutely nothing to help her cause. Wendy Clark had described William Desjardin as being stubbornly proud. The apple didn't fall far from the tree.

"Who came up with the extortion idea?" I asked.

"I honestly don't remember," Wendy said, shaking her head. "It started out as one of those wistful, feeling unappreciated rants —'I could rob this city blind and they'd have no idea'—kind of things. Eventually it turned into a reality. I fixed the books, and he applied for the external grants. No one in City Hall cared to oversee those kinds of details. We were able to secure funding for a lot of programs," she noted, "but we took our cut."

"Why did you do it?"

"It was free money, and we never thought we'd get caught."

Her candor was impressive, but this was also a woman who believed she had nothing left to lose.

"What about the affair? Whose idea was that?" I asked.

"There had been a string of tragedies. Jonathan's death. Olivia's diagnosis. William started spending more time in City Hall than at home. We were facing a budget crunch because of the Recession. All of that stress. And I guess he found in me someone to vent. It didn't turn physical for a very long time. I think we both acknowledged that would be the point of no return."

I quietly ate the sandwich she had made me while she revealed the details of her affair with Julia's father. I wondered if she'd ever said these words out loud to another person.

"When's the last time you and he spoke?"

Wendy sighed and looked out the window. "Just before the custody hearing. I had been placed on administrative leave, but I was still in Embarrass. I thought the guardianship trial was the perfect situation. He could leave his wife, but still save face if Julia got custody. But instead of leaving Olivia, he dug in his heels." She shook her head. "Stupid, prideful man. He wasn't going to let the courts take Olivia from him."

"Do you think it was pride, or the money that made him do that?"

"Money?" She blinked a few times. "He returned all the money."

"Not the stolen city funds," I clarified. "Mrs. Desjardin's family money."

The confusion on Wendy Clark's features deepened. "Olivia had a lot of money? This is the first time I'm hearing about it."

William Desjardin considered himself a self-made made. He might had tried to "self-make" himself even more through illegal channels, but at least he appeared to have considered his wife's money off-limits. It was a small concession, a small victory, but I knew every little bit of knowledge would help Julia reconcile her father's final days. William Desjardin might not have been her role model or someone whose approval she'd sought, but he'd still been her dad.

I considered telling Wendy that she'd been excluded from William Desjardin's will, but it felt too cruel to pile on to this woman's misfortunes and misery. It was too easy to blame the Other Woman in these kinds of scenarios, but it took two to tango. William Desjardin was just as culpable for the affair if not more.

"Thank you for your time. And the sandwich," I remembered to add.

"You're welcome."

Wendy Clark walked me out to where I'd parked Julia's black Mercedes.

"Why did you agree to talk to me?" I questioned.

"It gets lonely out here," she shrugged. "Besides the police, no one has bothered to visit. And no one's really asked for my side of the story."

I nodded slowly, understanding. "Will you stay out here?"

"This is only a rental," she said. "I'll probably head back to Illinois at some point. I haven't really been back since my divorce, but at least I have family there. And who knows—maybe a few friends."

"Good luck," I wished her in earnest.

"Good luck to you, too, Detective."

I offered Wendy Clark a small smile. "It's just Cassidy."

Chapter Fifteen

I sat on the floor of Julia's master bathroom while my girlfriend showered. The steam from the hot shower had fogged up the glass door, obscuring my view of her figure. I had to use my imagination to picture the contours of her naked body. Beyond the foggy glass plane, I visualized the fullness of her hips and the modest swell of her breasts. In my mind's eye, I saw her hands lather up her smooth, feminine figure. I imagined her arching back and her proud, firm breasts as she rinsed the shampoo from her nearly black hair.

"I called Chief Hart while you were out," she told me.

I cleared my throat as if she'd caught me doing something forbidden. "Oh yeah?"

"I told him about the $10,000," she said. "He's sending someone to my fertility doctor in St. Paul to confirm that's where the money went."

"That's great, babe," I enthused. "I'm really proud of you for doing that."

"Too bad they aren't ready to eliminate me as a person of interest," she remarked, having buried the lede. "So I've opened up my personal life for nothing."

"What?" I sharply questioned. "Why would they still suspect you?"

"Because I brought my father to court to get custody of my mother and lost."

"Circumstantial evidence," I rejected.

"And because I'm the sole beneficiary of a $1.5 million dollar life insurance payout."

"But you had no idea he'd done that!"

"And there's no way to prove that," she said.

The water in the shower turned off.

"So now what?" I asked. I stood up from my seated position on the floor.

"I honestly don't know, darling," she said. "But in the meantime, we'll have to find another way to communicate. After I called Chief Hart, David Addams came to the house to confiscate my cellphone."

I pulled down on my face. "Are you serious?"

I knew the action was standard procedure when building a case against someone, but it was startling when it was happening to someone I knew—someone I loved. The knowledge elevated the seriousness of the situation. This wasn't something to laugh away or casually dismiss.

"They'll be sending someone to search my condo as well, I'm sure," Julia remarked. I could hear her wring out her wet hair in the shower. "The public defender office. Confiscating my computers. Digging up all of my dirty little secrets." She seemed to be speaking to herself, not me. "I sent Alice an email about what's going on so she can relay that to the others in the office. I didn't want them to be alarmed when police show up to take away everything in my office."

I rubbed at my forehead. "This is such a disaster."

Julia opened the shower door and stepped out onto the bath mat. "It's routine police procedure; you know that," she said evenly. "And I can't expect special treatment."

It was an abstract concept—routine police procedure—something that I didn't invest too much thought on because it hadn't touched me personally. I knew how private Julia was, and her composure continued to amaze me. Soon, cops would be trampling in dirty boots across her condo's white carpet. They'd be pawing through her underwear drawer, medicine cabinet, and keepsake boxes. Nothing was sacred or off-limits.

I thought about my recent dogged resolve to get access to Kennedy Petersik's personal journals. I'd thought myself unthreatening—one of the Good Guys—who was only trying to solve Kennedy's death, but her mother had repeatedly refused me access to her daughter's private thoughts. I couldn't understand it at the time, but now that I was on the other side of an investigation, now that my girlfriend was under the microscope, a phrase like routine police procedure left a sour taste in my mouth.

I unfolded the thick, plush towel that Julia had placed on the bathroom vanity. I used it to enveloped Julia's body like a warm hug.

"I'm sorry," I breathed.

"It's okay," she routinely dismissed.

I released my hold on her and used the towel to wipe at the water droplets that clung to her torso. "Here, let me," I urged. "You've had a long day."

"I can handle drying myself off, dear." Her words said one thing, but she made no attempt to take the towel from me.

I brushed the towel across the tops of her shoulders. "They aren't going to arrest you."

"It's a charming thought." She smiled, small and sad. "I

suppose I should be thanking Tony Pond for starting this investigation against me. Now I don't have to waste time weighing the pros and cons of taking that *pro bono* position with Grisham and Stein. They won't touch me with a ten-foot pole after this."

I temporarily stopped drying her off. "You really think they'd rescind the job offer? What happened to innocent until proven guilty?"

Julia shook her head. "Criminal law firms tiptoe the ethics line just by existing. A prominent firm like G & S wants their associates and partners to be squeaky clean."

I should have felt relieved that Julia wouldn't be taking the job she'd warned would be a major time suck. Instead, I felt disappointed for her that she hadn't had the opportunity to decide her future for herself.

I needed to do more. I needed to be more helpful. Stanley was going to see if he could procure a copy of the case file, but there had to be something else I could do in the meantime. "They're doing digital forensics on you, but has anyone thought to do that for your father?"

Julia slipped into a short silk robe and continued to towel off her hair. "What are you thinking?"

"I don't know. I'm just kind of talking out of my ass," I admitted. "But what if his death was premeditated and only made to look like a break-in? Maybe there'd be some clues on his home computer or his cellphone."

"My father didn't have a cellphone; he abhorred the technology," Julia noted. "He only got a home computer so he could do research and email with doctors when my mother was first diagnosed."

"Where's his computer? Do the police have it?" I tried to remember the layout of the Desjardin home. I'd only been in

William Desjardin's home office briefly, when Julia had broken the ceramic ashtray.

Julia blinked. "We sold it at the estate sale."

"Shit," I cursed. "To whom?"

"I-I don't remember."

"*Think*, Julia. This is really important," I urged.

"Randolph," Julia said slowly. "Pamela Randolph. She and her husband live close to downtown. She said she was buying it for her son."

"Did you reset it to factory settings?" I was nearly giddy with panic and the prospect of this missing link.

Julia shook her head. "I didn't even think to. I'm such an imbecile," she scowled, frustrated with herself. "All of his personal information would still be on there."

"Or you might have just saved your ass," I observed, my excitement continuing to spike. "Maybe they haven't wiped it yet. Hurry up and finish getting ready; we've got to go."

~

Pamela Randolph lived in a modest ranch home not far from Embarass' small downtown. The home was well maintained with pale yellow vinyl siding and tidy boxwood shrubs beneath the home's front facing picture windows. A thin whisper of smoke plumed out of the chimney, filling the air with the pleasant scent of burning wood. Julia parked in the Randolphs' paved driveway and was out the driver's side door before I'd even unfastened my seatbelt. I clambered after her with haste; she was moving too fast. All of my military training and police instincts were screaming for us to slow down and strategize. We hadn't even brainstormed ideas about what we were going to tell the Randolphs so that they would let us dig around on her dad's old computer.

The heels of Julia's black ankle boots hit sharply against the sidewalk that led to the Randolphs' front stoop. A rubber welcome mat with an embossed cartoon turkey covered the top concrete step. Julia bypassed the glowing doorbell, opened the screen door, and knocked briskly on the wooden front door.

A middle-aged woman in a sweatshirt and jeans answered the door. I didn't recognize her from the estate sale, but then again, I'd spent a good portion of that day in a closet. "Yes?" she greeted.

I wasn't prepared, but apparently Julia was. She launched into her explanation for our unsolicited appearance: "I'm so sorry to be bothering you at home, Mrs. Randolph, but is there any chance I could retrieve some documents from my father's old computer?" Julia's voice had taken on a warm and apologetic tenor. "I didn't even think to back-up his files. Everything happened so quickly, you know."

I had no idea how well Julia and this woman knew each other, but I was willing to bet Mrs. Randolph—and probably most of Embarrass' small population—had never heard her speak in such a kind tone. She had softened considerably over the course of our relationship, but my girlfriend could still be abrupt, direct, and even standoffish. We needed something from this woman, however; Julia spared no charm.

"Oh, of course," Mrs. Randolph readily agreed. "Come on in." She took a step backwards to allow our entry.

The Randolphs' mudroom was packed tight with winter jackets, snow boots, and bulk home supplies like toilet paper and paper towels. Julia mindfully slipped out of her boots and left them in the tiled entryway, and I did the same.

"I was so sorry to hear about your father's death," Pamela Randolph started. She wrung her hands together. "You see terrible things on the nightly news, mostly about the Sin Cities, but you never expect that kind of thing to happen in Embarrass."

"It was very unexpected," Julia concurred.

"Do the police have any leads?"

Julia and I shared a quick look. Pamela Randolph would have only been asking out of curiosity, maybe hoping for some inside information to share with her friends; she couldn't have known that Julia herself was being investigated.

"No arrests have been made," I supplied, "but I know Chief Hart is doing his best to find out who's responsible."

Pamela Randolph's grey-blue eyes landed on me as though she was only just registering my presence. I couldn't blame her for not really noticing me before though; Julia tended to command people's undivided attention.

"The computer, Mrs. Randolph?" Julia gently reminded her. "We'll only be a minute."

"Oh, right! It's in my son's room," she revealed. "He'd been bugging us to get him his own computer for the longest time. I know he would have preferred something new, but I don't work and his dad's hours keep getting cut."

"I'm happy to know that my father's computer is getting a second life rather than sitting in a landfill," Julia noted in that same warm, indulgent tone.

Mrs. Randolph led us down a long hallway to her son's bedroom. Various "Keep Out" signs warned us against entry, but she pushed the door open without hesitation. The offensive scent of Axe body spray and dirty gym socks invaded my nose as I crossed the threshold. I took a moment to take in my surroundings. Posters of professional athletes covered the walls. The blankets of an unmade twin-sized bed spilled onto the carpeted floor. A small TV sat on a wooden bureau, connected to the tangled cords of a video game console. A wooden desk faced the room's only window. An older computer monitor, keyboard, and mouse sat on the desk's surface. The screensaver—a multi-colored geometric pattern—bounced around the blackened screen.

Pamela bent over to collect various t-shirts and unpaired socks that littered the floor. I was surprised when she didn't routinely apologize about the state of her son's room, but we were unexpected intruders, not invited guests.

"Can I get you girls anything to eat or drink?" she offered.

"That won't be necessary," Julia dismissed. "You've been more than hospitable already. We'll let you know if we have any questions." Her words were generous, but they also indicated that she expected us to be left alone.

Pamela took the cue. Her head bobbed in understanding. "Well, if you need anything, just holler."

She vacated her son's bedroom, shutting the door behind her.

Julia sat down in the cracked leather office chair in front of her father's old computer. I could see the displeasure on her refined features as she sank into the cushioning. I knew what she was thinking without have to ask because they had been my immediate thoughts as well: who knew how many times this kid had jerked off in this chair.

Once the initial disgust passed, Julia swirled the mouse on its pad and the computer monitor turned on. She clicked on one of the internet browsers and waited for it to load.

"I'm not quite sure what I'm looking for," she admitted.

I hovered over her right shoulder so I could see the screen as well. "Anything out of the ordinary on your father's search history."

"I don't suppose we'll get lucky and discover he searched the phrase 'how to plan your own murder.'"

"Probably not," I said, cracking a smile.

Julia clicked into the browser's settings preferences to identify her father's most recent internet searches. We simultaneously made a disgruntled noise when the cache turned out to be empty.

"No browser history," Julia sighed in defeat. "He cleared it." She spun slightly in her chair to appraise me. "Any other ideas?"

"Hold on." I dug my cellphone out of my back pocket. "There's got to be a way to get that stuff back."

I wasn't sure if Stanley would be in the cold case office or at the off-site evidence warehouse that day—his schedule was irregular—so I tried his cellphone. He picked up after a few rings.

"Hello?"

"Hey, Stanley," I greeted. "Is there a way to recover the deleted search history of someone's internet browser?"

I appreciated my relationship with Stanley. I didn't have to beat around the bush; we could get down to business without the need for small-talk.

"Nothing is ever really deleted on a computer," he told me. "It could still be stored in obscure files in the hard drive or operating system. Unless you scramble the computer with a powerful magnet, it'll still be there."

I flashed Julia a quick thumbs up to let her know there was still a chance of retrieving her father's browsing history. "So how do we find it?"

"Can you bring the computer here? It'd probably be a lot easier that way."

"No can do. It's stuck in the bedroom of a teenaged boy."

"You want the deleted search history of a teenaged boy?" Stanley deadpanned.

"The computer is in his room. But it's not *his* browser history. I have a pretty good idea what that would look like," I chuckled.

Stanley blew out a breath. "Okay. This will be a little bit more difficult over the phone, but it's totally doable."

I put Stanley on speakerphone and set my cellphone next to the keyboard.

"Alright," I told him. "I'm ready."

"The easiest method is to do a system restore," he said. "If the internet history was deleted recently, system restore will recover it. Go to 'Start,' click on 'Programs,' and then 'Accessories.'"

I used the attached mouse and followed Stanley's directions.

"You'll see a 'System Tools' option and 'System Restore' will be in there."

"Got it," I confirmed.

"Select the date you'd like to restore your computer to."

I glanced in Julia's direction. "Any ideas?"

"Some time before he took out the insurance policy," she shrugged.

"Can we mess this up, Stanley?" I asked my remote friend. "What happens if we pick the wrong date?"

"Then we'll all be trapped in a time loop continuum from whence we'll never emerge."

The phone was silent as he waited for his joke to land. It never did.

I cleared my throat. I didn't want to be rude, but we really didn't have time to fuck around.

"Nothing bad will happen," he said. "You don't want to go too far back though. You don't want to restore the system to a date where the computer user hasn't done the incriminating internet search."

I pulled up the computer's built-in calendar and scrolled back to the date the insurance policy had been issued. "A week before?" I suggested.

Julia nodded. "And if that's not far back enough we can keep restoring the system to an earlier date."

"Okay, Stanley," I pulled my colleague back into the conversation. "What next?"

"Pick your restore date, sit back, and wait until the computer does its thing. The computer will automatically reboot when it has finished restoring settings. Check the browser; the internet history should be in there."

"That's it?"

"That's it," he confirmed.

"You're a treasure, Stanley," I enthused. "Thanks for the assist."

"It's no problem. That's what they pay me the big bucks for," he brushed off. "On another subject, though, any idea when you'll be back in the office?"

"Miss me that much?" I teased.

The computer monitor blinked off and the hard drive tower grumbled and beeped as it reloaded. It was an older desktop; the longer it took to fully reboot, the more cognizant I became of the passing time.

"We can't hang out here all day," I thought aloud. "The Randolphs are going to get annoyed."

Julia's eyes remained trained on the monitor as it flashed through its opening sequences. "Fuck the Randolphs," she uncharacteristically swore.

My eyes widened at her language, and I had to stifle my laughter.

Stanley cleared his throat, almost as if to remind me that he was still on the phone. I turned off the speaker function and brought the phone to my ear. "I'll call Captain Forrester to check in soon," I promised.

I knew I was probably taking advantage of the department with my extended absence, but there was no way I was leaving Julia to deal with this on her own.

"It's not so much him I'm worried about," Stanley admitted. "But Sarah Conrad is getting bored."

"Truth or Dare?" I grinned into the phone.

"Let's just say I've been spending a lot of time at the Freezer lately," he said, identifying his nickname for the evidence warehouse. "Oh! And I meant to call you earlier—Celeste Rivers was able to get the BCA's files on the Desjardin homicide."

"And?" I felt my heart pump a little harder. "Break-in or something else?"

Stanley's training was in forensic pathology, but over the years he'd had much more experience in looking at photographs of crime scenes than myself.

"It looks like a standard home invasion—like someone came home and interrupted the thief. There were some bloody footprints on the carpet that indicate you're probably looking for at least two intruders. The treads look like Carhart work boots."

My initial excitement flat-lined. "So basically all of Minnesota could be suspects."

"Sorry I couldn't be more helpful," he apologized.

"It's okay; you've been more than helpful. Thanks for trying. And thank Celeste for me, too."

Julia took control of the mouse as soon as the computer had fully rebooted. She pulled up her father's browser history. Instead of a blank box, a new list of keyword searches now appeared.

"The system recovery worked, Stanley," I told my colleague.

"Just remember to use your powers for good," he replied.

"Understood," I laughed. "Thanks again."

I ended the phone call while Julia scrolled through her father's old internet searches. I tucked my phone into the back pocket of my jeans and leaned over Julia's shoulder to get a better view.

"Anything of interest?" I asked.

"How To searches for fly fishing."

I scanned the random list of words and phrases for something incriminating or at least a little nefarious. I wasn't necessarily rooting for William Desjardin to be a crook, but I was eager for something that might steer the attention away from Julia.

"Double indemnity?" I read aloud. "What's that?"

"I'm not sure," Julia said. She opened a new browser tab and typed the words into the browser and did a search herself. "*Double Indemnity*. 1943 novel by James M. Cain," she read from the screen. "1944 film."

"Was your dad into old movies?" I asked.

"Mmhmm," she confirmed. "He wasn't a big TV watcher, but when he did, it was typically the evening news or the old movie channel."

She closed the open tab and returned to the other search terms.

One particularly long phrase caught my attention. "Pancreatic adenocarcinoma," I read aloud. I was sure I'd probably butchered the pronunciation. "Carcinoma," I repeated, thinking aloud. "That's cancer, right?"

Julia nodded and turned around in the office chair.

"Who has cancer?" I wondered.

"My mother's doctor says she's in good health besides the dementia."

"Could your dad have had cancer?" I posed.

In lieu of a response, Julia shut down the computer and ducked her head beneath the desk.

"What are you doing?" I asked.

Julia detached the computer tower from the various cords that connected it to the keyboard, mouse, and monitor.

"Collecting evidence, Detective."

. . .

Mrs. Randolph was watching television in the living room when we finally emerged from her son's bedroom. She sat on an over-stuffed EZ-chair with her legs and feet propped up. She promptly sprung to her feet when she saw us.

"Find everything you needed?" she asked. I watched her eyes drop to the computer tower cradled in Julia's arms.

"Mrs. Randolph, I'd like to buy back my father's computer from you," Julia said.

"What? Why?"

Julia didn't respond to her questions. She turned to me instead. "How much do laptops cost these days?"

I shrugged. "Hell if I know."

Julia set the computer tower on the floor long enough to remove her checkbook from her purse. "How about $600 or $700?"

Mrs. Randolph stared in wonder. "But I only paid $50 at the estate sale."

"I know. But I'd like to compensate you for the inconvenience," Julia noted. Her voice had once again taken on a sugar-sweet quality to charm the middle-aged woman. "We barged into your home, and your son will be without a computer again."

Julia uncapped an expensive-looking ink pen and scribbled figures and cursive words onto the paper check. She tore the check from the larger booklet and handed it to Mrs. Randolph.

"Thank you again for your hospitality," Julia said before parting.

"O-ok," Mrs. Randolph eventually conceded.

I could tell she was wrestling with her instinct to refuse the money altogether. But at the same time, who was she to turn down a new laptop for her son?

. . .

The computer's electrical cord dragged behind Julia as she quickly strode toward her parked car. There was an urgency to her gait, perhaps with worry that Mrs. Randolph would change her mind. She opened up the rear driver's side door and set the computer tower in the empty space behind her seat. She shut the door, securing it inside her car, before I heard her deep, rattling breath.

Julia leaned against the driver's side door with one hand covering her face.

I rubbed my hands up and down her arms. "Hey, it's okay."

"That bastard," I heard her mumble. "That stupid, selfish bastard."

She righted herself and tugged open the driver's side door.

"Wait. Hold on a second," I urged.

Julia wiped her fingers under her eyes and sniffed loudly. "I'm not going to fall apart on Sycamore Street for half the town to see."

"Will you just talk to me?" I pled.

"At home," she promised. She opened the driver's side door and slid behind the wheel. I had no choice but to get into the car as well.

Chapter Sixteen

J ulia and I sat on the couch in her den, staring at the computer tower. It sat like an odd award or trophy on the coffee table. We'd left the monitor at the Randolphs' house, which meant we couldn't dig through her father's files any further. It was probably preferable, however. I knew just enough about computers to get myself in trouble. I feared accidentally erasing William Desjardin's recently recovered browser history.

The adrenaline surge from retrieving William Desjardin's hard drive and internet searches had waned as we drove closer to Julia's house. Julia had been noticeably quiet since we'd left the Randolphs' home. She'd just learned that her father potentially had had cancer, a diagnosis he'd kept from her. But beyond that bombshell, I could sense that there was something else on her mind.

"We need to turn this over to Chief Hart," I said.

Julia stared intently at the computer hard drive. She cradled a crystal rocks glass with bourbon between her cupped hands.

"Double indemnity," she mumbled. She sounded like she was talking more to herself than to me.

"Let's drop off the computer at City Hall and be done with this," I tried to reason. "We've already done enough work for the police; they can handle the rest of the investigation."

Julia twisted on the red velvet couch to appraise me. "One and a half million dollars, Cassidy. Do you know what kind of care my mother could get for that kind of money? If my father really had cancer, that all goes away. No insurance company is going to payout if they know the person they insured was terminally ill."

"So your mom could be shitting on a gold toilet while you're in prison?" I snorted. "No thanks."

"You know there's no case against me," Julia scoffed.

"Do you really want to gamble with your life?" I challenged. I couldn't believe how stubborn she was being.

"We can't even be sure he had cancer," she rejected. "All we have is a keyword search history. He could have been looking that up for any number of reasons."

"Such as?"

Julia shut her eyes and sighed. "I don't know. This is a lot to process."

"Did your dad go to a doctor in town?" I asked.

Julia's eyes opened. "Yes. Dr. Meyer. He's been treating both of my parents for years. He would know." She started to stand from the couch, but I grabbed her wrist and gently pulled her back down to me.

"It's been a long day," I hushed. "Dr. Meyer will still be there in the morning."

Julia must have been exhausted because she nodded and gave up pursuing the doctor without additional protest. She let her body sag against mine on the couch and folded her legs beneath her body. Her dark eyes shuttered and silent tears began to roll down her cheeks.

I didn't bother with empty assurances that everything was going to be okay. But I diligently wiped away each individual tear, making sure none of them got away.

∼

Embarrass was the kind of town that had one of everything. One bank, one grocery store, one public library. That extended to healthcare as well: one dentist, one ophthalmologist, and one family physician. Dr. Steven Meyer was a relative newcomer to Embarrass. He hadn't been Julia's primary doctor growing up, but he had treated both of her parents in recent years. His practice was located in a single-story building, not much different from the modular homes in the trailer park on one side of town. He wasn't at liberty to discuss William Desjardin's health over the phone, so Julia and I had made an appointment to see him in between patients. Doctor-patient privilege tended to extend beyond the patient's lifetime, but some extenuating circumstances existed— particularly in legal matters—where that confidentiality clause was overruled.

I knew that nothing about the situation was easy. No one wants to learn that a parent has been diagnosed with cancer, but more than that, if our hunch was true, William Desjardin might have falsified official documents in order to obtain a life insurance policy. If that was the case, the insurance company would refuse the $1.5 million dollar payout. Julia could always take the company to court, but that was a task for another day.

We met with Dr. Meyer in his private office during his lunch break. Laminate posters of the human anatomy covered the white walls and a realistic, but plastic model of a headless human torso stood in one cover of the room.

Julia crossed one elegant leg over the other. "Dr. Meyer, we appreciate you taking the time to see us today."

The doctor folded his hands and set them flat on his desk. "No trouble at all. Kind of a slow day today between diagnosing indigestion and arthritis."

"Do you know the last time you saw my father?" she asked.

Dr. Meyer stroked his salt-and-pepper beard. "It might have been at the grocery store—."

"I'm sorry," Julia cut him off. "I should have been more clear. I meant as a patient."

"Oh, right. Well, that probably would have been for his annual exam. Your father was really good about his regular check-ups. Not like most of the men in this town. Half of them will probably die from heart attacks from poor diets and the other half are drinking themselves to death."

"So my father was healthy?" Julia asked carefully. She flicked her eyes in my direction.

Maybe we'd been wrong? Maybe he hadn't had cancer? But then why had he been conducting internet searches for such a specific kind of cancer?

"Let me jog my memory."

Dr. Meyer pushed his wheeled office chair back from his desk and spun in the direction of a metal file cabinet. Still seated, he opened one of the pull-out drawers. His fingers ticked over the tops of folder files until he found the one he sought.

"Desjardin, William," he announced, pulling the file from the drawer.

"Did the police come to talk to you?" I abruptly asked.

Dr. Meyer's eyes slightly widened behind his thick glasses. "About William's death? No—should they have?"

"No, no," I quickly dismissed. "I was just curious."

With a gunshot wound to the gut, there'd been no need for a proper autopsy, so it didn't surprise me that no one from the police department had inquired about the Mayor's health with his regular doctor.

Dr. Meyer looked over the top of his glasses to read Mr. Desjardin's charts. "Can't read a damn thing with these glasses on," he spoke, more to himself than to us. "My wife keeps telling me to get my eyes lasered, but if I'm not the one making those adjustments, I don't trust it. Hazards of the occupation, I guess," he openly mused. "No good doctors except myself."

Julia pressed her lips together. I could tell she was growing impatient, and was struggling to not offend the town's only doctor.

"Alright. Your father had lost some weight since his previous exam," Dr. Meyer told us. "He said he hadn't had much of an appetite, but I figured it was because of ..." His sentence faltered. "Well, you know."

Julia hummed. "He'd been arrested for embezzling city funds and almost lost custody of his wife."

The doctor cleared his throat, clearly uncomfortable. "Right. I wasn't too concerned. At this age we're more concerned with weight gain and diabetes." Dr. Meyer's lips pursed. "Actually..." He tapped his pen against the mayor's health chart. "His glucose level came back a little elevated. I would have followed up with him to make sure it wasn't a sign of pre-diabetes but..." He trailed off again.

"But then he died," Julia finished for him. "Were you the physician who examined my father when he took out his life insurance policy?"

Dr. Meyer shook his head. "No. That doesn't sound familiar."

"But he would have had to get an examination before he could get the policy, right?" Julia pressed. "They want to be sure they're insuring healthy people who won't die the moment they sign the dotted line?"

"Not necessarily," the doctor said. "Depending on the size of the policy and the age of the person being insurance, you might not need a paramedical exam. You'd be surprised; insurance companies these days are more interested in credit scores and how many parking tickets you've had. It's less about blood tests or peeing in a cup. How much was the policy for?"

"$1.5 million dollars," Julia said, unblinking.

Dr. Meyer whistled under his breath. "That's quite a chunk of cheese. In that case, yes—he would have needed an exam. Typically, anything over $750,000 tends to require a physical. Otherwise, it's just a phone call."

"It was actually for $1,499,998," Julia noted.

Dr. Meyer's features pinched. "That's a funny number," the doctor observed.

"Which is double $749,999," Julia continued.

"Yes. That math checks out." Dr. Meyer appraised Julia over his glasses as if she'd just grown a second head.

"Double indemnity," Julia muttered under her breath.

"Double what?" Dr. Meyer questioned.

My girlfriend shot to her feet. "Thank you so much for your time, Dr. Meyer. You've been incredibly helpful." She turned to me. The muscles in her neck strained. She looked ready to explode. "Cassidy—we have to go."

Julia all but sprinted out of the doctor's office. If not for her high heels and the thin layer of ice on the blacktop surface of the doctor's parking lot, she might have run back to her car.

"Julia!" I called to her. "What's going on?"

She unlocked her car doors without waiting for me and slid behind the steering wheel.

I climbed into the passenger side of the car and shut the door behind me. I felt like I'd been chasing after her nonstop these past few days. "Jesus, woman," I complained. "Do you have to go to the bathroom really bad or something? I'm sure Dr. Meyer would have let you use his."

"Double indemnity," she said.

"You're like a goddamn parrot with that phrase," I protested. "Yeah—it's an old movie or something."

"It's also an insurance term," she said, turning to me in her seat. "I looked up the movie's plot last night while you were sleeping."

"What?" I hadn't realized she'd left the bed at any point the previous night.

"You were totally knocked out, probably from that extra glass of bourbon," she observed. "I love you, darling, but you can't hold your liquor."

I opened my mouth to defend myself, but Julia cut me off.

"In the movie," she continued, "a life insurance agent and a woman plan to murder the woman's husband. They make it look like an accident so they can capitalize on the double indemnity clause in his life insurance policy. If your death is an accident—you fell from a moving train, for example—your insurance policy payoff doubles."

"Or if you're killed during a home invasion," I noted, starting to catch on.

"Exactly," Julia confirmed. "I wasn't able to put the pieces together until Dr. Meyer told us about the insurance policy cut offs. The total of my father's payout had always seemed too random to me. But the base policy is one dollar shy of him requiring a medical exam."

"Double indemnity." Now it was my turn to be a parrot. "Do you think your dad talked to your mom about the insurance money?"

Julia shook her head. "I can't imagine he would have. And even if he didn't there's a good chance she wouldn't even remember those conversations. You'd never call a woman with dementia to the witness stand."

"Did he keep any journals? Any kind of filing system?" I tried to brainstorm.

"When you're trying to get away with a scam worth $1.5 million dollars," she said in a bitter tone, "it's probably best not to leave a paper trail."

She was right, of course, but I was still hopeful we'd find some concrete proof that Mr. Desjardin had arranged for his own death. In his hubris, however, he hadn't considered his daughter would be accused of having him murdered.

"I have a suggestion," I said, "but I don't think you're going to like it."

"What's that, dear?"

"I think we should bring Special Agent Andrews into this. She doesn't have any skin in the game. She wants to close this case, but she has no incentive to pin it on you."

Julia worried her lower lip. "Do you really think Chief Hart and David Addams want it to be me?"

It had been the first recorded murder in Chief Hart's several decades of being Chief of Police, so there had to have been some internal pressure for him to solve the case. The Desjardin family had embarrassed the local police department—first through the mayor's embezzlement of city funds, and then by Julia's successful defense of her father's criminal case. It would have been all-too-tempting to get retribution with one tidy homicide prosecution.

I felt myself wincing. "Kind of. Yeah."

Julia hollowed out her cheeks. I watched her silently struggle with my suggestion before finally exhaling. "Okay. Let's do it."

"Really?" I was shocked she hadn't put up more of a fight.

"It may surprise you that I'd like to avoid being charged with my father's murder. I like infamy, but not that much," she qualified. "Besides, if it'll get you back to Minneapolis sooner, I'm willing to do just about anything."

Chapter Seventeen

W e called ahead to let Special Agent Andrews know she should expect us the next morning. It felt like a smarter strategy than blindsiding her by showing up announced. We met again in her office in City Hall. The first time the three of us had met, the situation had been tense and unproductive. I hoped for a more civil second meeting.

"Coffee?" Agent Andrews repeated her offer from our initial meeting.

Again, both Julia and I politely refused the nicety.

Agent Andrews poured herself a cup of black coffee into the same plain ceramic cup. When she sat behind the mahogany desk, she reached into a drawer and pulled out a cardboard coaster. She set the coaster on the expensive desk before placing her coffee cup down. I glanced in Julia's direction and saw the unmistakable small, but pleased smile. It was progress.

"You asked for this meeting, ladies," Special Agent Andrews began. She leaned back in her office chair. "How can I help you?"

I lifted William Desjardin's computer tower from the floor and set it on Agent Andrew's desk. "We think Mr. Desjardin hired someone to kill him, but made it look like an accident so his wife could benefit from a large life insurance payout."

To her credit, Special Agent Andrews didn't look taken aback by my wild speculation. I wondered if she had a talent for poker. "And why do you think that?"

"First, the burglary was totally random," I started. "Embarrass doesn't have that kind of crime, and I bet your investigation hasn't turned up similar crimes in the surrounding communities to suggest this was part of a larger crime ring, otherwise you wouldn't still be considering Julia as a person of interest."

I could feel myself starting to lose my temper. Only Julia's solid, assuring hand on top of my knee prevented me from spiraling out of control about their tunnel vision on this case. This was more than Julia being a suspect; this was simply bad policing.

"Second," I continued, "Mr. Desjardin took out an unexpected life insurance policy on himself. He chose a level of coverage that wouldn't require a medical exam. We also have evidence from his internet browser that he'd been doing searches about pancreatic cancer."

I glanced in Julia's direction to gauge her reaction to my admission. For all of our leg work and detailed discussions about the case, we still hadn't really talked about her father's possible diagnosis at length. Her stony features revealed no emotions, however.

"We spoke to his regular physician," I noted. "Dr. Meyer believed that Mr. Desjardin was healthy, but noted that he'd lost weight recently and that his blood sugar levels were off—all symptoms of that kind of cancer. We haven't explored if he was seeing a local oncologist to confirm he'd been diagnosed with cancer, but it's a possibility."

Agent Andrews folded her hands on the desk. She was silent

as her gaze shifted from my face to Julia's and then back to mine. "You've been busy," she said evenly.

I held up my hands. "I'm not trying to step on your toes or butt into your investigation, but I'm also not going to sit back when my girlfriend is being accused of a crime she has nothing to do with."

Agent Andrews looked back in Julia's direction. "Chief Hart shared with me what the $10,000 was for. I'm sorry," she said, sounding genuine with her apology. "I understand why you wanted to keep that private."

Julia cleared her throat and sat up straighter in the high-backed wooden chair.

"The Mayor cleared his browser search history," I said, "but we were able to perform a system reboot. Not long before he took out the life insurance policy, he was doing internet searches about pancreatic cancer. We haven't dug very deeply into his browsing history beyond that, but maybe your forensics team can see if he solicited an assassin on the dark web."

The words sounded absurd coming from my mouth, but I also didn't believe in coincidences. What were the chances that someone with cancer had had an accidental death?

Agent Andrews shook her head. "Chances are he wouldn't know how to get to the dark web; it's not something you just accidentally stumble onto. The dark web is the name given to websites that you can't find doing a simple Google search. You need special software to even be able to access it. It's mostly scams; you pay money for something illegal and you never get it. It's not like you can report it to the police," she noted.

"How about Craigslist?" I proposed. "Doesn't a bunch of shady shit happen on that site?"

"Typically crimes on sites like Craigslist are people getting targeted for selling big ticket items. You meet someone who wants to buy your fancy watch, but they steal it from you instead," Agent

Andrews explained. "If Mr. Desjardin had posted an ad on Craigslist or some similar site about wanting to arrange his own death, it would have been flagged and taken down by the website's administrator. You can't post services or requests that are against the law."

"What about secret codes? Like a special language—you post that you—I don't know—want a dozen eggs, but that's code for a contract killer." I felt like I was grasping at straws. I was certain of the Mayor's culpability, but I didn't know how to prove it.

Agent Andrews appeared nonplussed. "I've heard of code words for drugs and prostitution, but not for a hit man."

"But it could be possible?"

"Possible, sure," she admitted, "but did William Desjardin strike you as the kind of person who would have been savvy to that lingo?"

"Probably not," I admitted. "But he also hadn't struck me as the kind of guy to embezzle hundreds of thousands of dollars from his hometown."

Agent Andrews nodded. "Your point is well taken. Is there anything else I should know?"

I looked to Julia for confirmation. She shook her head, apparently satisfied with the conversation.

Agent Andrews slapped her hands to the tops of her thighs and stood up. It was the unofficial Midwestern signal that it was time to go. Our meeting was apparently over.

"Thank you for coming in today," she said. "You've given me a lot to look into. I'll be in touch."

Julia was silent as we descended the stairs from the second floor. I cast furtive glances in her direction, trying to gauge her reaction to our second visit with Special Agent Andrews. Just as I had remained silent in our initial meeting, Julia hadn't been an active participant in the second. She didn't speak until we were outside. She pulled sunglasses out of her purse and slipped them on. "That wasn't terrible."

"Are you suggesting I was right about something?"

Julia curled her lip. "Even a broken clock is right two times a day, dear."

Her reluctance only made me laugh. "You're welcome."

Julia glanced back at the cream brick building. "Now let's see what she does with that information."

"We dropped a lot on her," I observed. "But she also has the resources to move things along more quickly than we could on our own."

"Will you get a big head if I admit that investigating with you has been kind of fun?" Julia revealed. "It's not often lawyers get to experience the ground work that goes into building a case. You're very good at your job, Cassidy. You have great instincts."

I jerked to a stop. "Uh oh."

Julia stopped and turned back to me. "What is it?"

I puffed my cheeks out. "Head ... inflating .... Can't ... be stopped!"

Julia shook her head, but chuckled at my antics.

We started to walk in the direction of Julia's parked car. Parallel parking was limited in front of City Hall, so we'd parked in the small lot behind the building. Most of the spaces were assigned parking with small metal signs that indicated which City Hall employee was allowed to park where. When Julia had parked in the space designated for the city prosecutor, I hadn't commented.

"So what do you want to do now?" I asked. The sun was out and I felt infinitely lighter now that we'd dropped off the computer tower. "Back to the house?"

Julia reached out and grabbed my hand. Our fingers reflexively intertwined. "How about a date?"

~

My eyes greedily scanned the laminated menu and its offerings. Mickey's Diner in the Twin Cities had been my go-to destination for greasy-spoon food, but Stan's diner ran a close second. I couldn't believe Julia had suggested the location. I supposed it was her nonverbal way of showing her appreciation for me. The fact that she'd called it a date instead of just lunch confirmed that as well. Early on I had been obsessed with us going on dates and having labels for whatever we were doing, but every day with Julia was better than any date I'd been on before her.

"Are you getting a salad?" I asked. My eyes didn't leave the menu.

"Probably," she said, "but don't let that stop you from ordering an early heart attack for yourself."

I licked my lips as I considered my choices. "Don't worry; I won't."

After making my culinary decision, I set my menu down and scanned the diner's interior. Julia and I were some of the only patrons. It was too late for the breakfast regulars, but not yet time for the lunch rush.

A dark-haired woman who wore her hair in a high ponytail stopped by our table to take our orders. She routinely flipped over the ceramic coffee cups on our paper placemats and filled them with black coffee. She started to recite the day's lunch specials, her eyes glazed over from the monotony of her job, before she realized who were were—or at least who Julia was.

The bored look on her face brightened. "Julia!" she chirped. "I didn't know you were still in town. I read about your dad in the paper. I'm sorry. You always think that kind of stuff can't happen in our little town, but I guess there's bad people everywhere, huh?"

The woman rattled on, practically without breath. To Julia's credit, she bore the attention and barrage of words with grace. In an earlier time, she might have cut the woman off and told her our lunch order.

"Thank you for your concern," Julia smiled placidly. "It was a shock to us all."

The waitress looked in my direction for the first time. Nothing on her face registered recognition; I'd never seen her before either, so she took our lunch order and left the table.

I watched Julia spoon an ice cube out of her plastic water glass and drop it into the steaming coffee. The ice immediately disappeared into the hot liquid.

"That's Maggie Holstrom," she said. "She's worked at Stan's forever."

I nodded, but didn't say anything.

Julia picked up her coffee mug and gently blew across its murky surface. "I've always liked the coffee here," she continued to consider aloud. "I'm sure it's not organic or fair trade, but it's good."

"Better than the mud they give us in the Fourth Precinct," I opined.

"We used to hang out here in high school all the time," she said. "Back when you could smoke in restaurants. We'd smoke stolen menthols and drink coffee all night, feeling like rebels."

I wanted to ask who *we* had been. Both Grace Kelly and David had led me to believe that Julia hadn't had many friends when they'd done to school together.

Julia pulled a non-dairy creamer container from a small ceramic bowl on the table. She flicked a manicured fingernail against its top, making it flip over. She continued the motion, over and over, sometimes flipping the pre-packaged creamer container over entirely, sometimes simply knocking it on its side. It was another wall, another layer being let down. Julia was funny—she made me laugh all the time—but I'd never seen her be goofy or silly. I was as ridiculous as they came; Julia, however, never did anything juvenile.

I plucked a creamer container from the shallow bowl and mirrored her motions. I flicked my finger against the slightly beveled lid of the coffee creamer, making it flip and hop across the table.

"Can't do this at *L'étoile Blanche*," I couldn't help remark. I'd probably butchered the name of the high-end French restaurant, but she knew what I meant.

Our food didn't take long to prepare. Maggie was back at our table with Julia's salad and my cheeseburger and fries. She produced a third, smaller plate and grandly set it between Julia and me.

"Key lime pie," she said with a sly wink. "On the house. Just don't tell Stan."

Her words were too loud and the diner too quiet for Stan—the man working the flat-top grill—to have not heard. He only rolled his eyes, however, and returned his attention to the open grill.

I bypassed my burger and fries and stabbed a bite of pie with my fork and took a generous bite. "Oh God, that's good," I said, covering my mouth with one hand.

Julia took a smaller, more respectable bite for herself. "I suppose there's some advantages to small-town life where everyone knows who you are."

"Yeah—free pie!" I exclaimed. "Food is always better when it's free."

"I imagine you get a lot of free food when you're in uniform," Julia remarked.

"I used to," I confirmed. "Free coffee. Donuts. Sub sandwiches. But now I'm just a chick in a dress shirt and ugly dress pants."

Julia took another measured forkful of pie. "I have it on high authority that your ass looks luscious in those pants. Far better than those polyester police pants."

Julia's playful comment fell on deaf ears. I was too distracted by movement beyond the front plate glass window of Stan's diner to hear the compliment.

I wiped at my mouth with my paper napkin and stood up.

Julia's eyes followed my rising form. "What is it?"

My eyes didn't leave the view beyond the window. "Nothing. I'll be right back."

Without another word of explanation, I strode toward the diner's front entrance. The brass bell above the door rang with my exit.

Outside of Stan's diner, Julia had parallel parked her black Mercedes in one of the available spots on Main Street. The parking meter associated with her spot had expired and my old coworker David Addams stood beside the meter with a thick pad of parking tickets. The familiar brown patrol car idled in the middle of Main Street, forcing other drivers to circumnavigate the police vehicle.

I fished into the front pockets of my jeans, but came up empty. All of my money was back in the diner in my leather jacket.

"Hold up, Addams," I called to him. "I've got change for the meter."

David didn't look in my direction. "I already started the ticket."

"And you can stop it, too."

David finally looked up. His icy blue eyes glared in my direction. "Julia's illegally parked."

"Dude, the meter *just* ran out. I've got change inside."

"Your girlfriend broke the law," he grit out. "And it's my job to make sure she's held accountable."

His tone told me this was bigger than a parking violation.

"You don't seriously believe Julia killed her father," I challenged.

"We have to investigate everything and everyone."

I found David's non-answer to be threatening.

"William Desjardin wasn't exactly the most popular guy in town," I pointed out. "Are you so hell bent on closing this case that it doesn't matter who you pin the blame on?"

"You're not a cop here anymore, Miller. We've got this handled."

"I'm *a* cop. And, yeah, it's a conflict of interest because I'm dating the person who you think is the mastermind behind all of this. But you also once believed she was the mastermind behind laundering money from the city, remember?"

"What did Julia say about the $10,000 she withdrew from savings?"

I hesitated before the lie came out: "She didn't."

If Julia had told Chief Hart, who'd then relayed that information to Special Agent Andrews, it was probably only a matter of time before Addams and the rest of City Hall learned what the $10,000 withdrawal had been for. But I wasn't going to announce Julia's personal business on the sidewalk in front of Stan's Diner.

"And you're okay with that?" David accused. "You're not the least bit curious about what that money was for?"

"I'm not. It's her money. That's not my business."

"That's bullshit," he barked. "You want to know. I bet it's eating away at you not to know what that money was for."

"How about you actually work the case and not take out old vendettas on Julia?"

"She's not one of us."

"One of us?" I burst out. "What the fuck does that even mean?"

We'd started to attract the attention of not a few bystanders, but I was beyond caring.

"She's not a badge; she showed her true colors when she defended the Mayor."

"She defended her *father*," I corrected. "You seriously wouldn't have done the same thing?"

"And then she had him killed," he spat out. "So much for loyalty."

I barely registered the sound of the diner door opening behind me and the small bell ringing. If I'd been a boxer, I would have probably started swinging.

Instead, I flinched when I felt fingers touch my elbow.

"Cassidy." I heard Julia's careful voice in my ear. "Let it go."

How sound-proof was the front window of Stan's Diner? How much of our conversation had she overheard?

I remained in my place, rooted to the sidewalk, my fists clenching and unclenching at my sides.

"Sergeant Addams," Julia reverently greeted. "Thank you for your service." She held out her outstretched hand to the man, palm facing the sky.

David looked momentarily confused. He quickly recovered, however, and ripped the top ticket off of his pad.

"Come on, darling," Julia spoke to me. "Your food is getting cold."

Chapter Eighteen

Afghanistan, 2012

I nudge the two fallen bodies with the toe of my boots to make sure the men are dead. Deader than a doorknob, my dad would have said. The old saying never made any sense to me, and it still doesn't.

Pensacola remained where I'd left him, not that he had a choice in the matter. I hustle back to his position, not wanting to waste more time. There's no telling how long it will be before another vehicle comes along.

He smiles through obvious pain. "Did I get them?" he wheezes.

"Yeah, buddy. You fucking wasted them."

He shuts his eyes. "Cool." His body visibly slumps; he's fading fast.

"Oh no you don't," I growl. "I didn't fucking drag your flat ass halfway across Afghanistan for you to die on me now."

Pense swats at invisible flies. "Not dying. Just closing my eyes for a bit." His words sound slurred.

I can carry him faster than I can drag him in my makeshift sled. My adrenaline levels are a little more subdued, and I'll probably exhaust my energies by carrying him the distance to the Jeep, but if we're lucky, this will be the last time I'll need to expend any energy.

If we're lucky.

I grab a near lifeless arm and roll Pense onto his back. I don't let myself dwell on that detail. I get on the ground with him and lay with my head on his stomach. One of the knocks against women in the military is the fear that if a male twice the size of a female became injured, she wouldn't have the physical strength to pick him up and carry him to safety. That argument was bullshit; all you needed was a little creativity and momentum. To attempt a ranger roll—the technique to get a fallen body onto your shoulders for the fireman's carry—requires grabbing your partner's leg. Pense only has one of those left, and his remaining leg is shredded like pulled pork.

"This is gonna hurt," I warn him.

Pense doesn't respond. I curl my right arm under his leg, just above the knee. I rock my body, rolling on top of his legs, and then throw my momentum in the opposite direction. I hear Pensacola's piercing shriek, but at least I know he's still alive. He's also successfully draped over my right shoulder.

With a loud grunt, I'm able to pull myself to my feet. "No more Oreos for you," I grit out. "You're going on a diet."

My steps are unsteady and sweat pours from my forehead. I put one foot in front of the other as I hump the short distance to the Jeep. I'm able to sling Pensacola into the passenger seat and buckle him in.

With one final glance in the direction of the two dead men, I climb into the driver's seat. The keys are still in the ignition. The guys hadn't bothered to shut off the Jeep during their piss break.

I disengage the emergency brake and shift the vehicle out of neutral. The gears grind and whine as I shift into first gear.

"You know how to drive this thing?" Pense asks. Despite his exhaustion, I can hear the skepticism in his tone.

"My dad taught me to drive stick before I learned on an automatic," I say. "He wanted to make sure I could always get home safely."

I'm not so far removed from the situation to not realize the irony of those words. My dad had taught me to drive a manual in case a friend got too drunk to drive and I needed to get us home. He couldn't have known I'd need the knowledge for a scenario like this. My eyes start to sting and I swallow down the lump in my throat. I can't afford the tears; I don't have water to spare. There will be time to cry later.

"Parents are cool," Pense mumbles beside me.

I reach over and squeeze the top of Pensacola's injured leg. He shrieks again. "Don't fucking go to sleep on me," I warn him. "It's rude."

The tires spin and kick up sand and dust as the vehicle lurches forward. I take a quick look in my rearview mirror at the two dead bodies on the side of the road as I put more distance between us and them. I can't wait until this whole fucking country is behind me.

~

Julia held my elbow as we left the concrete sidewalk for the cemetery lawn. A light frost had settled overnight on the cemetery grounds. It melted wherever our feet shuffled across the trimmed lawn, creating little visual paths like the condensation trails that followed a commercial airplane. Only a handful of days had passed since her father's burial, but the cemetery grounds had transformed with the sudden dip in temperature.

Julia's grip on my bicep tightened. "Thank you for coming back here with me. The day of my father's funeral was such a blur, I didn't even think about visiting Jonathan."

We'd stopped in town at the local florist to buy a bouquet of flowers for Jonathan's grave. I made no comment that we could have gotten a second bouquet for her father's grave as well. I let Julia set the agenda.

"Of course."

I pressed my shoulder into hers as we walked across the cemetery. If I didn't have the words, I at least wanted my body language to convey the sentiment: I was there for her. Whatever she needed, I would do it.

As we approached her family plot, I noticed the fresh sod laid over William Desjardin's burial site. The grass was a little more matted and trampled around the Desjardin plot than the surrounding grave sites. A wreath of decaying flowers leaned against the large tombstone that bore the family's surname.

Julia temporarily released my arm. She crouched down and set the new bouquet of flowers at the base of the tombstone. She touched a gentle hand to the granite's surface, near her brother's engraved name. I looked away, feeling like a trespasser on the intimate moment. Julia stood back up and took her place beside me. I bowed my head, not quite sure what else to do.

It was me who eventually broke the reverent silence: "Why is your name on that tombstone?"

I stared at the shiny grey stone. The Desjardin surname was carved into the top of the horizontal slab in a somber, capitalized font. Beneath the last name were four others: William, Olivia, Jonathan, and Julia. With the exception of Jonathan's dates, the other entries only included a birth year.

"It's a family plot," Julia explained. "My parents purchased the spaces when Jonathan died."

"Was there was buy one, get three sale?" I tried to joke.

Julia brushed a gloved hand against mine. "Everyone has to die someday, darling."

"Sure, but someday far, far, *far, far* down the road," I insisted.

I continued to stare at the smooth, engraved contours that shaped the letters of her name.

"I don't like it," I announced. "I don't like that your name is already on a tombstone."

"It's just a formality. If you look around, you'll see many similar plots."

"Are you—do you really want to be buried here?" I asked. I was amazed I was able to get the question past the lump in my throat.

"I honestly haven't given it much thought," she told me. "My parents bought the plots and the grave marker without consulting me."

I let out a long breath. "At least now I know what year you were born."

Julia's mouth dropped open when she realized the oversight. The tombstone listed her date of birth, and contrary to popular opinion, I could do basic math.

A coy smile reached my lips. "You're looking damn fine for being—."

"Don't even say it," Julia testily warned.

I looped my arm into hers and laughed. Maybe our visit to Embarrass was starting to look up.

~

Several days passed with no word from Special Agent Andrews' office. I knew it would take her some time to follow up on the information we'd been able to discover along with sending William Desjardin's computer to the forensics office in the Twin Cities, but that knowledge did nothing for my anxiety. I hoped we'd done the right thing in handing over our discoveries rather than continuing to work the case ourselves. Unlike other cops I'd worked with in the past, I had no problems with collaborating and sharing resources. I was probably in the minority, however. I'd met a number of detectives and special agents who were territorial about their case work. We were all supposed to be on the same team though.

In the days since we'd dropped off her father's computer to City Hall, Julia had put on a brave front. If it turned out her father had cancer, his insurance company would cancel the nearly $1.5 million policy payout due to her. If it was a dead end, however, she was still a person of interest in his death. While we waited for Agent Andrews to give us an update, we stuck close to her house— no more impromptu dates to Stan's Diner—and spoke little about the case. When we weren't cozy by the fireplace in her den, we were visiting her mom in assisted living, playing dominos or assembling puzzles.

Julia continued to introduce me as 'her friend Cassidy,' and I started to get used to the idea that her mother might never learn the true nature of our relationship. And I was going to have to decide if I was okay with that or not.

But even with the boardgames and evening fireside cuddling, my mind still drifted to her father's death. I'd convinced myself that the search history on his computer was connected to his own failing health. The knowledge that he'd taken out a life insurance policy one dollar shy of needing a proper medical exam was even more proof of that. The search history for *Double Indemnity* might have been a coincidence, but I didn't believe that.

The final piece of the puzzle, however, was identifying the individuals who had broken into the Desjardin home. The bloody footprints were too generic and no fingerprints, fibers, or DNA had been found at the scene. We'd turned over Julia's father's computer, which might have produced contact information or at least the name of someone involved if William Desjardin had planned his own death.

I worked over the details of the case in my head while Julia made sandwiches for lunch.

"Did I ever tell you about this guy I met in Afghanistan—Brent Boyer?" I said. "He was in the field hospital with me and Pense before we got shipped back to the States."

Julia shook her head. "No. That name's not familiar."

"We thought he was a goner," I continued. "His insides got all sliced up from a dirty bomb. The doctors had to take out half of his guts even before we got on the plane to go stateside."

Julia set down a butter knife and wrinkled her nose. "I don't know if this is polite conversation, dear. At least wait until after lunch if you're going to be so graphic."

"I have a point! I promise!" I exclaimed. "Pense called me a few days back and reminded me about Boyer; he and Claire were in the cities, and he wanted to see if we could meet up for dinner while they were in town."

Julia frowned. "Oh, that's too bad we missed them. I'll have to give Claire a call—once Embarrass' finest decide to give me my phone back," she qualified with a roll of her eyes.

"Anyway!" I continued, refusing to be derailed. "It got me thinking; what if your dad *wanted* to be shot in the stomach?"

"Wanted?" Julia questioned.

"Yeah—*wanted*. The pancreas is located behind the stomach," I observed. "We all just assumed it was a sloppy shot by an amateur burglar. But what if it was actually *on purpose*? If the coroner had actually done an autopsy, the bullet wound could have destroyed signs of his cancer, but maybe not. I mean, the coincidences are too much to actually be a coincidence, right?" I waved my hands excitedly; I started to get agitated as I spoke aloud. "He gets the cancer diagnosis. He takes out the insurance policy, and then he gets shot by an intruder right in the cancerous organ?"

Julia licked her lips. "That's a very compelling hypothesis, Detective."

"I don't suppose you'd ever consider exhuming your dad's body? Maybe the coroner could actually do his job this time."

Julia swallowed. "I ..."

"Forget I said anything," I said quickly. "Agent Andrews has more than enough to wrap this up."

My phone vibrated and chirped on the kitchen countertop. I didn't recognize the number, but it had a local area code. Because Julia's phone was now property of the Embarrass Police Department, Julia had given my numbers to Joy and the administrators at her mother's assisted living facility in case they needed to get ahold of her. I was tempted to let the call go to voicemail, but something told me to answer.

"Hello?"

"Detective Miller?" A vaguely familiar female voice spoke on the other line.

"Speaking."

"This is Special Agent Rachel Andrews with the BCA. I'm following up on our meeting from earlier this week."

I held back my snicker at her formality.

"I wanted to let you know that I followed up on your hunch about William Desjardin—your belief that he might have had cancer."

I gripped the phone a little tighter. "And?"

"We called every oncologist registered in the state. Mr. Desjardin was seeing Dr. Meyer locally, but he was also a patient at Regions Hospital in St. Paul."

Regions. I knew that name. "That's, like, across the street from Julia's condo," I thought aloud.

At the mention of her name, Julia perked up. She cocked her head and looked at me expectantly. I held up a single finger with the promise that I'd catch her up soon.

Special Agent Andrews continued: "The doctor at St. Regions was able to confirm that Mr. Desjardin had been diagnosed with pancreatic cancer. Stage Four."

My mouth went dry. "And there's no such thing as Stage Five."

"Right," she confirmed. "Based on this new information, I've recommended that Ms. Desjardin no longer be considered a person of interest in this case. I've arranged for Sergeant Addams to return her personal effects to her home by the end of the day."

The reference to David made me grimace. The two of us probably had some mutual apologizing to do. Thinking back to my outburst outside of Stan's Diner brought a blush of embarrassment to my cheeks.

"What about the homicide case?" I asked. "Someone still killed the Mayor."

"I'm staying on in Embarrass for a little longer," Agent Andrews noted. "We've got forensics looking into his emails and phone records to see if he really arranged for his own death or if the home invasion was merely circumstantial. To be honest though," I heard her sigh, "without an active suspect to look into, I'll probably be back in Grand Rapids before the end of the week."

I nodded stiffly even though she wouldn't be able to see it. "Thank you for the call, Agent Andrews. I'll relay this information to Julia."

"Thank you for the assist, Detective Miller. We might not have the actual criminal locked up, but at least we didn't arrest an innocent woman."

I glanced in Julia's direction. "And me and my innocent woman thank you for that."

Agent Andrews quietly coughed into the phone. "Please relay my condolences to Ms. Desjardin. Not only was her father the victim of a violent homicide, but then she was put under the microscope. I'm sorry she had to go through that."

I ended the call after we exchanged our goodbyes. Julia continued to assemble sandwiches on the kitchen island. Her features were schooled, nearly disinterested, but I knew her curiosity must have been killing her.

"That was Special Agent Andrews," I announced, stating the obvious.

"What now? Does she need me to drop off a DNA sample?" Julia quipped. "A pair of used underwear perhaps?"

"Your dad had cancer. Just like we suspected."

Julia braced herself against the kitchen island and deeply exhaled. "Terminal," she guessed.

I nodded. "Andrews called every cancer specialist in the state. She finally found his patient records at Regions Hospital."

"Regions?" Julia echoed.

She, naturally, knew its significant. When her father had received his cancer diagnosis, he'd only been across the street from her condo.

Julia stood a little more erect. "So what's next?" she asked.

"Well—you're no longer a person of interest, so I guess that means we can go home. Agent Andrews will keep working the case here, but she suspects BCA will probably have her home soon enough, too."

"And my father's killers will go free," she said evenly.

"On the bright side, Stanley and I will probably be the next people assigned to the case."

"That wouldn't be a conflict of interest?"

I couldn't help myself: "Well, it's not like we're married."

Julia quirked an eyebrow.

I laughed and shook my head. "Sorry. I couldn't resist. If I was a homicide detective I'd pass the case to a co-worker," I said. "But because I'm the only one in cold case, there isn't anyone else to defer to. In situations like this, I just have to declare that I knew the victim and we move on from there.

Julia pursed her lips. "Don't get yourself in trouble."

"Me? Never. Besides, some new piece of evidence or tip would have to be introduced for us to reinvestigate the case. It's not even a cold case yet," I pointed out, "so let's not get ahead of ourselves.

Julia hummed, but said nothing more. She resumed her task of lunch prep.

I leaned forward on my stool. "How are you?"

She released a shaky breath. "Happy," she said with finality. "Happy we can finally go home."

~

It didn't take long after receiving Agent Andrews' update to pack our bags, close up the mansion, and load up Julia's Mercedes. We didn't immediately head back to the Twin Cities, however. Julia visited her mother one more time. And I had my own detour before we left town as well.

A small U-Haul trailer was parked in Wendy Clark's paved driveway. I found the woman in question in the home's attached garage, leaning into an almost comically large box. I announced my presence by shuffling the bottoms of my boots against the smooth concrete.

Wendy popped out of the cardboard container, startled by the sound. "Oh!"

I held up my hands and grimaced. "Sorry. I didn't mean to scare you."

"Detective Miller!" she gasped, still working through the initial alarm. "How can I help you?"

"Nothing," I said. "I just wanted to say goodbye before we left town."

I gestured out towards the street to Julia's parked car. Julia hadn't questioned my request to stop by Wendy Clark's on our way out of town, but she had remained with the vehicle. Despite the dropping temperatures, she'd gotten out of the car, but she hadn't ventured any closer to the woman with whom her father had had an affair.

"Sounds like a trend," Wendy observed. "I'll be leaving soon, too. Probably shouldn't have unpacked in the first place," she noted.

"Are you moving back to Illinois?" I asked, remembering our previous conversation.

"No real reason to stick around here," she confirmed. "Small-town life can be a living hell when you're the one everyone is gossiping around."

I nodded knowingly; it was a truth I knew all too well on so many levels. I hadn't wanted to stay in my hometown of St. Cloud when I'd come back from Afghanistan for good. St. Cloud was a medium-sized city, but the hero's welcome I'd been given had turned me into a kind of mini-celebrity. No one can survive that kind of scrutiny. Grace Kelly Donovan had put the microscope on me once again with her front page exposé about my military accolades, but she'd also kept Julia and my affair under wraps. But when I'd been betrayed by Julia in the city courthouse, I'd had to get away again. Luckily, the Twin Cities had turned out to be big enough for my secrets, my past, and my disability. But even then, the Minneapolis police department could be like a small town itself, requiring that I not divulge too much about myself except with my small circle of friends.

There was really no delicate way to get the information I needed. The purpose for my visit was more than a simple goodbye. "William Desjardin had an advanced stage of pancreatic cancer. Did you know about that?"

Wendy's eyes widened and her earlier smile disappeared. "What? No. William always bragged that he was healthy as a horse. Didn't drink. Didn't smoke. He hardly ate red meat either."

"A man with no vices," I idly observed.

"Except greed and narcissism," Wendy unabashedly added. She chewed on her lower lip. "The way you phrased that made it seem like it was a surprise to a lot of people. They didn't find it during his autopsy?"

"The man had been shot in the stomach," I pointed out. "I don't think the coroner was too concerned about cause of death."

Wendy hummed. "Good point."

With slow, measured steps, Wendy walked towards the open garage door. The day's sun was bright overhead, but a brisk winter wind reminded us of the late date on the calendar. She idly rubbed at her arms. Embarrass hadn't earned its reputation as The Cold Spot for no reason.

"Is she okay?" Wendy nodded in the direction of Julia, who

remained outside in a hostile position, leaning against her parked Mercedes. Dark sunglasses covered her eyes, so I couldn't be sure if she was looking in our direction.

"Yeah," I said routinely.

It was too simple of a response for such a complicated question. Julie still had to decide where her mother was going to next or if she should remain in the assisted living facility in Embarrass. The Embarrass police and the Minnesota Bureau of Criminal Apprehension no longer considered Julia a person of interest in the death of her father, yet her suspected involvement had necessitated opening up her private life to be explored and scrutinized. Her dream job at a leading criminal defense firm had probably been forfeited, or so she was convinced. And even though her father had left all of his estate and monies to her, the revelation that he'd had cancer and had knowingly lied about it on his life insurance application had negated a beneficiary payoff of close to $1.5 million dollars. And then there was the simple fact that her father had been diagnosed with terminal cancer and had kept that information private. Despite their estrangement, it would have been a lot for anyone to process.

So was Julia going to be okay? Legally, yes. Emotionally—that was still a work in progress.

I didn't have anything else on my agenda, and I knew Julia was eager to get on the road so we could make it back to the Twin Cities at a reasonable hour. We'd both been absent from our lives for too long.

"Good luck in Illinois," I said in earnest. "I hope you're able to get that fresh start."

"Thank you. And thank you for coming over again, Cassidy." Wendy shook my hand in parting. "It really means a lot that after everything that happened, you still took the time to come out here and tell me about William."

I hadn't made the trip entirely out of kindness, but rather to ascertain if anyone else had known about William Desjardin's illness. But I wasn't so cruel as to burst this woman's bubble. I'd already said enough.

"Safe travels," I said.

Epilogue

The St. Paul condo had been taken over by the sweet and savory scents emanating from the kitchen. Football played on the TV in the living room. It had been a compromise; Julia had wrinkled her nose at the suggestion that watching football on Thanksgiving was as traditional as pumpkin pie, but she'd conceded provided I keep the volume at a reasonable level.

Speaking of pie, a variety of freshly baked treats had been tormenting me for days. When you're a child and a Thanksgiving spread magically appears on the table, you don't realize the labor and coordination behind the elaborate meal. Julia had spent the previous days slicing fruit and rolling out pie dough. The turkey had had to thaw completely and then be brined in preparation for the holiday. I'd offered to help throughout the process, but Julia had only given me a patient smile and had assured me she had everything under control.

The woman in question was looking adorable in an apron cinched tight around her waist. She was overdressed for a casual

Thanksgiving with some of our closest friends, but I wasn't going to complain. The capped sleeves of her black wrap dress perfectly accentuated her long, lean arms. The neckline dipped demurely in the front; a string of iridescent peals draped her chiseled collarbone. The dress' silhouette drew attention to her narrow waist and her slightly flared hips. The bottom hem stopped just above her knee to reveal miles and miles of leg. Her black nylons were translucent enough that the definition in her slender calves was visible, all emphasized by her skyscraper heels. The eye candy she provided was an appropriate way to begin the food-themed holiday.

Julia was too preoccupied by the pots and pans of various sizes on the cooktop to notice my arrival in the kitchen. I slid my arms around her waist and rested my chin on her shoulder. "Something smells delicious," I approved. "And I'm not talking about dinner."

I felt her smile and her body relaxed against mine. "Been thinking long about that line, dear?"

"Can I help with anything?" I asked for about the billionth time that day.

"You can refill my wine. I seem to be running a little low."

"Yes, ma'am," I agreed, ecstatic for the task.

The wine rack was located in the formal dining room. We hardly used the room except for special date night dinners. It was far more convenient to use the breakfast nook for most meals. Julia had manifested an elaborate table-scape for the dining room table, complete with name tags at each of the chairs. I'd tried to remind her that my friends weren't that fancy and that we didn't need to impress anyone, but my words had promptly been dismissed. I had privately wondered if throwing herself into single-handedly preparing the elaborate meal was a way to distract herself from not spending the holiday with her mom, but I hadn't known how to approach the topic.

Julia would have preferred that her mother had returned to the Twin Cities with us, but she couldn't legally remove her from the assisted living home in Embarrass just yet. When her father had died, guardianship had passed to the State of Minnesota, not to Julia. I wasn't worried that a judge would refuse Julia conservatorship of her mom, but she still had to go through the proper legal channels to make it official.

Julia was planning on driving to Embarrass the next morning to spend a long weekend with her mom—the goal being to select a suitable senior care facility in the Twin Cities. I knew the move was a big point of stress for her—was she doing the right thing? Or was it simply the convenient thing? Should her mom remain in Embarrass? Would the move and transition to a new facility be too overwhelming? I knew these questions and more kept her up at night. But like preparing Thanksgiving dinner, she'd chosen to shoulder it all herself. I could only keep offering my help; I couldn't force her to accept it.

I uncorked a new bottle of red wine and returned to the kitchen just in time to see Julia pulling the cooked turkey from the oven. The room was instantly filled with the savory scents of rosemary, butter, and thyme, which I'd learned earlier she'd coated the turkey with.

I loved to eat, so Thanksgiving had always been one of my favorite holidays. Plus there wasn't the pressure of buying or receiving presents. It was only my second Thanksgiving out of the military. I'd spent the previous holiday with my Minneapolis cop friends. None of us knew how to cook, so we'd gotten a turkey dinner with all the trimmings from a local restaurant. This was better. Much better.

I topped off Julia's wine glass while she poked and prodded the bird with a meat thermometer to make sure it was suitably cooked through. I reached for the turkey, hoping to sneak a small nibble, but Julia was too quick and forced me to abort my mission.

"Leave that bird alone, Marine," she scolded. "It has to rest for an hour."

"How about we go rest in the bedroom while we wait?" I wiggled my eyebrows suggestively. "I wanna gobble, gobble you."

"You are impossible."

"Impossible to resist?" my voice lilted with hope.

"You need to call your parents before our guests arrive."

The cheesy grin fell from my face. "My parents are such a cock block."

"Don't worry, darling. I have every intention of helping myself to a second helping of you once your friends leave."

My mouth went dry. "Is it too late to cancel?" I squeaked. "Why are we even having people over?"

"Go call your parents," she smiled serenely. "People will be arriving soon."

I grumbled all the way to the back bedroom to make my phone call. I was such an idiot. Why would I ever invite people over if I could have turkey and Julia all at the same time?

I shut the bedroom door to afford myself a little privacy in case any of our friends showed up while I was still on the phone. I typed in the phone number I knew by heart—the landline at my parents' house. They each had their own cellphone, and I had those numbers programmed into my phone, but neither of them were very attached to the technology. My mom probably used her phone more to play games like Fruit Ninja or Candy Crush and my dad's cell was probably in the center console of his truck, the battery drained.

My mom sounded slightly breathless when she answered the phone after the third ring. "Hello?"

"Hey, Mom."

"Cassidy! Hi!" she exclaimed. "Sorry—I was in the basement doing laundry, otherwise I would have picked up sooner."

"It's fine, Mom," I chuckled. "I didn't have to wait long."

"What's going on? How are you?" she asked.

I could hear the opening and closing of kitchen cabinets in the background as she started to multi-task. My mom had never been good at just *sitting*. She always had some task or chore she believed needed to be done, right at that moment. Both of my parents were retired, but they were constantly on the move.

"Not much. I'm good," I said, answering both of her questions. "Julia's finishing up dinner, so I thought I'd give you a call. We've got some friends coming over soon."

"Oh, that's nice," she said warmly. "It's just your dad and me this year, so I scaled things back. Still having all the sides, but I'm only making a turkey breast instead of the usual twenty pounder."

"No aunts and uncles and cousins this year?"

My mom typically hosted the entire extended family for the holiday.

"No. They decided to go to Florida. I heard they're having fish for dinner." My mom's judgment was obvious in her tone.

I allowed myself a quiet laugh. "Well, that's just sacrilegious."

"What are you having?" she asked.

"Uh, Julia made a big turkey," I said. "There's mashed pota-toes, green bean casserole, stuffing, cranberries, and pie."

"Sounds like you lucked out finding a roommate who can cook," my mom observed.

Her word choice had me wincing. How could I be so critical of Julia not telling her mother if I hadn't Come Out to my parents either? I knew it was something I had to do—soon—but a Thanks-giving phone call didn't seem like the right time or place. This was a conversation that needed to be face-to-face.

"Yeah. I really hit the jackpot with Julia," I said instead. I cleared my throat. "Hey, is Dad around?"

"He's watching football in the other room."

"Can, I, uh ... do you think I could say hi to him?"

On any other year, for any other occasion, I wouldn't have bothered to ask. I would have talked to my mom for a few minutes, hung up, and crossed off *Talk to Parents* from my To Do list. My dad and I no longer had a close relationship. He thought I'd screwed things up with Chief Hart and he had no idea how to talk to me about Afghanistan and my condition.

"Oh! Okay!" My mom clearly hadn't been expecting my request. Hell, even *I* was surprised.

My mom had cupped her hand over the cordless phone's receiver, but I could still hear their conversation.

"The phone's for you."

I heard his distracted grunt. My dad was like me—if sports were on, it took a national emergency to pull me from the TV.

"It's your daughter," my mom revealed.

"Never heard of her."

"Oh, behave," my mom chided. "Talk to Cassidy."

There was some muffled rustling as the phone was passed from my mom to my dad. More muted noises came through the phone until I heard him clear his throat: "Hello?"

"Hey, Dad," I greeted. "It's me, Cassidy."

"So I hear."

He was being overly surly, even for him, but I supposed I was the one interrupting his football viewing.

"What's the score?"

"Detroit's getting worked."

"They'll come back," I said optimistically. "They typically over-perform on Thanksgiving."

"Not this year," he grunted. "Their china doll quarterback hurt the thumb on his throwing hand."

"Ouch. Sucks to be a Lion's fan."

"Not that the Vikings are any better," he observed.

I took in a breath. This was safe. This was the sweet zone with my dad: talk about the weather, the price of gasoline, and sports. I didn't want to rock the boat—to venture into uncharted territory—but Dr. Warren had suggested I try something to repair our relationship. When Julia and I had first returned to the Twin Cities she'd made me schedule my next appointment before our suitcases were even unpacked.

"Hey, Dad? Uh, thanks for teaching me how to drive stick shift."

He was quiet for a moment, clearly confused by the subject change. "You finally turning in that bike for a real car?"

"No. I've still got the Harley," I said. "I don't know if I ever told you, but in Afghanistan ..." I trailed off. I closed my eyes; they'd started to burn with unexpected emotion. "The guy I was with out there—Terrance Pensacola—he was hurt pretty bad," I eventually continued. I could feel my hands start to shake. "When we were getting out of there, I had to drive us. It was a stick shift. So, uh, I just wanted to say thanks. Thanks for teaching me."

My dad didn't say anything, but that was okay. My soliloquy was more for me than it was for him.

"Anyway!" I chirped, switching my own gears, "I'll let you get back to the game. Happy Thanksgiving, Dad."

"Happy Thanksgiving to you, too," he replied.

I was about to end the call when I heard him: "Hey, Cassidy?"

"Yeah?"

"Thanks for the call. I love you, kid."

I clapped my hand over my mouth and swallowed down the

overwhelming need to sob. The burning in my eyes intensified. "I love you, too, Dad."

I ended the call and wiped at my eyes. I didn't have time to truly digest the conversation with my dad; I heard the buzzer that indicated that someone was waiting to be let into the building. I exited the bedroom, still sniffling.

"Your co-worker Stanley is here," Julia informed me from the kitchen. Her lips pursed. "He's early."

She took in my appearance, and her annoyance shifted to concern. "Is everything okay?"

"Yeah," I nodded.

"Your parents?" she questioned.

"They're good," I assured her.

She gave me a look that suggested she'd ask me more later. But a knock at the front door put that conversation temporarily on hold.

"I'll get it," I volunteered.

Stanley shoved a dark glass jug into my hands when I opened the front door.

"I brought mead," he declared.

"Um, thanks?"

"I know a guy with bees," he explained. Stanley looked around the front of the condo. He wore a green turtleneck sweater that accentuated his full, red beard. His normally chaotic mop of ginger hair had been relatively tamed for the occasion. "I'm early," he observed.

"You are," I agreed, "but that's okay. You brought mead. Let's crack into this thing before the others arrive."

Stanley followed me from the front foyer to the kitchen where Julia had remained. I hefted the jug of mead above my head like it was the Lombardi Trophy.

"Stanley brought mead," I announced.

Julia wiped her hands on the front of her apron. "Mead? I don't think I've ever gotten to try that before. Thank you, Stanley. What a kind gesture."

Stanley stood in the threshold, and seemed to be frozen in place. "I know a guy with bees," he repeated from before.

"What kind of glassware does one drink mead from?" Julia wondered aloud. She turned to open the upper cabinet where she stored her glasses of various shapes and sizes.

"The Vikings traditionally drank mead from specially fashioned cattle horns." Stanley spoke robotically, noticeably more awkward than usual.

"Well, I don't think I have any of those," Julia lightly laughed.

"A wine glass is fine," Stanley said.

I cocked an eyebrow at my friend while Julia's back was turned to us. "Dude, are you okay?" I quietly asked.

"You didn't tell me your girlfriend was so attractive," he whispered.

"Is that a problem?" I whispered back. I'd forgotten the two of them had never actually met.

Julia returned with three glasses of mead served in three small wine glasses, effectively ending our strange conversation. "Here we are." She handed a glass to each of us. "How would the Vikings say cheers—*skol*?" she guessed.

A pleased grin formed on Stanley's goofy mouth. He jerked his glass in the air, nearly spilling its liquid contents. "*Skol!*"

Stanley drained his glass in one extended drink. Julia took a more tentative sip, barely letting the liquid touch her painted lips. I'd never had mead before either, but I took a larger drink than Julia. I tried not to gag on the honey-sweet booze.

"Oh ... that's... unique," I settled on the neutral appraisal.

Another knock at the front door saved me from elaborating. "I'll get it!" I eagerly volunteered.

I hustled to the foyer and threw open the door without checking the peephole first. I only caught a flash of pale skin and red hair before I found myself struggling to breathe. Two surprisingly strong arms wrapped around me.

A high-pitched voice shrieked in my ear: "Cassidy!"

I tried to match her energy, but she was starting to choke me out. "Michaela!"

Michaela McCarthy was one of Julia's friends from college, and one of the few who'd stayed in town after they'd graduated. I'd later found out she and Julia had been sorority sisters at the housewarming party for Michaela's downtown loft.

"I'm glad you could make it," I greeted when she finally relinquished her hug. "Come on it. Julia's in the kitchen."

I took Michaela's jacket and hung it up in the front coat closet. We made our way to the back of the condo where Julia and Stanley looked to be in the middle of an animated conversation. Stanley had started to loosen up, thanks to a generous amount of mead.

Michaela squealed when she saw Julia. "Jules!" she exclaimed. "That dress is *gorgeous!*" She charged her friend and wrapped Julia up in a tight hug that rivaled the one she'd given me at the front door.

While the two friends hugged it out and started to catch up, Stanley gave me a pained look that nearly made me laugh out loud. Now there were *two* attractive women at Thanksgiving.

I grabbed a beer from the refrigerator. "Do you like football, Stanley?"

My co-worker's face lit up. "I thought you'd never ask."

My friends Angie and Brent were the last two invitees to show up for dinner. Traditionally, Rich and Adan, who rounded out our law enforcement friend group, would have joined us, but both men were spending the holiday with their respective girlfriend's families. Adan was already a fixture at Isabella's family's holiday events, but Rich was meeting Grace Kelly's family for the very first time and was appropriately freaked out. When Julia had originally proposed the idea of hosting Thanksgiving for all of our unattached friends, I hadn't been sure how the group might interact. Surprisingly, the two women and the two men found common ground with each other. Angie and Michaela had bonded over wine and cute boys, and Stanley and Brent spoke passionately about their Fantasy Football leagues.

It was a tight fit around the dining room table when the meal was finally ready. Julia's carefully crafted centerpiece had to be relocated to the living room once everyone's glassware crowded the table's surface. I knew Julia would have preferred to be entertaining in the grandiose space of her Embarrass mansion, but the St. Paul table was filled with food and friends who were like family. Besides, Embarrass wasn't going anywhere. And maybe our trips would become more frequent whenever we needed an escape from the city, although I suspected our refuge might be a rustic cabin on a lake instead of the white columned mansion.

Serving bowls were passed around the table. Angie had brought a killer sweet potato pie to add to the mix. Viking had brought a raw canister of biscuits that Julia had politely but stealthily put in the refrigerator for later. Conversation rose above the clank of silverware against porcelain plates.

"Wait!" Michaela exclaimed. "Before we eat, everyone has to go around the table and say what they're thankful for."

Michaela's suggestion was met with a chorus of boos and groans.

"You guys!" she squeaked. "It's tradition! I'll go first—I'm thankful for Julia and Cassidy's generosity." She tipped her wine glass in our direction in salute. "Thank you for the invite. I'm thankful I won't be eating a sad TV dinner for one tonight."

"You're very welcome," Julia allowed.

"And I'm thankful," Michaela continued, "for..." She tapped at her wine-stained lips in thought. "For ... raw cookie dough!" she settled on. "Thank you to the person who decided to package that stuff up."

Viking raised his pint glass. "Amen to that."

Michaela looked around the table expectantly. "Who wants to go next?"

I purposefully avoided her eye contact like a student who hadn't done their homework.

"I'll go next," Julia offered.

I turned to my girlfriend with a curious look. I was mildly surprised that she'd volunteered. This seemed like the kind of touchy-feely, being-vulnerable-in-front-of-strangers thing that she typically detested.

She pressed her lips together, looking pensive. "First, thank you all for being here. You've saved my waistline from having to eat all of these leftovers."

"Hey!" I playfully interjected. "There'd better be some left-overs for me!"

Julia smiled placatingly and squeezed my knee beneath the cover of the tablecloth.

"Next, I'd like to thank Stanley Harris," she said.

Stanley straightened in his chair. His body jerked so violently, the tops of his legs collided with the dining table. "Me?"

Julia smiled in his direction. "Yes, Stanley. I'm thankful for your computer expertise."

The praise clearly confused most of those seated at the table, but Stanley blushed a deep red that nearly matched the color of his beard.

"This year I have so many things to be thankful for," Julia continued. "The list is too long, and I don't want to bore you or keep you from your meal, but I would be remiss if I didn't take this moment to thank *you*, Cassidy."

I could feel all eyes at the table shift to me. I tried to not squirm beneath the spotlight, but it was a challenge.

Julia shifted in her chair so she could address me directly. "You are the most doggedly stubborn and obstinate person I've ever met." She gave me a melting smile. "And I'm so thankful for that tenacity because it's the biggest reason we're together today."

"Don't forget my klutziness," I bashfully countered. "I would have been just another girl to you if I hadn't spilled our drinks so spectacularly."

"Yes, I'm thankful you're so klutzy, too," she grinned.

"Ya'll are gross," Angie interjected. "But good for you. Who's next?"

"That was nice," I quietly complimented while Viking started to recite what he was thankful for.

"And all deserved." Julia leaned close and pressed her lips against my cheek. She swiped the pad of her thumb across my cheekbone to remove the lipstick she might have left behind.

"Hey, in case I forget," I remarked. "Thanks for making dinner tonight. Everything looks delicious."

"Of course, darling." Julia dropped her tone for only my ears: "Just be sure you save some room for me later."

About the Author

Eliza Lentzski is the author of lesbian fiction, romance, and erotica including the best-selling *Winter Jacket* and *Don't Call Me Hero* series. She publishes urban fantasy and paranormal romance under the penname E.L. Blaisdell. Although a historian by day, Eliza is passionate about fiction. She was born and raised in the upper Midwest, which is often the setting for her novels. She lives in Boston with her wife and their cat, Charley.

Follow her on Twitter and Instagram, @ElizaLentzski, and Like her on Facebook (http://www.facebook.com/elizalentzski) for updates and exclusive previews of future original releases.

http://www.elizalentzski.com

Printed in Dunstable, United Kingdom